## REMO ON THE RUN

The beautiful blonde girl, Holly, looked at the corpse of her killer companion, whose back Remo had just broken as easily as a brittle plastic stick. She felt her limbs grow warm and a tingling took over her belly. She had never seen anything like it. This new one brought death with such speed and force.

Holly threw herself at Remo's feet and began kissing his bare ankles.

"Kill me, too," she said. She looked up at Remo, into his eyes, imploring him. "Kill me. For *Her*. Death is beautiful."

For the first time in his new life, Remo ran. He ran from the clearing and from something he did not understand. He did not even know what he was running from.

But run as fast as he could and as far as he could, there was no hiding from, no escape from—

## THE ARMS OF KALI

𝒪

## Exciting Reading from SIGNET

# The Destroyer #59

# THE ARMS OF KALI

## WARREN MURPHY & RICHARD SAPIR

A SIGNET BOOK

NEW AMERICAN LIBRARY

**To Rol,**
**For moments to remember**

## PUBLISHER'S NOTE

This novel is a work of fiction. Names, characters, places, and incidents are either the product of the author's imagination or are used fictitiously, and any resemblance to actual persons, living or dead, events, or locales is entirely coincidental.

NAL BOOKS ARE AVAILABLE AT QUANTITY DISCOUNTS WHEN USED TO PROMOTE PRODUCTS OR SERVICES. FOR INFORMATION PLEASE WRITE TO PREMIUM MARKETING DIVISION, NEW AMERICAN LIBRARY, 1633 BROADWAY, NEW YORK, NEW YORK 10019.

Copyright©1984 by Richard Sapir and Warren Murphy

SIGNET TRADEMARK REG. U.S. PAT. OFF. AND FOREIGN COUNTRIES
REGISTERED TRADEMARK — MARCA REGISTRADA
HECHO EN CHICAGO, U.S.A.

SIGNET, SIGNET CLASSIC, MENTOR, PLUME, MERIDIAN and NAL BOOKS are published by
New American Library,
1633 Broadway,
New York, New York 10019

First Printing, November, 1984

1  2  3  4  5  6  7  8  9

PRINTED IN THE UNITED STATES OF AMERICA

# One

He wouldn't take a tip for helping her home from the airport. No, not even a nice frosted piece of yellow cake or even a cup of tea from the old woman.

All he wanted was to put a pale yellow cloth around her neck, and he wouldn't take no for an answer. He also wouldn't stop tightening it.

The Chicago police found her body in the morning. Her bags had not been unpacked. A homicide detective thought he recognized a pattern he had seen before, and he thought he had read about another death like that in Omaha: a traveler found strangled to death with the luggage still packed.

The detective checked with the FBI clearinghouse in Washington to see if this might be some sort of pattern.

"The dead woman had a ticket with Just Folks Airlines?" asked the FBI voice from Washington.

"Yes, she did."

"She met someone on the plane? A nice young person, perhaps?"

"We don't know that yet," the detective said.

"You will soon enough," the FBI voice answered.

"So there *is* an M.O.," said the detective, referring to a repetitive crime pattern.

"Like a clock ticking," replied the FBI agent.

"A national pattern? Or just here?"

"National. She was the hundred and third."

"A hundred and three people strangled?" asked the detective. His voice rose in horror as he imagined that old woman back in her picked-clean apartment, her purse open, her furniture rifled. More than a hundred, just like that? Impossible, he thought. "But this one was also robbed," he said.

"So were all hundred and three others," the FBI agent said.

## Number 104.

Albert Birnbaum was in seventh heaven. He had found someone who was not only willing to listen to the problems of selling retail hardware but was actually enthralled.

His late wife, Ethel, may she rest in peace, used to say: "Al, nobody cares about the markup on a three-quarter-inch screw."

"That markup gave you Miami Beach every year for two weeks during the winter, and—"

"And the ranch house in Garfield Heights and the educations for the children and those charge accounts. I've heard it, but nobody else wants to hear it. Not even once do they want to hear it. Albert, precious, sweetheart, loved one, a three-quarter-inch screw lacks glamour."

Unfortunately, she did not live to see the day that she would be proved wrong. Because Albert Birnbaum had found a young woman, a beautiful young thing with pink cheeks and yellow hair and innocent blue eyes, and a little *shiksa* nose and she was fascinated about hardware markup. Truly fascinated.

Albert had thought for a moment that she might be after his body. But he knew his body, and what he knew about it was that no one as good-looking as this lovely young thing would have to listen to hardware stories to get it, if she even wanted it in the first place already.

She had the adjacent seat on the Just Folks Airlines flight to Dallas. She had asked him if he were comfortable. He had said he was, considering that this was an economy fare. For a reduced rate, he said, it was a wonderful flight. However, she could keep the sandwich and candy bar they had tried to hand out at lunch. "Cheap planes serve cheap food and it'll rot your stomach."

"Isn't that ever so?" she said. "You really have such a philosophy of life. Even something like a flight, Mr. Birnbaum, you turn into an object lesson of comparative values."

"Listen, I don't need big words," he said. "Life is life, right?"

"So well put, Mr. Birnbaum. That's just what I mean. *Life is life*. It has majesty. It rings."

"You're putting me on," said Al Birnbaum. The seat was pinching his hips. But the way he looked at it, everything but a first-class seat pinched his hips nowadays. And he wasn't going to pay five hundred dollars extra not to get a pinched hip. He didn't mention this. The girl couldn't see the few extra pounds he was carrying around, as long as he was sitting down, so why mention it, right? And as pretty as she was, she was allowed to exaggerate a little bit about his philosophy of life being so wonderful.

But when he talked hardware and she really listened, Al Birnbaum realized he had found someone who would not lie. You did not keep those big blue eyes transfixed on the speaker, without honestly caring, not when you were able to say:

"You mean a little three-quarter-inch screw is the backbone of hardware-store profits? The ones I used to apologize for, buying just a few and wasting the clerk's time? Those screws?" she said.

"Those screws, those nails, those washers," Al Birnbaum said. "They're the gold of hardware. A sixty-, maybe sixty-five-percent markup on every one of them, and next year they won't go out of style or be replaced, but the price'll go up. The screw and the nail are the backbone of the business."

"Not the big appliance? That's not your big money-maker?"

"God should never have invented them," said Al Birnbaum. "You take some six-hundred-dollar-ticket item, they see a scratch on it, they don't want it. Back it goes. You put one out for display, kiss it good-bye, you sell it for junk. Then you've got your markup. How you going to compete with a discount store? I saw a convection oven at a discount house selling for fifty-seven cents over what I purchased it for wholesale."

"My God," gasped the girl, clutching her breast.

"Fifty-seven cents," said Al Birnbaum. "On a hundred-and-fifty-dollar-ticket item."

The girl was close to tears hearing that. Al Birnbaum had found a wonderful young woman and his only problem was that he didn't know a young man good enough for her. Which he told her.

"Oh, Mr. Birnbaum, you're too kind."

"No. You're a very special young lady. I'm only sorry *I'm* not young enough."

"Mr. Birnbaum, you're just the sweetest man I have ever met."

"C'mon," said Al Birnbaum. "Don't give me that." But it was nice to think about.

Later on, when the girl had trouble getting her own baggage, Al Birnbaum offered to step in. Al Birnbaum wasn't going to leave a decent young girl stranded. He wouldn't leave someone he didn't like stranded, so why should he leave this young girl who didn't even have a way to get into Dallas to visit her fiancé? He hailed the cab. He rode in with her. He even said he would like to meet her boyfriend.

"I wish you would. I know you'll just love him, Mr.

Birnbaum. He's thinking of going into hardware too, and he could use advice from someone experienced."

"Tell him for me, it's a hard business but an honest one."

"Oh, you should tell him. You know so much more about it."

"He's got to watch out for buying, now. American tools are getting killed by Korea and Taiwan."

"Please, not me. You tell him. You just can't buy experience like yours."

"Oh, you can buy it," said Al Birnbaum. "It just won't be any good." He liked that.

Her boyfriend lived in one of the city's worst neighborhoods and the apartment had virtually no furniture. He wondered how he might be able to offer them some help in getting a decent place to live. But he had to be careful. You didn't just barge in on a nice young couple like this and insult them by offering to help with the rent.

He sat on a simple wooden box under a bare light bulb, smelling old coffee grounds and a mustiness as if the place hadn't been cleaned in a year or two. Then he remembered that the door hadn't required a key. This was an abandoned apartment. They had no place to live. He decided he would have to help them.

He heard a creaking of footsteps behind him and he turned to see another clean-cut young man with a yellow handkerchief that he held by each end, spinning it into a pale yellow rope.

"Excuse me," the young man said. "Can I get this around your neck?"

"Wha—" Al Birnbaum started to say. He felt hands grab his legs, pulling him off the box, while other hands grabbed his right wrist. It was the girl. She had thrown her entire body on his right hand, and his left was pinned behind him and the ropelike pale yellow handkerchief was around his throat.

The handkerchief tightened. At first it just hurt, like something cutting into his neck, and he thought: I can handle this for a while.

He tried to twist away, but they seemed to twist with him. At his first try for air, that helpless try to breathe, he gave a violent lunge and when no air would come into his body, he felt a searing, desperate lust for just one breath. For mercy's sake, one breath. Give him one breath and he would give them anything.

They were chanting. He was dying and they were chanting. Strange sounds. Un-English sounds. Maybe he was too far gone to understand words? Already that far gone?

Darkness, darkness in the room, darkness in his skull, darkness in his convulsing, air-desperate body. And he heard very English words.

"She loves it."

And then, strangely, in the darkness, the deep darkness, there was no need for air, just a great peace upon him with much light, and there was Ethel waiting for him and somehow he knew that now, at this time, she would never tell him he bored her with talk about hardware. Never again would she be bored. She was so happy to see him.

Then he heard a voice, far off somewhere, and it was a promise: "They will not get away with this, these players with the gods of death."

But he didn't care now in this place of light. He didn't even have to tell anyone about hardware. He had forever to be absolutely happy.

# Two

His name was Remo and they had not given him the right breathing equipment. They were going to kill him. He realized it even before the diving boat pulled out from the Flamingo Hotel in Bonaire, a flat jewel of an island in the Netherlands Antilles.

During the winter, Americans and Europeans came here to escape the cold and dive in the turquoise waters and watch the fish of the Caribbean reefs as the fish watched back.

Tourism had been quite profitable to the island, and then someone wanted more profit. So Bonaire became a pumping station in the cocaine pipeline into the United States, and there was so much money, people would kill to protect it. Local police had disappeared, Dutch investigators from Amsterdam had disappeared, but when American assistance personnel disappeared, America told the Antillean government that the United States would take care of it in another way.

Then nothing seemed to happen. No American investigators came down. No intelligence agents came down. And no one in America seemed to know what on earth America had promised. All anyone knew was that it would be taken care of.

A highly placed American assured the Bonaire governor who was his friend:

"I've seen things like this happen before. Usually with the CIA, but sometimes with the FBI or the Secret Service. It's usually something at crisis level and nothing seems to work. Then somebody says: Stop everything, forget it. It will be taken care of."

"And then what happens?" asked the Bonaire governor, his voice a stew of Dutch and English accents on a stock base of African dialects.

"It really gets taken care of."

"By whom?"

"I don't know."

"An agency?"

"I really don't know."

"It must be something," the governor said.

"I don't think it is like anything we know of."

"Then what is it?" the governor insisted.

"I heard of somebody who once had an idea what it was," said the highly placed American.

"Yes?" asked the governor.

"That's it," said the American.

"That's it? You just heard of someone who possibly knew what America was using to solve its unsolvable crises and then nothing more? Who was he?"

"I'm not sure. I just heard," the American said.

"Why didn't you try to find out?" the governor asked.

"Because I heard that they found a finger of his on one continent and a thumb on another. They didn't match prints when they found him, they matched fingers."

"Because he knew?" the governor said.

"I think — I'm not certain — that he was trying to find out who or what this thing was."

"Not certain, eh?" said the Bonaire governor, a bit exasperated at the American who knew so little about what he was talking about. "You don't know who. You don't know what. Would you please be so eminently kind as to tell me just what you do know?"

"I know that if America says it's going to do something to solve your problems, your problems are solved."

"Anything else?"

"Watch out for the falling bodies."

"We don't have any heights here," the governor said.

"Then watch where you step."

Nothing unusual had happened. The usual tourists came down for the usual summer vacation season, and no one noticed another white skin, a man around six feet tall with high cheekbones, death-dark eyes, and thick wrists. They might have noticed that in the three days he was there he ate only once and that was a bowl of unseasoned rice.

Someone did notice that he refused tanning lotion to protect his white skin. They were sure he was going to end up in the hospital, the color of raspberry soda. But no matter how long he stayed in the sun with his skin exposed, he did not burn, nor did he tan, and everyone was sure this man had some sun-blocking lotion, although no one had ever seen him use it and it certainly was invisible.

One cleaning woman who practiced the old religion, honoring African gods as well as the Lord Jesus, wanted to see what this lotion was, this lotion that did not glisten in the sun and did not look like cold cream lathered thick on a porcelain-white body. So she tried to touch him with a finger to see what it was that kept that white skin safe. Later, she would swear that she could not touch him. Every time she reached out a finger toward his body, the skin itself moved, the flesh pulling back away from her touch.

She had the voodoo and she knew the spells and she

knew her prophecy and she warned all those who would listen that no one would be harmed if they did not seek to do the white man harm. She said he had the power.

But since she was, after all, only a cleaning lady in the hotel, richer and more powerful men did not listen to her. They were sure, within a day, who that man was. Some sort of American agent setting up some sort of raid. He went to the old slave huts on the windward side of the island to try to set up a deal too large to be trusted. He asked questions that dealers wouldn't ask. He virtually set himself up to be killed. People who could make a million dollars in a week certainly were not going to listen to a warning of a woman who cleaned rooms not to harm him. They *were* going to harm him. And when he signed up to take the diving excursion, they knew *how* they were going to harm him.

Remo leaned against the railing of the boat, glancing once at the yellow air tanks set up like huge wine bottles in a wooden rack. One of them was supposed to kill him. He did not know how it was supposed to be done and he might not even understand if someone tried to explain it to him. Mechanical things always seemed to go wrong, and it had gotten worse with the years.

But he did know one of those tanks could kill. He knew it by the way the diving instructor had set it down into the rack. He had been taught to know this, in a learning so deep that he could not imagine not knowing it.

The diving instructor had set the heavy tank down the same way he had lowered the other fifteen tanks of air. Knees bent, arms close to his body, and, kerplunk, metal tank banging down onto wooden rack. So what was different?

How did Remo know that the third tank from the

right contained death? How did he know that the very loud diver from Indiana, who said he was part of a diving club, had never used that diving knife he kept waving about? Was it that the man talked too much about "how to disengage from an octopus"? Was rapid, loud talk the tip-off? Was that how Remo knew?

No. Others talked like the man who said he was from Indiana, and Remo knew that they *had* used their knives in diving. Remo thought about it and finally realized, there on that boat in the Caribbean sun, that he no longer knew how he knew some things. His training had been that good. And if it hadn't, if he had needed to think about such things, then perhaps he would not be alive today.

The two who would kill him were on opposite ends of the boat, one up front with the captain, the other at the diving platform in the rear, making jokes with a young woman who was trying to seduce him. They motored for twenty minutes, until they came to an island even flatter than the one they had just left.

"We are now at Little Bonaire, the best diving island in the world. The fish you are about to see represent the highest concentration of reef fish found anywhere," announced the dive instructor. He mentioned that there was a pair of giant French angelfish that would eat from the hands of divers. He warned about moray eels. He had seen them many times, and one of them was even named Joseph.

"But he doesn't answer to his name," the instructor said with a laugh. Remo laughed too. He laughed while looking at the man in the rear of the boat, who was also laughing. The man had a big gold tooth right in the front of his mouth and he was looking at Remo.

The diving instructor, on the other hand, did not look at Remo. Thus, Remo thought, men differed in the way they approached their victims.

The diving instructor was sure to give Remo the

third tank from the right. Remo let them strap it on and listened to all the talk of how to operate the air-demand valve, assured them he had done this before, which he had, but did not mention that he had forgotten all of it. None of it mattered.

With the tank on his back and flippers on his feet, he put the mouthpiece in his teeth and dropped into the glass-clear waters of the Caribbean. He allowed himself to sink, down as far as a man, then a story down, then a frame house down. Ten stories down into the deep ravine, he snapped the air hose to let air slip from the tank in goblet-size bubbles to imitate the breathing of a man. They rose like slow white balloons toward the great silver-white covering of air above him.

The other divers followed, more slowly, checking their gauges, equalizing the air pressure inside their lungs with the water pressure outside their bodies, counting on gauges and dials to do what Remo let his body do better. Man had come from the sea, and blood was basically seawater. Remo felt his pulse level drop as he let his body attune itself to the sea, feeling a harmony in a thin body a hundred feet beneath the sea, still as a cave shark: part of the sea, not just in it.

Two yellow fish swam up to this strange creature who moved as if he belonged here, and then swam away as if conceding that he did. Remo saw them quiver as they passed through his air bubbles. Then they convulsed in crazy circles and floated up, out of control, to the surface.

The air tanks held poison gas, he realized. Given that, he should be dead by now, so he let his arms float loosely, opened his mouth to release the breathing device, and floated like a corpse, slowly up toward the surface like the two yellow fish.

His two killers grabbed his wrists, as if assisting him, but slowly they stopped his ascent and then tugged him down with them, eleven stories, thirteen, sixteen, almost two hundred feet down, where the surface was just a memory in the hazy darkness of this clouded world.

They tugged him to a dark opening in a volcanic hole, wide as a door and tall as a doghouse, and pushed him through. They followed to make sure he got through all the way, then pushed him upward in dark waters broken by sudden sharp lights from their flashlights.

Remo heard the water break and felt the water drain from his body. It must be an underwater cave with a trapped pocket of air, he realized. The two men pushed his body along on a rocky ledge, but they did not take off their scuba mouthpieces while doing it. Remo realized why. He could feel it on his skin. There was death here, rotting human bodies in a cave beneath the sea, a stench like sour soup. He continued to hold his breath.

This was where all the bodies that disappeared from Bonaire went. This was where the dope smugglers put them. One of the divers' flashlights shone on a pile of bales in dark blue plastic, all of them sealed tight. Those were the drugs. The drug storehouse was in the body storehouse.

They left Remo's body on the ledge, food for the fish and the eels, and took one of the blue bags of drugs. But as they were about to leave, they felt something on their wrists.

Remo had them.

Before they could slip back under the water to exit from the cave, they heard Remo say: "Sorry, boys. Not just yet."

In shock, the man with the gold tooth opened his mouth. His mouthpiece dropped out and he tried to breathe without it but caught a lungful of stench without much oxygen. He gagged and vomited and tried to breathe, then reached under the water for his artificial air. Remo helped push him under. The rapid bubbling showed the he hadn't found his mouthpiece. Soon there was no more bubbling.

Remo said, very softly, to the diving instructor's two fear-widened eyes, visible through his mask, "You and I have a problem. Do you agree?"

The mask nodded with incredible sincerity, especially after Remo tightened his grip on the man's wrist.

"You see, my problem is if I stay here, I get bored," Remo said as he threw off the tank with the poison gas in it. "Your problem's different," he said. "You stay here and you get dead."

The instructor nodded again. Suddenly a knife flashed out from his leg sheath. Remo caught it easily, like a very thin Frisbee, and flipped it over onto the rock ledge, where it would not again interrupt their conversation.

"So how do we solve our problems?" Remo asked. "Your life and my boredom?"

The diver shook his head, indicating he did not know. He noisily sucked the air from his mouthpiece.

"I have a solution," Remo said, raising a forefinger in the air for emphasis. "You tell me your employer."

Tears formed inside the diver's mask. The sound of his breathing became louder.

"You're afraid he'll kill you?"

The man nodded.

"*I* will kill him. If I kill him, he will not kill you."

The diver made a motion with his hand that could indicate many things.

"Is that one or two syllables?" Remo asked. "Sounds like . . .?"

The diver pointed in despair.

"You'll tell me everything on the surface?"

The diver nodded.

"And you will be a witness against the survivors?"

The diver nodded again.

"Then let's get out of here. This place has nothing to recommend it. It's even more boring than the island."

Back on the boat, it looked as if the diving instructor had rescued Remo by sharing his mouthpiece and air after Remo had lost his tanks. Remo did nothing to change anyone's opinion, but after they left the cruise boat, they went down to the beach for a nice quiet chat.

The diver's employer was in Curaçao, a neighboring Dutch island, a piece of quaint Holland in a warm azure sea.

Remo went there and visited four very important businessmen who had suddenly become very rich. Remo wanted to inform them in person that first, their bodyguards and fences were useless; second, their careers in the commerce of the islands was over, since they had been dealing in drugs; and third, since they had killed American agents and other law-enforcement people, their lives were over. He explained that they wouldn't be needing their windpipes anymore, so he would take them with him and feed them to the beautiful ocean fish. He did and they died.

Later, he had one last favor to ask the diver who had led him to the four main drug smugglers.

"We've been together only a day now, yet I feel we're real friends," Remo said.

The diver, who had been held two hundred feet beneath the sea by a man who needed no air, by a man who seemed to melt over fences and virtually through radar beams, and who took out the throats of powerful men as though plucking fleas from a dog, expressed his desire that they should always be such friends. A barroom of drunks on Christmas Eve never felt such true depth of friendship.

"All I ask," Remo said, "is that no matter what happens, you will never tell anyone about me, what you have seen, or why you have decided to turn state's evidence."

"I promise. We are brothers," sobbed the man.

And Remo repeated a line from a dating club that advertised trips to the Caribbean. "You meet such nice friends here." And then his smile faded and he said, "And if you speak the wrong things, I will meet you again." The voice was ice cold.

He flew out on Prinair to Miami, and from there to a hotel in Boston which he had been calling home for the last month. He was a man without a place, attuned to the forces of a universe which did not contain one roof he could ever get used to.

Inside the penthouse of the Ritz Carlton, overlooking the Boston Common, the floor was strewn with posters, some of them in English, some with Korean lettering.

They all said either "Stop" or "Halt."

On a small table just inside the door was a petition with three signatures. One in Korean headed the list, and then there was the scrawl of the maid and the room-service waiter.

"We're growing," came a squeaky voice from the parlor of the hotel suite.

Remo walked inside. An old man in a sun-yellow afternoon kimono, embroidered with the gentle dragons of life, pored over the lettering on a new poster. The man had small wisps of a beard and parchment-yellow skin. His hazel eyes shone with joy.

"I didn't hear you sign the petition," he said.

"You know I am not going to sign. I can't sign," said Remo.

"I know *now* that you are not going to sign. I know *now* that gratitude has its limits. That the finest years of a lifetime have been for naught, that the very blood of life I poured into a white thing has proven again to be worthless. I do deserve this," the old man said.

"Little Father," said Remo to the only man in the world he could call friend, Chiun, Master of Sinanju, latest grand assassin of the House of Sinanju, keeper of all that house's ancient wisdoms which Remo too now had in his being, "I cannot sign that document. I told you that before I left. I told you why before I left."

"You told me why when we had only my signature," Chiun said. "Now we have others. We are growing. This city and then the nation will be the pioneer group of a new mass movement, returning the world to sanity and mankind to justice."

"What do you mean, justice?" Remo asked.

"All movements talk of justice. You can't have a movement without a call to justice."

"This isn't justice we're talking about," Remo said.

"It is just," Chiun said solemnly. His English was precise, his voice high-pitched. "The most just. And for the public good, for their safety and eternal freedom."

"What safety? What freedom?" Remo said.

"Read," said Chiun proudly. He handed Remo the rough copy of the new poster he had been drawing.

The English letters were scrawled like the writing of a palsied man, but the Korean characters were clean and artistic, with a clarity that approached grace. Remo had never been good at foreign languages, but he had learned Korean over the years as Sinanju had been drilled into his body and mind and soul. So he read.

The poster called for an end to amateur assassins:

"STOP WANTON KILLING," it read. "THE AMATEUR ASSASSINS LITTER YOUR STREETS WITH BLOOD, YOUR PALACES WITH CORPSES, AND RUIN A VITAL PART OF ANY ECONOMY. BRING BACK ORDER. BRING BACK A SENSE OF DIGNITY TO THE KINGDOM. END THE BLIGHT

OF THE AMATEUR ASSASSINS WHO KILL WITHOUT PAY
OR REASON. HIRE ONLY THE PROFESSIONAL FOR YOUR
NEEDS."

Remo shook his head sadly. "What do you think this
is going to do, Little Father? It's already against the
law in America to kill someone."

"Of course. And why? The amateur assassin, the
spouse-basher, the political murderer, the thrill-seeker
who does not care about professional standards. Of
course it is outlawed. I would outlaw it too. the way it is
done nowadays."

"It is killing, Chiun," said Remo, and he went to the
window overlooking a very old piece of real estate,
acres of lawns and gardens in Boston that once the
goodly citizens were allowed to use as common
pasturage, now called the Boston Common. Those
citizens had belonged and now their descendants belonged. A sharecropper from Georgia could come to
the Roxbury district of this city and belong. Someone
could sail in from Portugal and find a community
where he belonged. But Remo did not belong; he
would never belong.

"It's killing, no matter how well it's done," he said,
without turning around. "That's what it is and maybe
those old emperors feared Sinanju and paid Sinanju,
but they didn't want them around for breakfast or fun
or an afternoon party."

"They were emperors. They had their ways. Every
great emperor had his great assassin," said Chiun. He
smoothed his kimono and assumed the posture of
powerful presence, the one of dignity and respect
which another Master of Sinanju, many centuries
before, had demanded that the Ming Dynasty rulers
show him.

"They had them where no one could see them,"
Remo insisted.

"Where everyone saw them. Where everyone saw them," Chiun said, his squeaky voice rising to tea kettle shrillness from the indignity of it all. "For here is the truth. Only in this country is it a thing of shame."

Remo did not answer. How many hundreds of times, thousands of times, in fact, had he tried to explain that they worked for an organization which had to remain secret? Two decades before, the people who ran the United States had come to realize that the country could not survive the coming turbulent years while living within the strict confines of its Constitution. So they set up an organization that did not exist, because to admit that it did would be to admit that the basis of the country—the Constitution itself—did not work.

The organization was named CURE and it would operate outside the law to try to preserve the law and the nation.

Of course, eventually, there had to be an enforcement arm to mete out the punishment that the courts could not or would not mete out. The enforcement arm was Remo Williams, former policeman who had been framed for a murder he did not commit, and sentenced to die in an electric chair that did not work. It had happened a long time ago in a state Remo had once called home. A long time ago, when he had had a home. Now his only place was not a place at all. It was his training as an assassin, given in full measure by Chiun, the reigning Master of Sinanju, only because he expected Remo to follow him as the next reigning Master.

CURE thought it had paid, in gold, for Chiun to train Remo. It did not understand that what Chiun had given Remo could not have been purchased at any price. It had been given to Remo because Chiun had found no one in Sinanju, a rocky windswept village in North Korea, who had the character to become the next Master in the long unbroken line of assassins from

Sinanju. Chiun never admitted this in so many words
to Remo. Chiun did not admit such things to whites.

And there was another reason also. One of the
ancient scrolls of the House of Sinanju talked about a
white man who would be dead, but who would
nonetheless, be trained to become the Master of
Sinanju. This white man would become the greatest
Master of all, because he was more than just a man: he
was the enbodiment of Shiva, the Destroyer God.
Chiun believed that Remo was this white man. Remo
thought that this was a porcelain crock of crap. But he
did not tell Chiun that, one did not tell Chiun such
things.

Remo was still silent and Chiun said, "Sulking is
never a sufficient response to anything."

"I could tell you again but you wouldn't hear it."

"I have given the best years of my life, the sacred
years of my life, to breathe Sinanju into your soul, and
now you are ashamed of it."

"I'm not ashamed."

"Then how can you label what an assassin does as
killing? Simple killing. An auto kills. A fall kills. A
mushroom kills. We do not kill."

"What do we do, then?" Remo asked.

"There isn't a good word in English for it. It lacks
majesty."

"Because it's the right word," Remo said stubbornly.

"Never," Chiun spat. "I am not a mushroom. Maybe
you are but I am not and I never will be. I have tried to
take what was given me, ignoring the fact that you are
white. I have always ignored it."

"You've never stopped mentioning it, Little Father."

"You mention it and bring it on yourself. Ignoring
the fact that you were white, I gave all to you. I gave
you Sinanju."

"Nobody in Sinanju could get it right. That's why.
You thought you would teach me a few blows, pick up

a bag of gold, and go home. I know why you stayed on to really teach me. Because I was the only one who could learn. This century. Not in the Mings or the Fus or any dynasty from Persia to the golden blossom courts of Japan. Today. Me. I was the only one."

"Trying always to ignore the fact that I was dealing with an ungrateful white, I gave you what centuries have blessed only one house of assassins with," Chiun said solemnly.

"And I learned."

"And if you learned, then you cannot call what we do . . . that word."

"Killing," said Remo. "We do killing."

Chiun clasped his breast. Remo had used the word. Chiun turned his head away.

"Killing," Remo repeated.

"Ingrate," Chiun said.

"Killing."

"Then why do you do it?" Chiun asked.

"I do it," said Remo, "because I do it."

Chiun lightly waved a long-nailed, delicate hand into the air of the penthouse suite.

"Of course. A reason without a reason. Why should I have ever expected that you would have performed for the House of Sinanju or for me? What have I done to deserve the slightest inkling of respect from you?"

"I'm sorry, Little Father, but . . ."

Remo did not finish. Chiun had clapped his hands over his ears. It was now the proper time for sulking and Chiun was doing it. He had one last word for Remo before he went to the large picture window where he could best be seen sulking.

"Never say that word again in my presence."

Chiun lowered himself into a lotus position facing the window, his back to the room and Remo, his head in perfect balance with his perfect spine, his face a rhythmed stillness of poise and silence. It was a graceful sulk. But then again, he was the Master of Sinanju.

It was only when he heard the door to the suite slam shut that he remembered there had been a message for Remo from the head of CURE.

"I will come up there to meet him," Smith had said.

"We wait with delight your coming, O Emperor," Chiun said.

"Please tell Remo to wait there for me."

"It is inscribed in the stone of my soul," Chiun had promised.

"You'll give him that message, then?" Smith asked.

"As the sun informs the spring flowers of its presence," Chiun had said.

"That's yes?" Smith asked.

"Does the sun rise in the morning and the moon at night, O Emperor?" said Chiun.

Remo had often corrected him, saying that Dr. Harold Smith was not an emperor, and did not like to be called an emperor. He just ran CURE. He was a man chosen, Remo would explain, precisely because he didn't like such things as titles and because he would not use such a powerful organization for his own self-aggrandizement. Chiun had always smiled tolerantly, knowing that Remo would eventually grow out of holding such silly notions about people. He could not learn everything at once.

"So he will be told as soon as he gets there," Smith had said warily to Chiun.

"He shall not see my face before he hears your words," Chiun had said, and having taken care of Smith, he had gotten back to more important things, namely his posters assailing amateur assassins.

He remembered the message only when he heard the door slam behind Remo. But it didn't really matter. Smith shipped the gold for Chiun's services to Sinanju whether messages were delivered or not. Besides, even though he hadn't delivered the message, Chiun could always figure out something to tell Smith when the time came. One had to know how to handle emperors. Someday Remo would learn that.

Harold Smith arrived in Boston and almost had a heart attack at Logan Airport. In World War II he had been parachuted into France with the OSS, and even floating at the end of a chute in darkness over Limoges, he did not feel quite so helpless as he did now, holding this Boston newspaper. He hadn't even bought it to read the news, since he already knew the news, but for the sports section, hoping to find something on Dartmouth football.

His gaunt lemony face suddenly became white, and even the cabdriver noticed it.

"Are you okay?" the driver asked.

"Yes, yes. Of course," said Smith. He straightened the gray vest of his gray suit. Of course he was all right. He had been dealing with shocking situations all his life. That was why he had been chosen for this position.

But he had not expected this. Not in a newspaper.

Just three days before, Smith had been in the White House to assure the President that CURE was a secure organization.

"I'm sure you know how the press would treat something like this," the President said. "Especially in my administration. It wouldn't matter that I wasn't the President who started your little operation."

"Security, sir, is paramount with us," Smith had said. "Are you aware how we established our security arm?"

"No."

"We used a dead man. We framed someone for a crime he didn't commit. We altered the execution mode to let him live and then we trained him. He's a man who doesn't exist working for an organization that doesn't exist."

"If you framed him, why didn't he resent it?" the President asked.

"He did."

"Why didn't he just walk away?"

"He wasn't the type," Smith said. "That's why we picked him. He is a patriot, sir, and he can't fight that."

"And the older one? The one you said was well into his eighties?" The President smiled when he mentioned that.

"He is no patriot," Smith said. "Not to us, and I believe he would leave us if the gold stopped. But he has developed some form of attachment for his pupil. The pupil loves him like a father. They are always together."

"The older one is better?" the President asked with a melon-wide grin.

"I'm not sure."

"I'll bet he is," the President said.

"I don't know. Those two would know, but I don't, sir," said Smith.

"So there is no danger of exposure," the President said.

"There are no guarantees in this world. But I think you can rely on us. We are nothing if not secret," Smith said.

"Thank you, Smith. And thank you for doing what has to be the loneliest job in America. My predecessors were right. We have the best of men running that shop."

"May I ask you a favor?" Smith said.

"Of course."

"I will, of course, come here whenever called. But every contact, no matter how well executed, is another small danger of exposure."

"I understand," the President said.

"If you understand, sir," Smith said coldly, "then please refrain from asking for a contact just to be reassured that everything is all right and to give me compliments. If there is any danger, you will know about it because we will not be there anymore. I will collapse the organization as planned."

"I just wanted to tell you I appreciate what you're doing."

"We all have wants, sir, but with the responsibility for so many lives, it behooves us all to control them," Smith said.

The President realized his predecessors had been right about Smith in another way too. The coldest SOB ever put on this green earth, they had called him. And they were right. The President tried to smile.

Smith remembered that smile, trying to cover up the President's hurt at being so coldly rebuffed. Smith had not wanted to hurt his feelings, but secrecy *was* paramount. To be exposed was to be a failure in every respect; it was to admit that America could not work within its own laws.

Secrecy. It was everything.

And now Smith was in Boston and there on the page facing the sports page was an advertisement with a familiar face, the slit eyes, the wisp of a beard. It was a public appeal to stop amateur assassins. It was Chiun.

Chiun's face, right there in the newspaper. Hundreds of thousands of people looking at his face.

Smith realized he had read the advertisement several times before recovering. There was no mention of Remo and no mention of the organization. Chiun, fortunately, had never seemed to understand what they were doing anyhow. Smith saw that the paper was shaking in his hands. He tried but couldn't stop it. There was that face that was supposed to share secrecy, right there in the paper along with that insane appeal: "STOP AMATEUR ASSASSINS."

Smith put the paper on the cab's backseat. He could see the worst coming on. Television cameras surrounding Chiun. There in the background would be Remo. And that would be the end. To have Remo's face on the television news. It would all be over and it had started unraveling right here with this newspaper ad.

Smith tried to calm himself. He could not go directly to the hotel; his presence before the TV cameras would just make things worse. He changed his destination to a good restaurant named Davio's, a mile or so down Newbury Street. He ordered salad and tea and asked to use the telephone. He told the hotel operator that he wished only to speak person to person to the occupant named Remo. No one else.

"He's not in, sir."

Good, Smith thought. Remo must have seen the ad and understood that he could not be compromised.

Remo probably already was calling Smith's special number. Smith checked the small computer terminal inside his briefcase. No message had been received, according to his readout screen.

By evening, when Remo still did not make contact, Smith had a cab drive him to the Ritz Carlton. There were no television cameras in front, no newsmen in the lobby.

He had made a mistake, underestimating the ability of Boston newsmen to miss a news story. CURE had lucked up and maybe gotten out of this one alive. But no more. He was going to speak to Chiun. No. He would speak to Remo. They could not afford to keep Chiun in America anymore.

While Smith was planning his ultimatum to Remo, numbers 105 and 106 were about to unpack their bags in a small motel in North Carolina when some downright friendly travelers who had helped them with their luggage said something funny about a pale yellow handkerchief that they wanted to put around their necks.

"Well, sure, but don't you think you've done more than a good Christian service already?"

"We're not Christians."

"Well, if it's a Jewish custom . . ."

"We're not Jews either," said the young people, who did not wish to discuss their religion with people who were going to be part of the services.

# Three

"So?" said Remo. He handed the advertisement back to Smith.

"You know this compromises us," Smith said.

"Compromises," Remo snapped. "You compromise Chiun's honor every day. What have you given him? You ship gold to his village so that those deadbeats who live off him can stay alive. You tell him a few nice words and then you expect him to fall down all over himself. Listen, Smitty, this country has given him beans of respect."

"Respect?" Smith said. "What are you getting at?"

"You know, in the Ming Dynasty, there was a special chair for the emperor's assassin. The old shahs of Persia made their assassins nobles of the court. In Japan, they even imitated the walk of the old Masters of Sinanju. So he took out a little ad. So what?"

"I would have assumed," said Smith, "that you, most of all, would understand."

"Just give me the job," Remo said. "Who do you want killed?"

"You're sounding strange," Smith said.

"Maybe. So he bought an ad. What difference does it make?"

"The difference between whether this little island of law and democracy, this very small island in a very big sea of time, is going to make it. The world has never seen a place where so many people come from so many places to live so free. Do we help preserve it or not? That's the difference it makes."

"I'm surprised that you would be giving a speech," Remo said.

"I give it to myself sometimes," Smith said. The old man lowered his head. Remo saw that the years had taken their toll on him. He was not like Chiun, for whom time and pressure were only ingredients in a larger cosmos. To Smith they were burdens, and the burdens showed. Smith was old while Chiun would never be old.

"Don't feel bad," Remo said. "I give myself the same speech sometimes."

"But do you listen?" Smith asked. "You've changed, Remo."

"Yes, I have." He wondered how he could explain it. He still believed as Smith believed. But now he knew that Smith was carrying some kind of death in the left pocket of his gray vest, something to kill himself with. Probably a pill, should he be facing some situation in which he might be captured and talk.

In the beginning of his training, when Remo was still an American patriot first, last, and always, he would have known how he could tell that there was death in that vest pocket. He might have observed the tender way that Smith treated that pocket. There was always some obvious tip-off. People never forgot they had death on them, and they touched it. Their bodies moved differently. They sat differently. And at the beginning of his training, Remo noticed those things and knew what they meant.

Now he no longer noticed those things. He just knew. He knew that Smith had death in his vest and he did not know anymore exactly how he knew. This is what made him different from before.

What he did know was that although he was still an American, he was now also Sinanju. Chiun was the reigning Master of Sinanju, but Remo was a Master of Sinanju also. The only other one in the world. He was two things in one place. America and Sinanju. Oil and water. Sunlight and darkness. And Smith had asked him if he had changed. No, he hadn't changed. Yes, he had changed completely.

When he said nothing, Smith said, "We have a problem with airline travelers."

"What else is new? Get the airlines to spend less money on advertising and more money on baggage handling and you won't have any more problems with travelers," Remo said.

"These travelers are being killed," Smith said.

"Hire detectives."

"They've had them. All over the country. Travelers are being killed. They fly on Just Folks Airlines and then they're strangled."

"That's too bad, but what's it got to do with us?"

"Good question," Smith conceded. "This has been going on for a couple of years now. More than a hundred people have been killed."

"I haven't heard anything about it," Remo said. "I watch the news sometimes."

"You haven't been paying enough attention. They are always discovering somebody who killed fifty or sixty people and you've never heard of those killings either until the murderers are arrested. These killings are happening all over the country, so none of the newspeople have noticed yet. Every one of the victims is robbed."

"I still say, why us? So there are a hundred more deaths. So what? Nobody does anything about anything anymore anyhow. They just count the bodies." There was bitterness in Remo's voice. He had been with CURE for more than a decade, killing whoever

Smith said to kill, all in the service of some greater common good. And America didn't look one damned bit better than it had before he had started.

"The whole thing's endangering travel," Smith said. "It has that potential and it could be quite serious."

"So that's it. We don't want some airline somewhere to lose a buck," Remo said.

"No, that's not it," said Smith sharply. "If you look at every civilization that has collapsed, the first thing that went was its road network. The first thing a civilization does is to establish safe roads. That's what makes commerce and the exchange of ideas possible. When you give up your roads to the bandits, you give up your civilization. And our roads are in the sky."

"Another speech," Remo said sourly. "People will still fly. Why should our airlines be any safer than our streets?"

"Cities died in this country when they couldn't use the streets anymore. The whole country would die if we couldn't use the sky. It's important, Remo," Smith said, and the total sincerity of his voice was such that Remo said with a sigh, "Okay. Where do I start?"

"First things first. We can no longer afford to have Chiun in this country. You're going to have to tell him to leave. He's become a danger to our organization."

"Good-bye," Remo said.

"You won't do it?"

"If Chiun goes, I go. If you want me, Chiun stays."

Smith thought a moment, but a very small moment. There was no choice really.

"All right for now," he said. "You go to the corporate headquarters of Just Folks Airlines. They have been investigated before and nothing's ever been found."

"So why there?"

"Because people are getting killed all over the country and there isn't any other place to start. Maybe you can find something at Just Folks that other investigators have missed. Some of these victims have been killed for just thirty dollars. And please take Chiun with you. Maybe we can get him out of town before the Boston press wakes up."

"I don't think you've treated him very well," Remo said, glancing out the windows at the darkening Boston sky. Just then, Chiun returned. He had two more signatures. One was written as if it had been done during an earthquake. There were squiggles in the line. Remo thought that either a child or someone held upside down out a window until he saw the wisdom of stopping amateur assassins had signed it.

Chiun had heard Remo's last remark, and when he turned to Smith, he was all sweet oil and incense. His long fingernails made the gentle but flamboyant sign of the fan in Smith's honor.

"Emperor Smith," Chiun said. "We must apologize for the disrespect of our pupil. He does not know that an emperor cannot mistreat anyone. Whatever you did, we know was justified. It should be even more. Speak. Tell me who is this insolent one who has deserved even harsher treatment from your mightiness. Give me but his name and I will make him quake in honor of you."

"No one, Little Father," said Remo without taking his eyes off Smith.

"Silence," Chiun commanded him, and turned back to Smith. "Speak but the word, O Emperor. Thy will be done."

"It's all right, Master," Smith said. "Everything has been settled."

"I bow to your wisdom," said Chiun in English. In Korean he muttered to Remo: *"This is an emperor. Tell the idiot anything he wants to hear."*

"Thank you, Chiun," said Smith, who did not understand Korean. "You've been . . . uh, very gracious."

"Good-bye," said Remo.

"Good luck," said Smith.

"May the sun reflect your awesome glory," said Chiun in English; and in Korean: *"He certainly has a lot of work for us lately. Maybe we are not charging him enough."*

*"It's not that,"* Remo said in Korean.

*"It's always that,"* Chiun said. *"Should I ask him to sign my petition?"*

Remo's loud laughter followed Smith from the hotel suite. When he was gone, Remo told Chiun: "Smith is not an emperor. We don't have emperors in this country."

"They all like it, though," Chiun said. "It's standard in the vocation of assassins. Always call them Emperor."

"Why?" Remo asked.

"If I must explain it now again, then certainly I have wasted my time with you these many years," said Chiun, the squeaky voice again resonating with the magnitude of the offense.

Chiun was still offended when they reached Denver, Colorado, the headquarters city of Just Folks Airlines. Remo was to be identified as an agent of the NAA, the National Aeronautical Agency, and Chiun—if he would wear an American suit and take off the more extravagant wisps of hair around his chin and ears—could do the same.

Or, refusing that, Chiun could stay at the hotel. Remo explained this to him. Chiun had a choice. One or the other.

There was a third way available, Chiun explained, as without changing anything, he accompanied Remo to the offices of Just Folks. On the way, he explained the virtues of the kimono over the tight three-piece suits that white men wore and which Chiun called "caveskins."

Aldrich Hunt Baynes III, president of Just Folks Airlines, was wearing a gray "caveskin" with a dark tie. He had set aside up to ten minutes for the NAA representatives who wanted to see him.

A. H. Baynes had a smile with all the warmth of a giant salamander. His fingernails were polished and his light blond hair looked as if it were cared for by a nurse. He believed in the old adage that everything in life has its place. He had a time for emotions, too, all the emotions, as he often told key stockholders and others close to him. He even liked to roll around in the dirt once in a while. Usually, around late May, for seven minutes in the sunshine with a company photographer present to record his humanity for the company's annual stockholders' report.

A. H. Baynes was thirty-eight years old. He had been a millionaire since he was twenty-four, a year after he graduated from the most prestigious business school in America. When he had entered Cambridge Business School, he put down on his application under "goals": "I want to be the richest son of a bitch in the world and I have absolutely no qualms or inhibitions about what I do to get there."

He was told that sort of statement was unacceptable. Accordingly, he wrote: "I hope to be part of a community-based synergism, responsibly and effectively answering the deepest needs and aspirations of all people within the structure of a free-market economy."

It meant exactly the same thing, he knew. He was president of Just Folks by twenty-six and at thirty-eight, with two children, one white male, age eleven, one white female, age eight, a white female wife and a photogenic dog, he kept piling up money by answering the deepest needs and aspirations of all people.

A short while before, he had bought a company in a small Ohio town. The company was barely breaking even and was a prime candidate for closing down, even though everyone in town worked for the company. The town was so happy when Baynes bought the company that it held an A. H. Baynes Day.

He arrived with wife, two children, dog, smiled for the photographers, and two days later assured the department that made the cases for shipping the product that they would never lose their jobs if they worked for him. The cases continued to be made in the Ohio town; they continued to read "Made in the USA." The products that went into the cases, however, were subcontracted out of Nepal, Bangladesh, and Ramírez, Mexico, cutting labor costs to six cents an hour, seven cents if the workers got an extra bowl of rice.

When his secretary came in and told him that the two NAA men were here for their meeting and one of them was an Oriental, Baynes thought that there must be a mistake in his appointment book and that one of his subcontractors was visiting him. He decided to see them anyway.

"Hi. A. H. Baynes, and you two are from . . .?"

The white man looked at a card he took out of his pocket. Baynes thought it was a business card and reached to take it. But the white man was reading it.

"We're from National Aeronautic something," he said.

"I thought you were from Asia," he said, smiling to the old man in the kimono.

"Sinanju," said Chiun.

"North Korea?" said Baynes.

"You have heard," said Chiun serenely.

"Everybody has heard of North Korea," Baynes said. "A great work force. Even better than Bangladesh. They eat every other day in North Korea, I've heard. And they've got to like it."

"One does not have to gorge oneself on meats and fats and sugars if one knows how to make one's body work properly," Chiun said.

"I'm going to be renegotiating some labor contracts pretty soon," Baynes said. "How often does a person have to eat, would you say? I'm really interested."

"Once a week. It depends on how one stores one's food," Chiun said.

"Wonderful. Let me write that down. You're not making this up?" Baynes was scribbling frantically on a white pad with a gold pen.

"He's not talking about the same thing as you," said Remo.

"I don't care," Baynes said. "The concept is perfect. I just have to turn it into more human terms."

"Such as?" Remo asked.

"Once-a-week eating is good for people. For good people. And we want to make everybody into good people."

"It doesn't work for everybody," Remo said, and took the pad from Baynes's hand. Baynes lunged for it but Remo had it in the wastebasket before Baynes could reach it.

"That's an assault," Baynes said. "You, a federal employee. You have assaulted an officer of a corporation."

"That wasn't an assault," Remo said.

"That is a legal assault," said Baynes, sitting down in a formidably dark cherrywood chair from which he could, if he wished, menace his growing empire.

Remo took the arm of the chair and the arm of A. H. Baynes and blended them somewhat. Baynes wanted to scream but the white man's other hand was on his spinal column and all that came out was a barely audible peep from a desperately quivering tonsil.

Baynes could not move his right arm. He did not even dare to look at it. The pain told him it would be an ugly sight.

Tears came to his eyes.

"Now, that," Remo said, "is an assault. Can you see

the difference? The other thing with the pad was kind of a getting-something-out-of-the-way, not an assault. If you understand the difference, nod."

Baynes nodded.

"Would you like the pain to end?" Remo asked.

Baynes nodded, very sincerely.

Remo adjusted the spinal column where the pain-controlling nerves were. He did not know their names but he knew they were there. Baynes would not feel pain anymore.

"I can't move my arm," Baynes said.

"You're not supposed to," Remo said.

"Oh," said Baynes. "I suppose that's your leverage for getting me to talk."

"You got it," Remo said. "People are getting killed on your airline."

"No, they're not. That is wrong. That is a misperception and we have responded to that before," Baynes said.

"About a hundred people, all of them ticketholders on Just Folks, have been strangled."

"Unfortunate, but *not* on our airline, and we'll sue anyone who suggests such a thing," Baynes said. "Any one."

"I'm saying it," said Remo, making an obvious move toward the other arm, the one not yet blended with the cherrywood.

"Saying it among ourselves is not slander," Baynes said quickly. "We're just brainstorming, right?"

"Right. Why do you say they're not being killed on your airline?"

"Because they get killed after they get off our airline," Baynes said. "Not *on* it. *After* it."

"Why do you think somebody picked Just Folks to do this to?" Remo asked.

"What I hear is that they're cheap robberies. And we have the cheap consumer fares," Baynes said.

"What's that mean?"

"Lowest fares in the business. People Express took fares as low as they could really go. So we had to do something else to take them even lower. We're a semi-scheduled airline."

"What's semischeduled?" Remo asked.

"We take off after your check clears," Baynes said. "We also don't waste a lot of capital overtraining pilots."

"How do you train your pilots?" Remo asked.

"All Just Folks pilots have a working knowledge of the aircraft they fly. That doesn't have to mean count-less hours of wasting fuel in the sky."

"You mean your pilots have never flown until they fly a Just Folks plane?"

"Not so. Let me clear that up. They most certainly do fly. They have to fly to get their pilot's licenses. They just don't have to fly those big planes that use so much fuel."

"What do they fly?" Remo asked.

"We have the most advanced powered hang-gliders in the business. We have in-air training for our pilots."

"So you think it's the low fares that attract these robbers and killers to your semischeduled airline?" Remo asked.

"Exactly. May I have my arm back now?"

"What else do you know?"

"Our advertising department says there's no way we can capitalize on the fact that our fares are so low that even small-time killers fly us. They said an advertising appeal to hoodlums wouldn't help our ticket sales."

Chiun nodded. "Hoodlums. Killing for pennies. The horror of it. Remo, I should have brought my petition with me."

Remo ignored him. "Would any of your people rec-ognize any of the killers? Maybe they fly frequently."

"We wouldn't recognize our own employees,"

Baynes said. "This is a semischeduled airline. We don't go taking off on the button like Delta. You're not talking a Delta crew when you're talking Just Folks. We are semischeduled. We have to factor in some element of crew turnover."

"What do you mean, crew turnover?" Remo snapped. "In the course of a whole year someone had to notice something."

"What year? Who's been at Just Folks a year? You're a senior member of our line if you can find the men's bathroom," said Baynes. "My arm. Please."

"We are joining Just Folks," Remo said.

"By all means. Would you please separate my arm from the chair?"

"I never learned how," Remo said.

"What?" gasped Baynes.

"I am a semischeduled assassin," Remo said. "By the way, what I did to your arm . . .?"

"Yes?"

"If you were to talk about this to somebody, I might just do it with your brain and a potato," Remo said.

*"That's crude,"* said Chiun in Korean. In English he told Baynes, "There are many things we do not understand in the world. My son's desire for secrecy is one of them. Please be as solicitous of his feelings as he is of yours."

"You'll do to my brain what you just did to my arm," said Baynes. "Is that it?"

"See?" Chiun told Remo. "He understood, and without your being crude about it."

Baynes was thinking of how he would get his arm sawed free. Maybe he could walk around with a piece of cherrywood blended to his arm. He could live that way. Specially tailored suits could hide most of it.

Suddenly the hands that hardly seemed to move were at his arm again and he was free. He rubbed his arm. Nothing. It was slightly sore, but nothing was wrong. And the arm of the chair was just as it had always been. Had he been hypnotized? Had there been hidden straps holding him to the chair?

He thought he might have talked too much. He should have been tougher and just called the police. Maybe he would try it now, he thought.

The young white man seemed to know what Baynes was thinking because he took the airline president's gold pen and rubbed his finger very slowly over the clasp. First the gold shimmered under the fluorescent light as if it were waving, and then the metal melted on his desk, burning a smoking foul hole in the perfectly polished cherrywood.

"You're hired," Baynes announced. "Welcome aboard Just Folks Airlines. We have several vice-presidencies open."

"I want to fly," Remo said. "I want to be on board."

Baynes stuck a finger straight up in the air. "Which way is that?"

"Up," said Remo.

"You're now a navigator on a semischeduled airline."

"I want to move among the passengers," Remo said.

"We can make you a flight attendant."

"Sure," said Remo. "Both of us."

On the next Just Folks flight from Denver to New Orleans, there was no coffee, tea, or milk. The two flight attendants just sat all the passengers down and watched them. There were no complaints. When one of the pilots asked for a glass of water, he was thrown back into the cockpit and told to wait until he got home.

# Four

**Number 107.**

Holly Rodan's mother was delighted. When she heard that her daughter's new religion did not involve dating minorities, everything took on a positive glow. It was a real community kind of religion but Holly would not have to live there all the time. Just occasionally, for formal prayers and ceremonies, such as tonight, when Holly would be inducted, and then return home in a few days.

"Do you need any special dress like for First Holy Communion or something like that?" her mother asked.

"No," said Holly.

"I see you have an airplane ticket. Is your church far away?"

"Mother. I have found a meaningful involvement. Are you going to try to ruin it now?"

"No, no. Father and I are really happy for you. I just thought I might help. After all, we can afford to help. We would be happy to give you the price of a full fare on a scheduled airline. You don't have to be poor or anything for your faith, do you?"

Holly was a beautiful girl with a blond cherub's face, innocent blue eyes, and a ripe milkmaid's body.

"Gawd, will you ever leave me alone," she said.

"Yes, yes, dear. Sorry."

"I have found a place for myself in this world."

"Absolutely, dear."

"I have done this despite the oppression of wealth . . ."

"Yes, Holly."

"A family environment devoid of a meaningful sharing . . ."

"Yes, dear."

"And parents who have never failed to fail me. Despite all this, I have found a place where I truly belong."

"Yes, dear."

"Where I am needed."

"Absolutely, dear."

"So get off my back, bitch," said Holly.

"Absolutely, dear. Can I give you something to eat before you leave?"

"Only if you want to sauté your heart," Holly said.

"God bless you, dear," said her mother.

"She does," said Holly Rodan.

She did not say good-bye to her mother and she did not tip the cabdriver who took her to the airport. She took her Just Folks cardboard ticket to a counter, where someone checked it against a handwritten list of passengers, then made a mark on the back of her hand with a rubber stamp. She was then directed to a waiting area, where someone was renting stools to sit on.

Holly steadied herself and thought of the prayers she had been taught. She chanted silently to herself and then knew that whoever she selected would be a demon and deserved to be killed for Her. Because She was the mother of all destruction and required that demons be killed so that other humans might live. All it took was killing, Holly realized. Kill, she thought. Kill. Kill for the love of Kali.

She walked around the waiting room looking for a suitable demon to sacrifice.

"Hello," said Holly to a woman with a paper bundle. "Can I help you get that onto the plane?"

The woman shook her head. Apparently she did not believe in speaking to strangers. Holly smiled her warm smile and tilted her head winningly. But the woman wouldn't even acknowledge that she was there. Holly felt the first chill finger of panic. What if she couldn't get anyone to trust her? They had to trust you first, she had been told. You had to win their trust.

An old man was sitting on a rented stool reading a newspaper. Old men had always seemed to trust her.

"Hi," she said. "That's an interesting newspaper you're reading."

"*Was* reading," the man corrected.

"Can I help?" she asked.

"Usually I do my reading solo," he said. It was a cold smile he returned.

Holly nodded and walked away, frightened now. Nobody is going to let me help. Nobody is going to let me be friendly.

She tried to calm herself but she knew she was going to fail. She would be the first to fail. Every other initiate had passed. It was supposed to be so easy because people traveling were supposed to feel vulnerable, grateful for help, but there was no one in the sparse waiting room of Just Folks Airlines who would let her help.

She tried a young boy reading a comic book and he physically kicked her away.

"You're not my mommy and I don't like you," he snarled.

The world was like that. She was going to fail. She

had failed emotional development at the consciousness institute. All the marches for peace, for support to revolutions, to end all arms — they had all failed, because there was still no peace. Governments refused to sponsor and support revolutions, and there were still arms. All failures, and now, in the most crucial test of her life, she was failing again. She cried.

A young man with a face of acne that looked ready to harvest with a hard rub of a washcloth asked if he could help.

"No, dammit, I'm supposed to be the one helping," she said.

"Help any way you want, honey," he said, giving her a lascivious wink.

"Really?" said Holly. Her eyes widened. The tears stopped.

"Sure," said the young man, who was a sophomore at a large Louisiana university and was returning to New Orleans on Just Folks because it was cheaper than a bus. In fact, he said, when you considered what shoes cost today, it was cheaper than walking. While he was talking, he was recording everything in his mind to boast about back at the dorm if this pickup should turn out to be as successful as he hoped.

"Are you going to be met by anyone?" asked Holly.

"No. I'll just take a bus to the campus," he said.

"Do you need a lift or anything?"

"Well, I'll take one," he said.

"What is your name, where are you going, and why; is there anyone you really care about in your life; what are your main worries and hopes? Mine are to live happily," said Holly. Dammit, she thought. She was supposed to ask those questions one at a time, not all at once.

But the young man didn't mind. He answered them all. She didn't even bother to listen. She just smiled and nodded every few minutes and it was enough for him.

Every one of his jokes was funny, every one of his ideas profound. He discovered in this milk-skinned, big-busted blond beauty an approval the world had never given him before.

The two hardly noticed the two male flight attendants on Just Folks, one of them wearing a kimono. They must have been efficient, though, because everyone seemed to stay in his seat and there were no calls for anything. Once someone wanted to use the lavatory and the old Oriental in the kimono explained how to use bladder control.

But Holly and her new friend didn't mind at all.

At the airport outside New Orleans, Holly offered the student a lift. He thought that was a great idea, especially since she implied she knew of a lonely, secluded place.

The place was an old ramshackle building in a black section of the city. Holly led him inside, and when she saw her brothers and sisters in Kali, she could hardly contain herself. They were her prayer-mates. And there was the phansigar. He had brought the strangling cloth.

Holly smiled when she saw the yellow cloth in his hands. Tradition, she thought. She loved tradition. She loved calling the strangler "the phansigar," just as Kali devotees had done in the olden days. The cloth too was a part of that tradition.

"This isn't going to be a gang bang, is it?" The student laughed and all the rest laughed with him. He thought they were wonderful people. They thought he was as brilliant as she did.

He waited awhile for Holly to take off her clothes. While he was waiting, one of the others asked if he could get a handkerchief around the student's throat.

"No, I don't go for kinky stuff."

"We do," said the other man, and then they were all on him, holding his hands, his feet, and there was a cord around his neck.

He couldn't breathe, and then, after a point of incredible pain, he didn't even want to breathe.

"She loves it," said Holly, seeing the death struggles of the young man, his face becoming red, then blue with death. "Kali loves his pain. She loves it."

"You did well, Sister Holly," said the phansigar, removing the yellow cloth. There was a red welt around the neck, but no blood. He untied the sacred strangling cloth, which was called the "rumal." They went through the student's pockets and found forty dollars.

It barely covered the air fare, even the Just Folks consumer fare. The phansigar shook his head. He did not know what the Holy One would say.

"But isn't the important thing the death offering to Kali?" Holly asked. "Kill for Kali? Offer her up a demon? Doesn't Kali love pain? Even our pain? Even our deaths?"

The phansigar, formerly a stationery-store clerk in Kansas City, had to agree. "It was a good death," he said. "A very good death."

"Thank you," said Holly. "It was my first. I thought I wasn't even going to be able to say hello to anyone, I was so frightened."

"That's just how I felt my first time," said the brother phansigar, he of the strangling cord, he who offered up the sacrifice suitable to Kali, the goddess of death. "It gets easier as you go along."

On their way to the Holy Temple, where Kali received the kiss to Her followers, Her loyal servants ate the traditional raw sugar and said the prayers again. They wrapped the forty dollars in the holy rumal, and with songs of praise and the raw sugar still on their lips, went before the Holy One, who had been brought to America by Kali. They intoned prayers for Kali and recitations of the victim's pain, which was wine for Her lips.

Ban Sar Din heard the prayers, heard the recitations of devotion from the followers, and waited until the holy rumal was placed at his feet. Then he nodded sagely at the bowing devotees.

"Kali has tasted the sweetness of death again because of you, beloved followers," he said, and then added something in the language of Bangalore, his native Indian city. Americans liked that. Especially the kids. The kids were the best. They were complete jerks.

Ban Sar Din gave the holy strangler phansigar a fresh rumal and took the closed death cloth with a grunt of gratitude. A quick glance inside told him only forty dollars.

Impossible, he thought. Even on a Just Folks consumer-fare flight, they would be losing money on a forty-dollar take. And that was just one fare. What about the other fares? What about those times when there was no one for them to set up? The overhead was enormous. The lights alone for the temple cost $120 a month. What was the matter with these kids? Forty dollars. Impossible.

When Ban Sar Din retreated for private devotions into his solitary office, the cold brutal fact hit him when he saw three tens, a five, and five singles. It *was* forty dollars. This group of yo-yos had wasted a consumer-bonus fare for forty dollars. He wanted to run back into the temple and kick them out.

How the hell did they think he was going to meet his budget?

The yellow handkerchiefs were going up. He used to be able to get a gross for $87.50, and that included the printed likeness of Kali. Now a gross of something barely strong enough to strangle a neck bigger than a chicken's cost $110, and if you wanted printed pictures, forget the whole thing. And the other pictures of Kali. They went well, but prices were rising there too. And candles. Everybody in America was burning candles, and prices had gone up like smoke.

So with strangling cloths going up, candles out of sight, printing prohibitive, and it only a matter of time before Just Folks raised its fares to meet the competitors', Ban Sar Din realized he was going broke at forty dollars a pop.

But how was he going to tell these American hooples to at least look to see if the victim was wearing an expensive watch? Was that too much to ask? Look for an expensive watch before you send the demon on his way to Kali.

That didn't seem like a lot to ask. But he didn't know. He never knew about Americans or America.

He had come to the country seven years before, with only a six-month visa and his quick wits. Back in Bangalore, the ruling magistrate had let him know that he wasn't wanted on the streets of the city and if he were caught picking another Indian pocket, the police were going to take him into an alley and beat his dark brown skin purple.

Then a friend told him about the wonders of America. In the United States, if you were caught picking a pocket, you were given a room to yourself and three good meals a day. It was supposed to be punishment. Americans called it jail.

You could even get free legal help, and because Americans thought that any kind of punishment was too harsh, they were even experimenting with making the opposite sex available so that prisoners wouldn't be lonely. They had taken away the bars too, and given prisoners free education so they could make money outside jail by working if they chose to, although not too many did. And who could blame them, when jail was so good?

"I do not believe such a place like this exists," Ban Sar Din had told his friend.

"True. It is like that in America."

"You lie. No one is that stupid. No country."

"Not only do they do all these things, but if a person who is rewarded for killing and robbing kills and robs again, guess who they blame?"

"I don't know."

"Themselves," his friend had said.

"You lie," Ban Sar Din spat.

"They gave India fifteen billion dollars in grain, and look at how we treat them. Fifteen billion when a billion was a lot of money even for Americans."

"They can't be that rich and that stupid. How do they survive?" Ban Sar Din asked.

"They have a very big ocean on both sides of them."

Ban Sar Din crossed one of those oceans with his very last penny and immediately went about picking pockets, expecting to get caught and go to this wonderful place called jail. Then one day some white man on a park bench near Lake Pontchartrain spoke to him.

"Where did I go wrong?" the white man said.

Ban Sar Din would have left, but his hand was solidly inside the man's trouser pocket.

The man furrowed his brows. "We are a vacant, empty society," he said.

Ban Sar Din tried to get his hand out but couldn't, so he nodded.

"I am vacant, too," the man said.

Ban Sar Din nodded again. He was only five feet tall and weighed less than one hundred pounds. He did not have the leverage to just yank free.

He had black hair and eyes and dark brown skin and he had expected people in America to single him out because of that. Everyone in Bangalore had the same coloring, but in America people were different colors, but none of them ever died in the streets no matter what their color. In Bangalore, there were often demonstrations on behalf of the racially oppressed in America, and everyone marched, except of course the untouchables, who, when they tried to demonstrate along with the other castes, were beaten to death or flogged from the streets.

"What can I do to make amends?" the white man asked.

"Lean forward a bit to I can get my hand out of your pocket," Ban Sar Din suggested.

"Forward. Yes, of course. I've been looking at the past, turning in on myself and the tragedies of the past. I have to look forward."

"And twist a bit," Ban Sar Din said.

"Of course. Twist. Change. Are you telling me all change is possible?" asked the man on the bench.

Ban Sar Din smiled.

"You smile. Do you think my struggles ludicrous?" asked the man. "Or do they have a deeper, more transcendental meaning?"

The hand was almost loose from the pocket now.

"Up," said Ban Sar Din.

"Higher than transcendental?"

"Stand, please."

"You are beyond me in your wisdom," said the man, slowly getting to his feet. "I know money is meaningless to you, but here, let me give you something."

He took the wallet out of his rear pocket along with the limp brown hand that was clutching it.

Ban Sar Din knew now he had succeeded. The man would surely call the police. Then, glorious jail.

"You knew I wanted to give you everything, didn't ou?" the man said. "You understood my problem."

He kissed Ban Sar Din's limp hand and pressed he wallet forward. "Yours," he said.

Ban Sar Din backed away, suspicious, and the nan said, "No. Yours, please. I have been :nlightened. I have been freed from the bonds of naterialism. I am going to free myself from every-hing that binds, and I owe it all to you. What can I lo for you, friend?"

"Do you have any change also?" asked Ban Sar )in as he made a great realization: picking \mericans' pockets were not nearly as profitable as )icking their minds.

It was a revelation and it proved to be a turning )oint. Ban Sar Din found that in America nothing vas unsellable, no matter how stupid, if you put a owel on the head of a salesman and called it nystical.

The problem was which religion. Most of the good )nes were taken already and were doing land-office )usiness. One of them even had people paying good noney in the belief that they would be able to learn o levitate.

Then, on a rainy afternoon in downtown New )rleans, Ban Sar Din remembered the old robbers )f the highways.

Before the British came, an Indian could hardly ravel from one province to another without an army o guard him.

But during the British oppression, as he had earned to call it, schools were started, courts of law vere established, and roads to enable the peasants to :ngage in commerce were established.

But there was a problem on the roads. There were he servants of Kali, called the Thuggees. Their eligion told them to rob travelers, but never to spill blood. It was so successful that both Hindus and Muslims, in a rare sharing of a doctrine, formed Thuggee bands, from which the word "thug" came into use through the English-speaking world. The British Colonial Office, in their rigid backwardness, thought it improper to have bands of killers prowling the roads, preying on travelers, so after years of constant policework, they finally hanged the last of the lot.

Ban Sar Din checked around. No one was using Kali. He went to an old junk shop and found a statue of the goddess. The price was surprisingly low, and after paying it, and safely holding the statue in his arms, he asked the store owner why he had sold it so cheaply.

"Because the damn thing's haunted, that's why," the store owner said. "Came in on a ship a hundred years ago, and anybody who owned it died badly. It's all yours, my friend."

Ban Sar Din was no one's fool, and certainly not fool enough to believe in one god from a country that had twenty thousand of them.

He rented an old storefront for use as an ashram and installed the statue at the front of it.

And then things started to happen. Students made the first good converts. They told him stories of how before their conversion, they had been timid and frightened. But as soon as they had placed their first rumal around a throat, power had come to them.

The converts themselves taught Ban Sar Din, whom they called the Holy One, new intricacies of the cult of Kali, the goddess of death. He never knew where they were getting their information or how they were learning Indian words. Then, one horrible night, he had a dream and the goddess with all her arms talked to him.

"Little pickpocket," she said in his dream, "I have let you live because you have brought me to my new home. Little pickpocket, I have hungered these many years for the death struggles of victims again. Little pickpocket, do not interfere with the rituals of death. I love them."

He ran out into the deserted ashram and looked at the cheap statue, which he had not even bothered to repaint. It had grown another arm, and there was no seam, no paint, nothing to show that the arm had not always been there, nothing but Ban Sar Din's memory. It frightened him so much that he decided he had been wrong about the number of arms and put it out of his mind.

By this time, the little Indian weighed 240 pounds and looked like a giant M&M without the candy coating. He was also wearing one-thousand-dollar suits and driving a Porsche 911SC. He was wintering in Jamaica, summering in Maine, and hitting the French Riviera twice a year in between, all for handing out little yellow handkerchiefs and getting them back with money in them.

He knew, therefore, to leave well enough alone. So when forty dollars came back in a rumal, he gave the little jerks the Indian hocus-pocus they wanted and took the money. Although forty dollars in New Orleans would not even buy him a top-of-the-line meal.

He did not know, during that evening of despair, that his money troubles would soon be over and that he would become far more dangerous than any little band that had ever terrorized an Indian highway.

And as he went to sleep at his luxury penthouse that night, he did not know that back at the ashram, the chants were reaching a hysterical pitch.

Holly Rodan, who had just that day made her first offering, noticed it first. That was her privilege for pleasing Kali.

"It's growing, it's growing," she cried. A small brown nub was sprouting from the side of the statue, so slowly it looked as if it had always been there, so very slowly, but yet, when one blinked, one could see several smaller bumps, little things, like the beginnings of fingers on the beginning of a new arm.

Kali was speaking to them, they all realized.

She was growing another arm.

And it too would have to be fed.

# Five

Just Folks Airlines was making a few adjustments in flight-attendant profile-performance packages. Remo didn't understand what that meant, and a supervisor told him:

"When someone has to go to a lav, you don't give him a lecture on bladder control."

The supervisor was an attractive dark-haired woman with a pleasant smile and that sort of helpless determination people get when confronted by the reality that things are not going to work out well. She had already adjusted to Just Folks no-frills consumer fare, and far from being embarrassed at the airline's policy of charging to use the bathrooms, she now regarded it as somewhat of a sacred duty.

"We get a quarter every time they use a lav," she told Remo. "Four dollars near the end of the trip. So please don't have your partner give instructions on how *not* to go to the bathroom."

"Why do you charge four dollars at the end of the trip?"

"Mr. Baynes figures that people have to go worse at the end of a flight, so you can get a premium price. There's a lav-increment scale. Twenty-five cents on boarding, fifty cents right after takeoff, and so forth."

"That's robbery," Remo said.

"No one is forcing them to take our lav-time."

"Where else are they going to go?"

"They could plan ahead and use the johns at the airport."

"What are we supposed to tell them when we ask for four dollars to use the bathroom?" Remo said.

"We always suggest saying that fuel consumption increased near the end of the flight and mumble something about flush-to-fuel comparative expenditures."

"I am not charging someone for a bodily function," said Remo.

"Then the loss comes out of your pay."

The first thing Remo did on the next flight was to give away the snacks and the sodas. He ripped the pay locks from the lavatory doors. He lent out the pillows without cost and urged the passengers to take them home as souvenirs. Then he carefully tried to see if anyone was setting someone up for a kill. He had learned that a college student who had been on his previous flight had been found murdered, strangled and robbed.

Yet, on that flight, there had been no one giving off any sense of death.

He asked Chiun about it later. "Do you give off a sense of death, Little Father?"

"For me, death is not evil. So I do not," Chiun said.

"Perhaps, then, there are others who don't think death is evil," Remo said. "Maybe they don't give off the sense of death either."

"Perhaps."

"I can't believe there are that many trained assassins who are petty robbers too," Remo said.

"Perhaps they are not trained assassins. Perhaps there is another reason," Chiun said.

"What reason?" asked Remo.

"We will see," Chiun said, and turned away to check

the passengers on the plane. He liked being a flight attendant, provided passengers did what they were told. What he liked best was ensuring their safety, telling them what they should do in the event of a crash.

"The wings are always falling off planes like this," he would say. "When it happens, make your essence not part of the plane, but part of the pull of the planets."

"Yeah? And just how do we do that?" asked a rotund woman in the smoking section.

"Change your filthy eating habits first," said Chiun, who then decided that there would no longer be a smoking section on his Just Folks flights. Instead, he told them to occupy their time with reading material. He passed out petitions and brief excerpts from an Ung poem praising the first petal of the first flower on the first morning of the new dawn.

"I don't like that flowery crap," said one young man. "I'd rather smoke." Chiun showed him how he really didn't need a seat bealt to stay transfixed to his seat. He did it with the young man's spinal column, and instantly the youth's appreciation of poetry rose. He loved the poem.

Chiun said he did not want the young man to appreciate the poem because he was being forced to appreciate it, because then he would not really appreciate it at all. The youth swore over and over again that he was not being forced. There were tears in his eyes.

Chiun visited with passengers. He especially appreciated parents' tales of their children's ingratitude, and called Remo over to listen to many of them.

And then Remo noticed a young blond woman with milkmaid skin, very interested in an elderly gentleman who was going on about the meaning of spastic fabrics in a nonspastic world, as he called it.

Everyone around that seat was dozing, having been

put under by the interminable Ung poetry. Except for the girl. Her blue eyes were wide, gaga with the wisdom of not trying to market nonspastic fabrics in a spastic world, and vice versa. The man was obviously a salesman of some sort. Remo knew this because the man talked in terms that could have been used reasonably only by Napoleon or Alexander the Great.

The man had New England and South America. He would control Canada. He wouldn't move into Europe because that was held too tightly.

Remo figured out that these were the man's sales areas. He never did quite figure out what a nonspastic fabric was, although he got the impression that it was used somehow in zippers.

Remo thought he recognized the girl. He looked at the passenger list and saw her name was Holly Rodan. He asked to speak to her privately.

"Don't be too long, honey," said the salesman.

Remo brought the young woman up to the well between the cockpit and the seats. The copilot came out to talk to him.

Remo said, "I'm busy."

"Look, I'm a pilot and you're a steward. You're not even in uniform. You are going to make me a cup of coffee, do you understand?"

Remo twisted the copilot's arm in the shape of a handle, stuck his head into the coffeepot, then delivered him back to the cockpit soaking wet.

"You are now a cup of coffee," Remo said.

Remo tried to talk to the young woman, but a passenger came up into the well wanting a drink.

"Speak to the other one," Remo said.

"He said to talk to you."

"What do you want?"

"I want a rum fizzle. Do you have a rum fizzle?"

"Take whatever you want," Remo said.

The passenger poked around in the liquor bin. Holly

said she wanted to go back to her seat. She asked nicely and she was answered nicely. No.

"I don't see any rum fizzles," the passenger said.

"Take what's there," Remo said.

"Can I have a vodka and rum?"

"Sure. Take it and go," Remo said.

"Can I have two?"

"Take them. Go."

"Two of them?"

"All of them," Remo said.

"Are you really a steward?" Holly asked Remo. She was not afraid. She had Her on her side.

"Sure," said Remo. "I've even seen you before. On this flight."

"Not on this flight," said Holly. "This flight only began a half-hour ago." It was a perfect answer. She liked putting people in their places. Mother had taught her how. It was the only thing her mother had ever been good for.

Remo suggested that now, since the coffeepot wasn't using the hotplate, she might like to sit there.

"You can't talk to me like that. There are regulations. You'll get fired."

"All right," said Remo.

"That's it?"

"Yup," he said.

"Nothing else?"

"Go back to your seat."

She did, and Remo watched her go. There was something wrong with this young lady. He wondered if Chiun had noticed it, but Chiun was busy with several people who were agreeing with him that workmanship throughout America was becoming shoddy. The true professional was a thing of the past. Chiun nodded sagely and pulled another petition from his kimono: "STOP AMATEUR ASSASSINS."

Remo let Holly Rodan get off the plane with the man

she had been fawning over, but just as she was about to
be picked up by some young friends, Remo moved in
on the car and told the salesman to get lost.

The man threatened to call the police. Remo
noticed his wedding ring and said, "Good. And call
your wife too."

"Talk about a semischeduled airline. I've never seen
such bad service," the salesman said.

"He has a right to come with us," said Holly. "We
want to give him a lift."

"Give me a lift," said Remo.

"We don't want to give *you* a lift."

"We'll give him a lift," said the man in the front
seat.

"We're not giving this son of a bitch a lift," Holly
said. "I've got the other man who wants to go with us
and we're not giving this one a lift. He's a lousy
stewardess and I wouldn't give him a lift to hell in a
handbasket."

The young man in the front seat did not try to
reason with her, as her mother had, nor did he seek, as
her father had, to understand the deeper meaning of
her complaints. He did not attempt, as her teachers
had, to establish a bridge of understanding.

What he did was far more effective than anything
else that had ever been practiced on her. He slapped
her in the mouth. Very hard.

"We would be happy to give you a lift, traveler," she
told Remo.

"Much obliged," he said. "You people travel much?"

"Only when we have to," said the man next to the
driver. The airport was Raleigh-Durham and they
asked Remo if he wanted to go to Duke University or
Chapel Hill.

"I just want to talk," Remo said.

"We like to talk too," said the passenger in the front
seat. His hand rested over his shirt pocket and Remo

knew that the pocket contained a weapon, although all that he could see was a yellow handkerchief.

They stopped the car near a small woods to have a picnic. They said they were hungry and had, in fact, been describing the odors and tastes, the crispness of fried chicken, the succulence of lobster in butter, the smooth richness of chocolate in the throat. When Remo thought about these things, his stomach became queasy, but he said nothing because they obviously were trying to work up his appetite.

They parked the car and walked with Remo along a little path to a clearing, where they opened a picnic basket.

"Excuse me," said the man who had been sitting next to the driver. "Can I get this around your throat?"

"Sure," said Remo. So the handkerchief wasn't hiding a weapon. It was the weapon. The others grabbed his legs and hands. The handkerchief became a cord and circled his neck and then closed and tightened. Remo counteracted the contraction with neck pressure. He did not fight it with his muscles. He just lay there with people sprawled across his arms and legs.

The strangler pulled. Remo lay there.

"She loves it, She loves it," said Holly Rodan.

"The hell She does," said the driver. "Look, he's not even turning red."

Remo let the blood pressure rise in his head so his face reddened.

"There it goes," said the driver.

"Now She loves it," said Holly.

"Why isn't he struggling? Pull harder," the driver said.

The noose tightened. The phansigar's forehead broke out in perspiration. His knuckles whitened and his wrists strained. Holly Rodan dropped an arm to help pull on the other side of the rumal. She pulled and the phansigar pulled. The demon about to be offered up to Kali smiled and then the rumal snapped in half.

"Hi," said Remo. "Let's talk about strangling and robbery."

"You're not dead," said the phansigar.

"Some people might give you an argument about that," Remo said.

The diver made a break for the car. Remo caught one leg, then the other leg. He whipped the body into a tree, where it folded up neatly with a snap of the spinal column, then convulsed once and was still.

The phansigar opened his mouth, and then breakfast came up as he looked at the driver. The body was bent in two, backwards, with the nape of the neck touching the heels.

"Don't make bodies the way they used to," Remo said. "Now, the Neanderthal, that was a man. Solid. You hit a Neanderthal against a tree and the tree would break. Look at this guy. Never going to fix him. He's done. Just one little bang on a tree and he's done. What do you think, sweetheart?"

"Me?" said Holly Rodan. She was still holding half of the yellow rumal in her hand.

"You, him, I don't care," Remo said. "What's going on?"

"We're practicing our religion. We have a right," said the phansigar.

"Why are you killing people?"

"Why do Catholics say Mass? Why do Protestants sing or Jews chant?"

"It's not nice to strangle and rob," Remo said.

"That's what you say," the phansigar said.

"How would you like it if I killed you?"

"Go ahead," said the phansigar. "Long live death." Remo felt himself hesitate. He looked at the girl, and she was just as calm as the other young man. That was why he had sensed nothing about the girl on the Just Folks flight.

"Go ahead," said the young man.

"Sure," said Remo. "If you insist," and dropped him like a loose marble onto the picnic basket.

"Long live pain," the young man gasped as he expired.

"What is all this about?" Remo asked the girl.

Holly Rodan stared at the broken body. It had been so fast, so forceful, the body breaking like a brittle stick. She felt her limbs grow warm, and a tingling look over her belly. It was beautiful. This new one brought death in such speed and force. She had never seen it like this. She had a taste for death now. It could be beautiful, she realized, beautiful if it were strong enough. Not some limping off into eternity, but the gigantic crash into a tree. She looked at the phansigar, dispatched by Remo like a gum wrapper.

Then she looked at Remo, the handsome dark-eyed man with high cheekbones. His sharp gaze sent gushers of passion through her body. She wanted him. All of him. She wanted him in death, in life, his body, his hands. Death or passion, it was all the same thing. She now knew the secret of Kali. Death was life itself. They were the same.

Holly Rodan threw herself at Remo's feet and began kissing his bare ankles.

"Kill me too," she said. "Give me death. For Her."

The feet moved away and she crawled after this beautiful force of death. She crawled down the path, her knees scraping on stones, bleeding. She had to reach him. She had to serve him with her life.

"Kill me," she said. She looked up into his eyes, imploring him. "Kill me. For Her. Death is beautiful."

For the first time in his new life, Remo ran. He ran

from the clearing and from something he did not understand. He did not even know what he was running from.

Back at the airport, he met Chiun, who was stopping passersby and asking them to sign his petition. But when Chiun saw Remo, he knew something was wrong and put the petition away inside his kimono.

All the way back to New Orleans, Chiun made no criticism, expressed no annoyance at having had to train a white man, and on leaving the plane, even paid Remo a compliment. "You move and breathe well, Remo."

"I'll be all right, Little Father. I just have to think."

"Of course," said Chiun. "We will speak when you are ready."

But that night, at their new hotel, they still did not speak. Remo looked at the stars and could not sleep. Chiun watched Remo, and late, during the night, he put away the petitions in one of his large steamer trunks.

They would have to wait; something more important had happened, he knew.

# Six

Ban Sar Din ate his way through the forty dollars before breakfast. And it wasn't even at his favorite restaurant; he couldn't afford that.

He left the restaurant and wandered the streets. Something was wrong with America. If you bought a plane ticket and sent three people out to do a job and then all you earned was less than the price of a full meal with dessert, something was seriously wrong. With the economy. With everything.

People were making fortunes on fund-raisers for revolutionary movements that were little more than bandit gangs. There was one yogi who was even selling a secret word for two hundred dollars a pop and he had the suckers lined up waiting.

Some cults had mansions. Others had corporations that came close to being listed in the Fortune 500. Some yogis bought their own towns, drove around in Rolls-Royces, and the suckers threw flowers at their feet.

And what did Ban Sar Din have?

He had an ashram full of crazies who thought nothing of killing someone for forty dollars just to see the victim wriggle a bit. And he was losing money. The Kali thing had started out all right, but now the crazies seemed more interested in the killing than in the robbing, and he was going bust.

In a land of opportunity, if you couldn't make money through murder and theft, how could you make money?

He felt like taking one of those bonus-fare coupons from Just Folks Airlines and flying off somewhere. But his hands had gotten too fat for picking pockets and he had gotten used to being a spiritual leader to America's youth. What bothered him most of all that troubling evening was that he knew there was a fortune to be mined somehow, somewhere in that ashram. He had free personnel and a cult that seemed to have caught on.

How to make a buck out of it? A reliable buck.

He couldn't send out more of the killer teams. If each one showed a loss, increasing the volume just meant increasing the loss. Expenses? He couldn't cut any more than he had already. Handkerchiefs any cheaper and they wouldn't be able to hold a throat. He had tried white handkerchiefs once, but the faithful insisted on the yellow, and how could you argue with people you weren't paying anyway?

He couldn't even cut expenses by going to a totally unchartered airline. Who knew what kind of poverty-stricken passengers that kind of line might be carrying? His loonies would wind up killing and come home with a handful of food stamps.

He was in a circle growing smaller and there was no way out.

And then, in his despair, Ban Sar Din heard voices, a beautiful song rising with faith and gusto toward the heavens. He looked around and saw he had wandered into a poor black neighborhood. The voices came from a church. He entered and sat down in a rear pew.

The minister sang with the chorus. He preached of hell and he preached of salvation, but most of all he preached of the magic prayer cloth that would answer problems, and when treated with the magic blue juice, would cure the gout, rheumsey, cabob disorder, and lung cancer.

After the prayer meeting, Ban Sar Din went up to the minister.

"What ails you, brother?" asked the Reverend, Tee Vee Walker, a boom of a man with a rutted black face and large hands that glistened with gold and diamonds. His was the Church of the Instant Savior.

"Business is bad," said Ban Sar Din.

"What business you in?" asked the Reverend Walker.

"Religion business," said Ban Sar Din.

"You in the life, then?" chuckled the Reverend Walker, and when Ban Dar Sin explained he was running an Indian religion, the Reverend Walker asked his weekly take.

"It used to be good, but costs have gotten out of hand."

"Don' know how to handle costs, excep' don' have none. What I always do is take the ugliest woman in the choir and give her some heavy lovin' and then make her in charge of all the costs. She figure out how to pay. Learned from my Daddy, he be a preacher too, one of your basic no-frills yell-in-their-face gospel preachers. You can go anywhere with that. Yell in their faces."

"I have a different sort of gospel," Ban Sar Din said.

"They all the same. It be what people buyin'."

"It's *not* the same. I'm afraid of my congregation."

"Pack one of these," said the Reverend Walker. It was a little silvery automatic. He explained that it was unseemly for a minister to carry a large pistol, but a pearl-handled automatic could fit in a jacket or trouser pocket. His father, he said, used to carry a switch-blade.

"But mine are crazy," Ban Sar Din said. "I mean

real crazies. You just can't yell in their faces. You don't understand."

"Listen, little fat fella. I'm not rescuing yo' congregation for nothing. I'll show you how to work the pulpit," the Reverend Walker said. "But I get the day's offerings."

"You can yell in their faces?"

"I can whip yo' congregation into a pack of little puppies. And when I got them where you want 'em, remember . . . give the ugliest woman some loving and let her solve yo' problems for you."

Ban Sar Din gauged the big man's size again. Perhaps. Perhaps he might get them in line. And once they were in line, Ban Sar Din might be able to get them into more profitable areas, might be able to convince them that coming back with forty dollars in a rumal was a sin, especially in these times when forty dollars didn't even get you a first-class meal with dessert.

"All right, nigger," Ban Sar Din said. "A deal."

'What's that word yo' say?" asked the Reverend Tee Vee Walker.

"It's wrong?"

"Only a nigger can use the word 'nigger.' "

"Everybody calls *me* 'nigger,' " Ban Sar Din said, in great confusion. "I thought that made us blood brothers or something."

"Not you. You brown enough, but you talk funny."

"The British imperialists forced us to learn this funny talk," said Ban Sar Din, catching in a single sentence the basic doctrine of the third-world theology, namely that no matter what happened, one had to blame it on some white men. That done, anything was acceptable.

The Reverend Walker did not find a pulpit in the ashram. There was a bare wood floor, well polished, a statue of their saint, which had too many arms and an ugly face, and not even the smell of something cooking somewhere. Just some very quiet, very white, very young people walking around.

"When do services begin?" the Reverend Walker asked Ban Sar Din.

"I don't know. They begin them themselves most of the time."

"This has got to stop right heayah. You run the church, or the church runs you. Let's lay some gospel down on their heads."

He noticed a blond girl, quite excited, her cheeks flushed with joy. For this occasion only, for his pudgy brown brother only, he would make an exception about the ugliest woman in the congregation. One had to take care of the good-looking ones too.

Reverend Walker flashed his broadest smile and stepped in front of the statue at which everyone was looking.

"Brothers and sisters," he boomed. He wished he had a pulpit to bang. He wished he had chairs to look at, faces to look back at him. But half these people had their heads down on the floor and the other half were only trying to look past him toward the statue.

"We got to move on to be right on," yelled the good Reverend Tee Vee Walker. "Man can't walk, man can't talk. If you pray, you pay."

People still didn't look at him. He thought that that should have worked. It hardly ever failed. One black preacher had even run for president by trying to reduce the nuclear-technological age to seven-year-old rhymes.

The reverend didn't know why these whites weren't responding.

If he couldn't get them with preaching, he would try singing.

His rich voice boomed out over the throng, calling

for sweet understanding, bemoaning suffering, calling for trust. He liked the way he could bring it all up from his toes. But they still didn't respond. And it was good singing, too.

The Reverend Walker began to clap. No Walker had ever lost a congregation, not in four generations of preachers, and he wasn't going to be the first. He stamped his feet. He yelled some more at their heads, and no one even noticed him.

Then the pretty little blond girl smiled at him and nodded him into a side room.

The Reverend Tee Vee Walker did not miss that smile. So there were other ways to bring a congregation into line. He knew them all. He winked back and followed the girl into the room.

"Hi," she said.

"Hello there," said the Reverend.

"Can I just get this around your neck?" came a voice from behind him.

So these whites did groups. "Any neck you want," he said with a broad smile.

And there was number 108.

Ban Sar Din was waiting in his private devotion office when he heard a knock on the door. They were calling him to appear before Her.

Good, he thought. The reverend has finally gotten them into line.

But there was no Reverend Walker. Just a small group holding one of those silly yellow handkerchiefs. He didn't remember any groups going out now, but then again, they weren't telling him everything anymore either. He wondered what they had in the rumal this time. Loose change? He looked around the ashram, but saw no sign of the minister. Maybe he had done his job and left.

"She loved it," said one of the followers.

Ban Sar Din reached into his pocket. No cloth. He looked at the upturned faces of his followers. The crazies were going to kill him if he didn't have a fresh rumal. Maybe strangle him with their bare hands.

"We await, Holy One," said the kid from Indianapolis who had taken to calling himself the phansigar. There were several of them now.

"Right. Waiting," said Ban Sar Din. "Waiting is perhaps the fullest way of service to our holy Kali."

"Did you forget the rumal?" asked the kid from Indianapolis.

"Forgetting is a form of worship. Why does one remember? That is the question we must all ask ourselves," said the pudgy little man. He felt sweat forming in his underpants, and his mouth was dry. He tried to smile. If he smiled, they might not think he was getting ready to run for it.

He made a sign of blessing he had seen somewhere. Oh, no. It was the sign of the cross, and he carefully did the motions again, backward, as if erasing his previous moves.

"Thus Kali erases false doctrine," he said unctuously. If he ran for it, could he get away? he wondered.

"You have forgotten the rumal, the holy blessed rumal with which we serve Her," said the yellow-haired girl from Denver. She was the one who frightened him most. He had gathered indirectly that she loved the death throes even more than the male followers did.

"Let us all praise Kali now," said Ban Sar Din. He backed toward the door. If he could get a jump on these crazy white kids, he might make it into the alley and then out of New Orleans. He could always lose weight and pick pockets again. And even if he failed, there was always jail. At least, he would still be alive. It was an incredibly appealing thought.

Ban Sar Din's little legs began running toward the thought before he could stop them. They were moving, and moving fast.

They were not fast enough.

Hands had his ankles, his arms, and he knew his throat was next. He felt his legs still going through the motions of running, but he was not going where he wanted to go. He was being carried to the base of that statue, which apparently was a new one, because it had more arms now than when he bought it. This was religion out of control, he thought, and somebody ought to do something about it.

"Kali. Kali." The chants began, first as two screams, then as drumrolls, and the feet began hitting the floor and the whole ashram building shook with the chant of Kali. Kali the divine. Kali the death giver. Kali the invincible, goddess of death.

The floor shook underneath his back from the stomping, and his fingers grew numb because his wrists were being held so tightly. He could smell the floor wax and feel the fingertips of young worshipers dig into his ankles.

The chant continued: "Kali. Kali."

It occurred to Ban Sar Din at that moment that if he heard the chants and smelled the floor wax and felt the pounding of feet, he was still alive. And if there was one thing he knew about the cult of Kali, it was that they never did the chanting before a death. It was always *after* a death had occurred. Of course, he did not know all that much about the cult. He had only bought the statue and given the white kids some Indian names.

Ban Sar Din felt something funny on the soles of his feet. At first it tickled.

"Please don't torture me," he cried out. "Have mercy."

"It's kissing," said the phansigar from Indianapolis.

Bar Sar Din opened his eyes. He saw lots of yellow hair near his feet.

"Head north," he said.

"It is so. It is ever so," said the yellow-haired girl. "He does not have the rumal."

"If you say so," said Ban Sar Din.

"We were told you wouldn't," she said.

"Who told you? Get him out of here, whoever he is," said Ban Sar Din. "What does he know?"

They were all looking down at him. He pulled his feet away from the yellow-haired girl and rose. He pulled his upper tunic tighter around his body.

"Do you have the rumal for us?" asked one youth.

"Why do you ask?"

"Tell us you don't. Please," said the blond girl. Tears of joy filled her eyes.

"All right. Since you asked, I don't. Now, step back. Holy men don't like to be crowded."

"Kali the grand. Kali the eternal. Kali victorious," chanted three young men. Their feet began stomping on the wooden floor of the ashram.

"Right," said Ban Sar Din. "I am going to get another rumal. I knew that this time I shouldn't bring one."

"She told us. And we knew," said Holly Rodan.

"Only the Holy One should predict and know," said Ban Sar Din as he looked around at the cult members. No one seemed to object, so he repeated it with more force. "Only one should predict."

"She did. She did," repeated Holly Rodan. "She said that two must be brought before Her. He who has not the rumal will be the Holy One, the leader. And that one is you."

"And the one who has the rumal?" Ban Sar Din asked.

"He will be Her lover. And we will send him to Her in death," Holly Rodan said. "And that one is not you," she said. The blond-haired girl smiled at Ban Dar Sin. "Do you not wonder who that one is?"

"The Holy One never wonders," Ban Sar Din said, wondering what she was talking about.

"Did you not notice that we are now fewer?" Holly Rodan asked him.

The pudgy Indian looked around. There were two faces missing. What had happened to them? Probably they took off for some other wacko cult.

"Here today, gone tomorrow," he said. "Lots of people leave for fly-by-night cults, and we are well rid of them. We just have to make sure that they don't leave with the offerings in the rumals. Kali needs our offerings. It's part of our faith, faith of our fathers, now and certainly through November," he said, thinking of the disconnect notice of the electricity.

"No. They did not leave. They were faithful. They tasted death. It was beautiful. Never have we seen death so strong, death so quick, death so powerful," said Holly Rodan.

"Wait a minute. You mean we lost people to death?" asked Ban Sar Din.

"Long live death. Long live Kali," said the girl. "We have met the great one, the one She wants. We have met Her lover. And we will bring him to Her and he will be carrying the rumal."

Ban Sar Din took the yellow handkerchief that was shoved into his hands and left to go back into his office.

Over the edge, he thought. They had gone over the edge. It was one thing to kill for some statue with too many arms, but to talk about bringing Her some lover to die for Her, well, that was just too much. He broke out in a sweat when he realized that he had been only a yellow handkerchief away from being the one.

The pudgy pickpocket was thinking of packing and leaving when he opened the rumal and noticed the very thick roll of green bills. There was twenty-three hundred dollars in cash. There were four rings. Were they combining robberies now? Then he noticed that all the rings were for large fingers. There was a gold Rolex watch with a diamond-studded sweep second hand. There was a lapis-lazuli cocaine case with gold-inlaid initials, TVW, and a pearl-handled automatic pistol.

The reverend. They had killed the Reverend Tee Vee Walker.

Ban Sar Din would have run if he hadn't counted the bills again. Over two thousand dollars. And inside the roll of bills was an airline ticket.

He thought at first that it was one of the Just Folks cheapo tickets, but this was a first-class round-trip ticket to Stockholm, Sweden. Inside was a note with perfumed stationery. It read: "From your grateful congregation to the Reverend Tee Vee Walker."

On the inside of the ticket was another handwriting, much rougher and less refined. Ban Sar Din guessed that it was Reverend Walker's own writing. He had apparently jotted down something he didn't want to miss in Stockholm: "Madame Olga's House of One Thousand Pleasures."

Ban Sar Din looked at the ticket for a long time. He could use it to flee, but something told him not to. Some inner voice said the ticket was a gift and an opportunity, not to be wasted.

He wrapped the ticket in one of the old rumals with the Kali picture on it, the ones you couldn't buy for a decent price anymore, and went out into the ashram and placed it in one of the statue's many hands. The followers would know what to do.

Three days later, the rumal came back with

$4,383.47. Plus jewelry. Real jewelry. And Ban Sar Din learned a new lesson about economic success. You had to spend money to make money.

No more consumer flights. No more semischeduled airlines. From now on, first-class flights.

He called Just Folks Airlines and canceled his special year-round consumer fare with the free-use-of-the-bathroom option and the offseason three a.m. Anchorage to Tallahassee fare and told them where to send the refund.

## Number 109.

Comedienne Beatrice Bixby found someone who really thought she was funny. She found him next to her in first class headed to Stockholm, Sweden. He was not interested in her body or her fame or her money. He really gave Beatrice what she had always sought on the stage, approval. Everything she said was either brilliant or hysterically funny.

"I'm not that funny," she said, not meaning a word of it. She was as funny as she had always dreamed of being. When the young man invited her to stop off at a little restaurant and then later suggested they go someplace quiet, and then asked a simple favor about a handkerchief, she said:

"Of course. And if it's going around my neck, you can put diamonds in the handkerchief too." She waited for the laugh.

But he wasn't laughing anymore. And soon, neither was she.

# Seven

Dr. Harold W. Smith got the one answer he had always feared from Remo. It was two letters, one word, and the word was "No."

He had gotten a secure telephone hookup to call Remo from the CURE headquarters, which were hidden behind the large brick walls that surrounded Folcroft Sanitarium in Rye, New York. It had been many years ago that Remo had been brought to the sanitarium from the morgue of the prison and nursed back to life and to health and then to something more. He had been chosen by Smith because all the tests had shown that Remo's basic character would not let him fail to serve his country.

And now Harold Smith was getting that first "no" to a call for help.

"It's gone international," Smith said.

"Fine. Then America's safe."

"We can't let something like this go on," Smith said.

"Well, we are, aren't we?"

"What's wrong with you, Remo?"

"Maybe there are a lot of things that are wrong."

"Would you like to tell me about them?" Smith asked in what he tried to project as his warm voice. It sounded like ice cubes cracking in warm water.

"No," Remo said.

"Why not?"

"You wouldn't understand."

"I think I could," Smith said.

"I think you couldn't."

"That's it?"

"It," agreed Remo.

"Remo, we need you," Smith said.

"No," said Remo.

For the first time since Remo had gone out for the organization, Smith was forced to go to Chiun for an explanation. It was not something he relished, because he seldom understood the old Oriental. The only things he was ever sure of was that he was being forced to send more money to the old man's village in North Korea. Remo had explained to him once that the village of Sinanju was poor and that for centuries its people had lived on the earnings of the Master of Sinanju, the world's foremost assassin.

There had been many bad times, and in those times, Remo explained, the villagers had been forced to "send their babies home to the sea." This meant to throw them in the bay to drown rather than letting them starve to death. Remo felt it explained Chiun's insistence on large payment, frequent payment, and payment in gold, and seemed to think that it was a beautiful story.

Smith thought that it was basically stupid and that all the villagers had to do to prevent starvation was to find a job somewhere and work for a living. Remo told him that he should never mention this idea to Chiun, and Smith never did. The infrequent meetings of the two men generally degenerated into Chiun's fawning all over Smith as America's emperor and then proceeding to do exactly what Chiun wanted.

Not this time, Smith thought. He had to find out what was wrong with Remo. The meeting with Chiun was imperative, but where to meet someone in a kimono without attracting attention, someone who, for some insane reason, had blatantly taken out an advertisement in a Boston newspaper with his picture in it?

He thought about it a long while, then decided to fly out to Denver. He rented a car at the airport, picked Chiun up at his hotel, and drove off into the Rocky Mountains outside Denver. It was the best he could think of. And Smith was tired. And he was wondering if it all made a difference anymore. Maybe Remo was right.

Looking at the first snows on the peaks, Smith wondered if all he was trying to do, all the struggles and organization, were not just like those mountains. The problems were here today, and like the mountains, they would be here tomorrow. Nothing had been lost, but what had been won? He had been at this for twenty years and he was getting old and tired. Who would replace him? And would it make a difference? Could anything make a difference anymore?

He saw Chiun's long fingernails reach over and appear as though they moved a button on Smith's chest.

"Breathe as if a melon is stuck in your throat," Chiun said. "As if you must force the air into your stomach. Hard."

Smith, without understanding why, complied and pulled air deep into his body, and suddenly things felt light. The world was light. Problems were solvable. This sudden change unsettled Smith. He was a man who ran everything by his intellect, and he did not want to believe that his perspective on the world could alter because of the way he took oxygen into his system. And yet it hadn't changed. He knew everything he knew before, all the problems and worries. It was just that he felt stronger, more able to deal with them, less tired of the world.

"Chiun, you have trained Remo magnificently."

"A reflection of your glory, O Emperor."

"We are, as you know, engaged in an operation yet to be completed," Smith said.

"How wise," Chiun said, and nodded, and his beard fluttered in the breezeless car. He was not sure what Smith had said. He assumed that he had just stated that they were all working on something, but Chiun never knew with Smith. He never quite understood him, so he nodded a lot.

"Remo seems to be having troubles," Smith said. "Do you know what they are?"

"I know that he, like I, lives to serve your wish and enhance the glory of the name Smith, greatest of Emperors."

"Yes, yes. Of course. But have you noticed something bothering him?"

"I have. I must admit, I have. But it is nothing that your glory should concern itself with."

"It does concern me," Smith said.

"How noble. Your grace knows no bounds."

"What is bothering him?"

"As you know," Chiun began, "the yearly tribute is delivered to Sinanju, as was agreed in our contract of service. Your submarine delivers onshore a seventeen-weight of silver, a five-weight of gold, and fragrances of great value."

"Yes, that's the contract," said Smith suspiciously. "Since the last time you renegotiated it. What's that got to do with Remo?"

"Remo's adoration for you, Emperor, is so strong that he cannot bring himself to share with you his true worries. He said to me: 'Gracious Master, teacher of Sinanju, devoted servant of our great Emperor, Harold W. Smith, how can I rest my head knowing that a five-weight of gold is all that comes from my country to Sinanju? How can we be so disgraced as a race and a people to give a paltry five-weight of gold and a mere seventeen-weight of silver?'

" 'Still your tongue,' I said. 'Has not Emperor Smith through these many years delivered the correct amount? Have we not agreed to this amount? Is it not according to the contract?'

" 'Indeed, noble teacher, true servant of the Emperor Smith,' Remo said, 'it *is* according to the contract and I should still my tongue.'

"And this he did," said Chiun. "But the hurt remains. I tell you this only because of my great trust in you."

"Somehow, I can't see Remo worrying about Sinanju's yearly tribute," Smith said.

"It is not that. It is the honor of his nation. And yours."

"I don't think Remo's mind works like that," Smith said. "Not even after all your training."

"You asked, Emperor, and I but told. I await your command."

Smith could easily add more gold to the payment. The cost of having a submarine enter North Korean waters to deliver the tribute to the house of assassins far exceeded the tribute itself. But the problem with giving Chiun more money for a special emergency, as this was, was that it became the new base price for everything else in the future.

"Another weight of gold," said Smith reluctantly.

"Would that it were enough for Remo's heavy heart," Chiun said. "But in my foolishness, I told him that even a small king in a small poor country paid a ten-weight of gold to Sinanju."

"Seven," said Smith.

"It is not seemly that a servant argue with his emperor," Chiun said.

"Does that mean that seven is acceptable? That we have a deal at seven?" Smith asked.

"It means I dare not negotiate with you."

"You're standing at ten?" Smith asked.

"I am yours to command. As always," Chiun said.

"Eight."

"If only I could convince Remo."

"I know he isn't going to serve any other country," Smith said. "He isn't that much Sinanju yet."

"I only follow your will," Chiun said calmly. His hands were folded and he looked out at the mountains.

"Nine. And that's it."

"For this special emergency, your will overrules the very tides," Chiun said.

"Something is wrong with Remo," Smith said again, "and we need him. This danger has just gotten worse, and he's not willing to do anything about it."

"It will be done," Chiun said.

"What will?"

"What is needed to be done," Chiun said, and such was the authority of his voice and the grace of his body and movements that Smith, at that moment, believed him. Why not? This was Sinanju, and it had not survived for thousands of years because these people did not know their business.

"Did Remo tell you what this case is all about?" Smith asked.

"In his halting way," Chiun answered. "He is only eloquent when speaking about injustices done to my village."

"Someone is killing people who fly aboard aircraft. Now, you might think the number of deaths small—"

Smith did not get a chance to finish the sentence because Chiun spoke first.

"The deaths themselves are unimportant. Robbers and murderers do not make roads unsafe or impassable. They kill only a few at worst. What makes a road

impassable is that people believe it is. If travelers come
to believe they cannot move with safety, they will cease
to use your roads. And this country's roads are in the
sky."

"It is a danger," Smith agreed.

"More than a danger," said the Master of Sinanju.
"It is the end of civilization. Goods would not travel,
and neither would ideas."

"We've just been lucky so far that the news media
haven't picked up on it," Smith said. "Do you think
you can get Remo to understand why this is
important?"

Chiun said, "I will try, Emperor," but he did not
know if he could. However, he did know he would not
be the one to let this civilization die, because he was the
Master of Sinanju who had been contracted to save it.
Failing would be too much shame to bear and would
humiliate him in the eyes of all the ancestors who had
gone before.

Chiun would have to tell Remo something that he
had hidden for all these years. He would have to tell
him about the shame of Sinanju, about Master Wu,
who lost Rome.

And then he would have to find out exactly what was
bothering Remo.

A. H. Baynes liked to run a tight ship, and his staff
had standing orders to show him any paperwork that
was out of the ordinary. So when the request was
received in the mail asking for a refund on the year-
round consumer-fare ticket, he thought it was worth
looking into. It was the only year-round consumer-fare
ticket that had been sold by Just Folks, and he looked
at the letter and saw it had been bought by a small
religious community in New Orleans.

He instructed his New Orleans area manager to find
out why the refund was being sought.

A week later, the area manager had not been heard from. When his paycheck remained uncashed, this strange incident came up on Baynes's computer terminal.

For the first time, Baynes noticed the area manager's name, and wondered where he had seen it before. He checked it with his computer and found out.

The area manager had advised him once by note that he was going to track the stranglings just in case anyone tried to sue Just Folks Airlines for the deaths.

Baynes was about to put it out of his mind and forget it when his attention was called to a news clipping. The area manager's body had been found. His face was blue from the last horrible moments without air, his pockets had been emptied. He left five — his wife, three children, and an ailing mother.

Another murder, and there had been nine others in the past few weeks of people who had not been flying Just Folks. Quietly, Baynes programmed his computer to find out who had purchased tickets on overseas flights after which passengers had been strangled and robbed.

On every flight after which there had been a murder, Baynes saw the name of the same ticket purchaser: it was the little religious group in New Orleans that had just asked for a refund on its Just Folks tickets.

It was immediately clear to Baynes. He had found the passenger killers. It was someone connected with that religious group. And what they had done was equally clear: first they had flown Just Folks, killing passengers. And then they had moved up in the world, flying bigger and more expensive airlines, and killing and robbing richer passengers. Since the first death involving an overseas airline, there had been no more murders of Just Folks's passengers.

He felt exultant. He had figured it out, and those

two idiotic investigators from the NAA were still out there somewhere flying Just Folks, and they hadn't figured out anything yet. So much for free enterprise versus government, he thought.

For a moment he considered letting the government know of his findings immediately, and then he paused and considered some more. He certainly wasn't going to rush toward some public acclaim before thinking everything through. He had not gone to Cambridge Business College so that he could forget its most important lesson: how can I make some profit out of this?

He phoned the ashram in New Orleans and asked to speak to its spiritual leader.

"We are most sorry. The Holy One cannot answer the telephone. He is communing in his holy office."

"Tell the Holy One that if he doesn't commune with me on the phone, he'll be communing with the police in person. I know what you people are doing to airline passengers."

"Hello," came the high-pitched voice of an Indian a few moments later. "How can the blessings of cosmic unity be bestowed upon your consciousness?"

"I know what you're doing with airline passengers," Baynes said.

"We bless the whole world with our mantras."

"I don't want your blessings," Baynes said.

"Have a mantra. No charge. I'll give you a free one over the phone and call it even."

"I want to know how you do what you do," Baynes said.

"Dear kind sir," said Ban Sar Din. "If I should be doing something of an illegal nature, I certainly would not discuss it over the telephone."

"And I certainly wouldn't put my neck within grasp of any of you people."

"Stalemate," said Ban Sar Din.

"The police can probably break the stalemate," Baynes said.

"We fear no police. We serve the cult of Kali," Ban Sar Din said.

"A religious thing?" Baynes said.

"Yes."

"Then you don't pay taxes. Everything above overhead is profit."

"How American to think of money in connection with holy work," said Ban Sar Din.

"How Indian to turn holy work into murder," said Baynes. "Do you know the number of the New Orleans police? Save me a dime."

A compromise was struck. Baynes would come to New Orleans and he would meet Ban Sar Din, alone, in a public restaurant, and they would talk.

Agreed. "Travel safely," Ban Sar Din said.

"You better believe it. I'm flying Delta," said Baynes.

In the restaurant, Baynes got right down to business: "Your gang is killing travelers so they can rob them."

And Ban Sar Din, who recognized a kindred spirit when he encountered one, said, "You think this is easy? You don't know what the hell I've been living with. These people are nuts. They don't care about anything except a statue I have in the ashram."

"They're your people, aren't they? They call you the Holy One."

"I can't control them. They don't care about money, they don't care about living well, or even, damn it, about living. All they want to do is kill."

"Why do you hang around, then?" Baynes asked.

"I do make a small profit, a living so to speak, sir," said Ban Sar Din.

"You mean you have people who will go out and kill

for you, risk their lives for you, take money off corpses, and give it all to you."

"I guess you could say that," said Ban Sar Din. "But it is not all as rosy as it might seem to be."

"Ban Sar Din, you now have a partner."

"Someone tried that before. He said he was going to yell in their faces, and now he has earth in his face," said the Indian.

"I'm not him," said A. H. Baynes.

"You're going to get killed."

Baynes gave him a tolerant smile.

"How much of the take do you want?" Ban Sar Din asked.

"It's all yours."

"You mean we're partners, but I get to keep all the money?"

"Yes. And I'll provide the plane tickets for your people too," said Baynes.

"Okay, partner," said Ban Sar Din.

The next day, fifteen thousand dollars' worth of first-class airline tickets arrived by courier pack. They were all for one airline, International Mid-America, a medium-size carrier that served the Midwest and South America.

At first, Ban Sar Din thought that Baynes must have gotten some incredibly reduced rate, but then, something on the tickets appeared odd. None of them had a name written in. Were they stolen? Was that why the American executive had given them to him free? A thing to think about, reflected the Indian.

He heard the chanting out in the ashram. He knew he had to go out there and pass out the handkerchiefs soon. They were beginning their frenzy.

Ban Sar Din had always lived in fear that one day the chanting would stop and they would come into his office after him. When he had forgotten the handkerchief the other day, he had thought he was done for. But it had all worked out for the best. Somehow Kali had told them—who could believe these American kids?—that since Ban Sar Din didn't have the rumal on him, he was the Holy One. The one who came with the rumal was going to be Kali's lover. Which was another word for dead. All in all, it had worked out well. He was stronger than ever in the ashram.

He stood up, ready to take some of the tickets outside, but stopped. Something was wrong with a stack of first-class airplane tickets as high as a phone book, and all without the purchasers' names.

He phoned International Mid-American Airlines, IMAA.

"I have some tickets that I think were stolen," he said.

"Just a minute, sir."

The chanting from the ashram grew louder. He could feel the walls hum with the name of Kali, and he could hear the joyous, almost orgasmic frenzy of the young people. Even his desk calendar was jumping. If they weren't all crazies, he would have liked to join them. But they might turn on him. Who knew with these people?

He watched his calendar jump and vowed that when he could afford it, he would line the walls and doors of his office with steel, put in a lock that could stop a tank, and build a secret rear exit to the alley and keep a very fast car parked outside. He would not necessarily have the motor running.

He heard a pounding on his door and changed his mind about the motor running.

IMAA finally came up with the right person. No, those tickets had not been stolen. They had been purchased the day before for cash. No, they did not know the name of the purchaser. Yes, anyone who had such a ticket could use it.

"Thank you," said Ban Sar Din, and stuffed two round-trip first-class tickets into two yellow handkerchiefs. He had the tickets, why not use them? At least it would keep the crazies busy a little longer.

They were thumping on his office door. He opened the door and with a flourish of his holy robes ducked the knocking motion of one of the followers and strode out in the ashram. He thought it was a bit crowded today. That accounted for the extra strength of the chanting.

Was the cult growing? Ordinarily, when he presented the sacred rumal, there were, at most, seven kneeling before him. Today there were closer to fifteen. There were faces he didn't recognize. Older people. Younger people. He was happy he had thought to bring double handkerchiefs and double tickets. He spoke in the Gondi tongue as he normally did and told them that Kali was proud of them but that She was hungry for Her offerings.

But before he had a chance to tell them that this day he had brought twice the normal instruments for the offerings, two phansigars presented themselves for the rumals.

"She knew. She knew. She knew," chanted the followers.

Ban Sar Din only nodded knowingly. Then he got out of there fast.

**Numbers 120, 121, 122.**

The Walford family was taking its first vacation trip outside the country and they found that international travel was more problem than pleasure, at least when they needed help with the baggage. IMAA personnel were absolutely worthless, they thought. Fortunately, some decent young people were there not only to help them but also to give them a lift to Acapulco.

\* \* \*

**Number 123.**

Deeter Jackson was the only man ever to be selected by the Grain Society of Troy, Ohio, to visit the Argentina Feed and Utility Show with all expenses paid. Of course, he didn't expect someone as lovely as the passenger next to him on the IMAA flight to be interested in that. But not only was that beautiful young woman interested, she said she wanted to visit Troy, Ohio. It had always held a fascination for her. Maybe Deeter could take some time and tell her all about it. In her hotel room in Argentina.

**Number 124.**

Mrs. Pruella Nascento thought that if IMAA charged so much for a first-class seat, the least they could do was coddle an egg properly.

"She's right," a passenger across the way told the stewardess. "I hope you don't mind my butting in. But I think that I just wouldn't want to fly again in an airplane where they can't even coddle an egg correctly."

Mrs. Pruella Nascento did not mind the passenger butting in. She was found dead along a roadside the next morning and the time of her death was fixed at one-half hour after she left the aircraft. The coroner could tell because the yolk of the egg had been only partially decomposed by her stomach acid.

**Number 125.**

Vincent Palmer Grout did not speak to strangers on airplanes, did not like to discuss his business, did not even politely answer inquiries about his opinion of the weather. There was always some kind of weather and Vincent Palmer Grout saw no need to discuss this fact with strangers.

Oh, well, somebody was willing to give him a lift into

the city? Well, he would accept that, if the person did not presume to be too friendly.

When they asked if they could put a handerchief around his throat, he said, "Absolutely not. Who knows where it's been?"

When they did so anyhow, he became enraged and he would have given them a piece of his mind, but he couldn't very well talk if he couldn't get air into his throat, could he?

**Number 126.**

Who said there still weren't nice young people in the world who cared about the elderly and were willing to help also?

**Number 127.**

"Are you from Dayton too? Really?"

**Number 128.**

"I collect watch chimes. Wife doesn't think anybody else in the world would be interested in watch chimes. Boy, will she be surprised."

Ban Sar Din was ecstatic. The rumals were coming back stuffed with money and jewels. Better airlines produced better passengers, and better passengers produced better corpses with fuller wallets. He still did not know what was in it for A. H. Baynes, but he knew what was in it for him. It was only the best restaurants from now on.

He ordered nylon-reinforced rumals and he insisted on a full four-color picture of Kali on each one. He even ordered two gross, just in case, and threw out the old cheap ones.

He had contractors set steel plates around his office, install double-bolt locks, and cut in that secret exit

door to the alley, where he parked his new Porsche
911SC.

A newspaper reporter at a wire service got a telephone
call late one night, just before he was ready to go
home.

"I have got the greatest story of your career. How
would you like to hear about multiple murders, ritual
murders? Huh? Is that a news story?"

"Who's this?"

"Someone who wants to help."

"I can't just take information over the phone. Who
are you?"

"Someone who can tell you where to look. There
have been a dozen murders recently. All of the victims
had just gotten off an International Mid-America Airlines flight. All strangled after they left their airplanes.
It's the airline of death. Do you hear me?"

"How do you know this? Why haven't I heard of it?"

"Because reporters cover a murder here and a
murder there and they don't know it's one story. Now
you do. One story. Many murders, all the same." And
the caller gave the cities the deaths had occurred in.

"How do you know?" asked the reporter, but the
caller hung up.

The next day, every newspaper on the wire-service
line carried the story. IMAA became the Airline of
Death. By the time the television news department got
through with the story, a viewer got the impression that
to fly on IMAA meant certain death by strangulation.

Reservations were canceled as people switched to
other airlines. IMAA flew half-full flights, then
quarter-full flights, then empty planes.

Then IMAA stopped flying at all.

It took two days, and in Folcroft Sanitarium, behind
the one-way glass shielding him from the untidy outside world, Harold W. Smith knew that what had

happened to IMAA could happen to every airline in America. Every airline in the world.

So did the President of the United States.

"What's happening?" he asked over the special red telephone line that ran from the White House directly to Smith's office.

"We're on it," answered Smith.

"Do you know what this means?" asked the President.

"I do know, sir."

"What am I supposed to tell the heads of the South American countries? What about Europe? They know what it means too. If it spreads, are we going to close the airways to passenger travel? I don't care what you do. I don't care if you're exposed and have to go under, stop this. Stop it now."

"We're working on it."

"You sound like an auto mechanic," said the President disgustedly.

Smith held the red phone in his hand and stared out through his windows at Long Island Sound. It was a dark autumn day and storm warnings were up for all the boats. He put that phone away and took another and tried to reach Remo. He got Chiun instead.

Chiun was in the hotel room, and with relief Smith heard him say that Remo had not only been told about the serious problem but also now understood its magnitude and had come around again. Both he and Chiun were very close to putting the perpetrators out of business, all for the glory of Emperor Smith.

"Thank God," Harold W. Smith said, and hung up.

Across the country in a Denver hotel room, Chiun gave a formal little bow to the telephone and set out to find Remo. Not only had he not spoken to Remo, he had not even seen him for a week. But he knew he could make him understand.

For now he was prepared to tell him of the greatest

failure in the history of Sinanju, and he was not going to see it repeated here in a little 200-year-old country, doomed even before it began to grow up.

# Eight

Remo saw the snow of the Rockies and did not care. He sat in a lodge by a fireplace and did not answer questions about what he did for a living or if he liked Vail this year of if he preferred Snow Bird in Utah. One of the young women flocking around him mentioned that she hadn't seen his skis.

"I ski barefoot," he said.

"Are you being insulting?" she asked.

"Trying my best," Remo said.

"I think that's cute," she said. She gave no sign of leaving, so Remo got up, left the fire and left the lodge, and began walking in the snow. It was a sun-crisp day in the Rockies and the autumn snows had begun and the world was alive, so incredibly alive.

And there were people out there who welcomed death. Young people. Killing happily and dying happily, in some nightmare of a world.

He saw skiers use the edges of their skies to turn, the better ones in tighter control, knowing that when they put pressure on the edge of the downhill ski, the skis would turn. But what would they do, thought Remo, if they cut with their downhill ski and there was no turn? Like him, with those crazies off the Just Folks Airlines. Everything he had been trained for, things that had become instinctive, suddenly were no longer useful. It was like leaning on a downhill ski but not turning.

He paused to think about that and squatted in the snow and idly let the fresh powder sift through his fingers. He had met religious fanatics before and he had killed them when he had to without even a look back. He had fought and killed political zealots, maniacs who were sure their cause was right to the point of death.

Why was it different this time? What was it that had stopped him from simply killing that little bubble-headed blond girl and closing the book on that particular assassination squad?

He didn't know the answer, but he knew he had done the right thing outside of Raleigh-Durham airport. Somehow, he knew, it would have done no good to finish off that girl. She really did love death. So did the two young men he killed. They all loved death. And something inside Remo was all knotted up and he knew he could not give them all the death that they lusted for. Some reason, some instinct, something stopped him. And he didn't know what it was.

He headed across the slopes, past warning signs of deep powder and unmarked trails. He wore a light jacket but did not need it. He knew the temperature was low; he did not feel the cold as pain but instead as something that automatically made his body generate its own heat. Everyone's body could do the same thing if it were trained properly. In bed, it was never a blanket that made heat; it only kept in the heat that was made by the body. Remo could do the same thing, but he didn't need a blanket. His blanket was his skin, and he used his skin the way all men did before they invented clothing.

This was Remo's explanation to himself of why Sinanju worked; it harnessed all those vestigial powers in the animal body, all the powers that man had let die, and the ability to do that was the major accomplishment of an ancient house of assassins from a village on a west Korean bay.

It was colder now and Remo walked into deep snow and his body began to swim through it, without his knowing it, moving like a fish, a shark of the airy snow. His mouth breathed in the air in the snow and it tasted of the fresh pure oxygen no longer found in the cities. He lost track of time. It was perhaps only minutes, or maybe hours, before he was out of the snow, standing on rocks, and then he found the place. It was a small cave, an opening in the great stone mountain, and when he entered, he realized he was retreating from everything.

And there he sat, his body quieted, waiting for his mind to work out for itself just what was going on.

He had sat for several days when he heard movement outside the cave. It was not the sound of feet compressing snow, but a pure gliding movement, as soft as a breeze.

"Hello, Little Father," Remo said without looking up.

"Hello," said Chiun.

"How did you know I was here?"

"I knew where your body would take you when you were frightened."

"I'm not frightened," Remo said.

"I did not mean fear of being hurt or being killed," Chiun said. "I meant another kind of fear."

"I don't know what is going on, Chiun. All I know is I don't like it and I don't understand it." He looked up at Chiun for the first time and he was smiling. "You know how you're always saying we should leave this country and go to work for this king or that shah, and I've always said no because I believe in my country the way you believe in your village?"

"Not the village. The village is just where the House of Sinanju is," Chiun corrected. "The house. The house is what we are and what we do."

"Whatever," Remo said. "Anyway, let's do it. Let's go to another country. Let's just pick up and go."

"No. We must stay," Chiun said.

"I knew it," Remo said with a sigh. "All these years, you've just been waiting for me to say 'go,' so you could say 'stay.' Right?"

"No," said Chiun, sitting down in the cave, spreading his thin white winter robe beneath him. "Today we stay not for your foolish loyalty to this foolish country. We stay for Sinanju. We stay because we must not let it happen again."

"Let what happen again?" Remo said.

"You have heard of your Western empire, Rome?"

"Sure. It conquered the world once."

"How white of you to think of it that way. Only the white world was conquered by Rome, and not even all of that."

"All right, all right. It was still the greatest empire the world has ever known."

"For whites," Chiun said. "But I have not told you about . . . about Lu the Disgraced."

"Was he a Roman emperor?" Remo asked.

Chiun shook his head. The wisp of beard hardly moved in the icy chill cave, where no wind cut or sun entered.

"A Master of Sinanju," Chiun said.

"I know all the Masters of Sinanju. You made me learn them and I never heard of this Lulu."

"Would that I never had to tell you of Lu the Disgraced."

"I take it he screwed up," Remo said, and Chiun nodded.

Remo said, "No reason to keep him a secret. Sometimes you can learn more from what's wrong than from what's right."

"I did not tell you because you did not have to know. I did not tell you because you might mention his name one day to someone."

"Who would care?" asked Remo. "I care, but who else would care?"

"Whites would care," said Chiun. "Whites would never forget. They are a treacherous gang, just waiting for Sinanju to fail."

"Little Father," Remo said patiently, "they don't care."

"They do," Chiun said.

"No," said Remo. "The line of assassins of Sinanju is not exactly a major study course at American universities."

"Rome is. The fall of that empire is," Chiun said.

"What are you getting at?"

"Rome fell because we failed it. Sinanju failed Rome. Lu the Disgraced failed Rome."

He folded his long-nailed hands in front of him as he often did when about to begin a lecture. Remo clasped his hands behind his head and leaned back against the cold wet rock wall of the cave.

As Chiun began to tell it, he slowly started slipping into the familiar phrases of old Korean, the language of the older legends with its sharper cadences.

He related how Sinanju had discovered the Romans many centuries before their prime and marked them as a coming civilization, although in those matters no one ever really knew. So much was left to chance, and this was the way of nations too. The only sure thing about kingdoms and empires was that they came and they went.

Still, the Masters of Sinanju put Rome on their list as a place worth watching, because if it grew and prospered, its emperors would want assassins to prolong their reign, and that was the business of the Masters of Sinanju.

Finally, in the year of the pig, Rome was growing. It had two consuls who ruled together, and one, because of vanity, wished to rule alone. So it came to pass that he employed a Master of the House of Sinanju and paid him, and soon he ruled alone.

Thus Rome became an important city, and often, when there was no call for their work among more civilized courts, Masters of Sinanju would journey to Rome and visit the Western city where people had strange eyes and big noses.

Now, it happened that Lu, in the 650th year since the founding of the city of Rome, which was roughly A.D. 100 by Remo's calendar, came to that city. Rome had changed. There was an emperor now, and the games, once small religious festivals, were now filling giant arenas. Men fought animals. Men fought men. Spears and swords and tigers. So great was their lust that the Romans could not see enough blood.

But because they did not respect life, they could not appreciate a professional assassin. Death was just death to them, nothing special, so there was no work for Lu.

Yet, Chiun related, it came to pass that the emperor heard of the one from the East and wished to see his eyes and his manner, and Lu appeared before him. The emperor asked what weapons Lu used, and Lu answered that the emperor never asked his sculptor what chisel he used or his carpenter what lathe.

"Do you kill with your funny eyes?" asked the emperor.

Lu knew that this was a new land, and so he did not show the disdain he felt. He answered, "One can kill with a thought, Emperor." The emperor thought this empty boasting, but his adviser, a Greek, who were at that time smarter than the Romans, although, Chiun said, it is now a tie for who is stupidest in the world, spoke to Lu and said that Rome had a problem.

The problem was with Rome's roads, Lu was told. Rome used them to move legions around the empire, to allow farmers to bring goods to market. The roads were the lifeblood of the empire, this adviser said, and Lu nodded. Masters of Sinanju had already noted that there was only one permanent truth about the prosperity of an empire. With roads, they flourished; without roads, they didn't.

Chiun now pointed out to Remo in the cave of the Rocky Mountains that China's great wall was no wall. The Chinese, Chiun said, are slothful perverts, but they have never been fools. They never thought that a wall would stop an army. It never had and never would. The secret of the Great Wall of China that no one understood these days was that it was not a wall at all. It was a road.

Remo remembered seeing pictures of it. Of course it was a road. It was a raised road, for moving armies and goods. People only called it a wall because they felt safer behind walls, although Remo knew that walls were only illusions of safety.

The Roman emperor's adviser told Lu: "We have bandits on our roads. We crucify them by the roadways so that will serve as a reminder to others not to rob again."

"Do they rob much?" Lu asked.

"What they rob is not important. That they rob at all is. It is the fear of the people we are concerned with. If they fear the roads, if they fear to travel, they will begin to mint their own coins, they will begin to withhold crops."

"But it is not a problem yet," said Lu, who could not help but notice that these barbarians with the big noses had floors of marble as fine as any Ming emperor had ever had.

"The best time to solve a problem is at the beginning," said the adviser. "The robbers know that only a few will be caught and crucified by the roadways. But if something they did not understand was killing them and it was said that it was the will of our divine emperor in Rome, then the robbers would diminish and we could make the roads of Rome truly safe for all."

And to Lu this was wise, so he set forth south toward the city of Herculaneum. Between Brundisium and Herculaneum, he sought out the robber bands and with swift and sure hand dispatched them, even some of them who were in league with local governments. For it happened then, as always, wherever there was money, it could find its way from the robbers to those who were supposed to stop them.

And from Rome the word went out. Divine Claudius had decreed that robbers would die by his will alone. They would suffer in the night the broken neck, the split spine, the crushed skull—all by the emperor's will alone. And none knew that Lu, the Master of Sinanju, was the emperor's secret power.

The sudden terrible deaths were more effective than even crucifixion. Robbers left the roads. Never had the highways been so safe, and travelers and merchants moved along them in confidence, making the empire even stronger and giving an unwarranted reputation for excellence to the fool emperor Claudius. So said Chiun.

And then, just as everything had become successful, the fool Claudius, who was a glutton for the blood arena, wanted more entertainment. He wanted the assassin from far away who was busy protecting the roads of Rome to perform for him.

Now, it is an emperor's right to be a fool, Chiun told Remo. But it is an assassin's everlasting disgrace.

Lu, remembering the fine marble floors and finding

boredom and hot winds between Herculaneum and Brundisium, accepted and did perform for the emperor. And also for the crowds in the arena. In three appearances, he made more than he had before in his entire lifetime, and he left. But not only did he leave Rome, he left behind his vow to protect Rome's roads. "He took material wealth and left," Chiun said.

"I saw Roman jewels in your village," Remo told Chiun.

"Those. And a baggage train of marble for the floors, and gold, of course. Always gold."

"So how did Sinanju cause the fall of the empire?" Remo asked.

"The roads went back to the robbers," Chiun said. "Soon the people knew that, and soon none would travel those roads."

"But Rome didn't end then. It took a few more centuries, didn't it?" Remo said.

"It died then," Chiun said. "It took a few more centuries to fall down, but it became a corpse the day Lu forgot his mission and left."

"But no one blames Sinanju for that," Remo said. "Only you know about it."

"And now you."

"I'm not telling anyone. So Sinanju doesn't have to be blamed for losing an empire at all."

"Blame is blame, but facts are facts. Lu lost Rome. I will not be the Master who loses America," Chiun said.

"What happened to Lu the Lunkhead?" Remo asked.

"Much more happened, but that will be for another time," Chiun said.

Remo rose and looked out at the cold whiteness of the Rockies. The sky was a delicate pale blue, cold, severe, and demanding. It reminded him of the code that bound him to Sinanju and to his duty. He knew he was returning to the battle. He was returning to those people who so unnerved him by their willingness to die. He would do it, but he didn't want to. He just knew he had to.

"What is troubling you?" Chiun asked.

Remo looked at him and said, as Chiun had said of the rest of Lu's story, "That will be for another time."

And Chiun merely smiled and took Remo's arm and led him from the cave.

In the ashram, Kali the goddess, Kali the invincible, stretched out a shining new arm and pushed it forward so that even the worshipers could see she was bringing something to her bosom. But there was nothing in the hand yet.

"He is coming. Her lover is coming," the disciples chanted. And Holly Rodan, the overprivileged child from Denver, was the happiest of all. She knew who the lover would be. She had seen him kill in North Carolina.

"What was he like?" the others asked.

"He had dark hair and dark eyes, and high cheekbones. And he was thin but he had very thick wrists."

"And what else?"

"You should have seen him kill," Holly said.

"Yes?"

"He was . . ." Holly Rodan gasped, her body quivering with memories of that day. " . . . he was wonderful."

# Nine

A. H. Baynes lived in days of honey and sunshine. If he could have whistled or sung or danced on his desk, he would have, but he had not learned any of those techniques at the Cambridge Business School.

What he knew was that the deaths had stopped aboard Just Folks Airlines and that International Mid-America Airlines was as good as dead. Its stock had vanished through the floor of the stock exchange, but Just Folks's was soaring and would go even higher when his new promotional campaign—"Just Folks, the Friendly, Safe Airline"—hit the newspapers in another week.

He thought that he had performed very well, even though, for some reason, his father's image popped into his mind and he knew his father would have called it cheating. "You've always been a smart-ass cheat, A.H."

But the Cambridge Business School philosophy that had directed the industrial thinking of America since the sixties and had remolded the armed forces according to its management systems was something that A. H. Baynes thought his father was ill-equipped to comment on. Daddy had run a little grocery store in Beaumont, Texas, and on his only visit to Cambridge had told A. H. that the school was filled "with a pack of pissants with the morals of rattlers and the brains of cactus weeds."

"Dad is such a card," A. H. had said, trying to laugh it off.

"You pissants don't know bucks and you don't know goods," his father had said again. "You know talk. God help us all."

When Cambridge graduates had redesigned the armed forces along modern management lines, Daddy had said, "There goes the army."

But his father didn't understand that it did not matter that the American military leadership was becoming more comfortable in Bloomingdale's than on the battlefield. That wasn't important. It wasn't part of the new code.

Armies didn't have to win and cars didn't have to run and nothing manufactured had to work to be a success, according to the new code. What had to be ensured was that the graduates of Cambridge Business School were always employed. That was a maximum-priority item and its graduates learned that lesson well.

The days of honey and sunshine that A. H. Baynes now enjoyed were due to that training. But lately he had begun to wonder if maybe there was something else involved. Maybe there was a god and maybe that god had singled him out for special success. And maybe, just maybe, that god had something to do with the ugly multiarmed statue in that storefront church in New Orleans.

Accordingly, one day, the entire A. H. Baynes family, except the dog, showed up at the ashram and presented themselves to Ban Sar Din.

Ban Sar Din did not like their looks. The woman had a mousy face and wore a neat white suit. The boy had on a little green blazer, white shirt, tie. His gray pants were pressed sharp and his black shoes were shined.

The girl wore a white skirt and carried a little white pocketbook.

"This is my family. We want to join your services," A. H. Baynes said. He wore a dark blue suit with a striped red-and-black tie.

"It's not Sunday, Daddy," said the boy.

"Shh," said Mrs. Baynes. "Not everyone worships on a Sunday, dear. There are other places to worship than in a big church."

Ban Sar Din took A. H. Baynes aside. "You're bringing your family into that ashram? Out there?"

"Yes," said Baynes. "I have searched my heart and I find that I wish to be a part of something meaningful and spiritually rewarding. I want to belong to Kali."

"They're crazy killers," hissed Ban Sar Din, louder than he wanted to. "That's your family."

"They're going to kill us, Daddy. They're going to kill us. I don't like it. I want to go to our church," cried the girl.

"Nobody is going to kill us, dear," said Mrs. Baynes soothingly. "Daddy would not permit it."

"He said so," said the girl, pointing to the balloon of a man in his white silk suit. Ban Sar Din blushed.

"Daddy says this is a rewarding faith, dear, and we have to give it a chance," said Mrs. Baynes, and turned to Ban Sar Din to ask if the ashram offered yoga programs, breathing, discussion groups, chanting, and had guest speakers.

Ban Sar Din did not know what else to do, so he nodded forlornly.

"See?" Mrs. Baynes told her children. "It's just like our church at home."

Mrs. Baynes did not mind that there was no minister talking about Jesus or salvation. There hadn't been much talk about that at her church back home for a long time either. Back home, there was usually some revolutionary leader giving a speech against America and then being invited to one of the homes, where if he hadn't talked about overthrowing America, he would not have been allowed in the neighborhood. It didn't matter to Mrs. Baynes, because she never listened to the sermons anyway. One joined a church to be with the sort of people one wanted to be with. These people did not seem to fit that category, but good old A. H. would never let her and the children join a religion that was not socially acceptable.

She heard about some man who was supposed to be coming for the goddess, Kali, to be Her lover. Not at all unlike the Second Coming her other church used to talk about before they got into revolution.

One thing she liked very much was the way this new church referred to God as She.

A. H. Baynes knelt in the rear with his family, and they all waved their arms and screamed when the rest of the ashram screamed to kill for the love of Kali.

"Kill for the love of killing," chanted the people as they bowed before the many-armed statue.

A. H. nudged his son, who had been silent.

"I don't like to yell, Daddy," said the boy.

"You yell enough at home," whispered A. H.

"That's different."

"You can yell here," Baynes said.

"I don't know the words."

"Move your lips," Baynes said.

"Who do they want to kill?"

"Bad people. Yell."

A. H. Baynes let his mind wander pleasantly as the chants began to roll: kill for the love of killing, kill for the love of Kali. This was a resource driven by a power he had never experienced before. In the rear of the ashram, he felt as if he had just discovered atomic energy.

There was one problem that he could see. If this

group kept growing, there would be an ever-growing need for travelers to kill. And that many killings might not just kill travelers; it might kill travel itself.

No more communications, no more commerce. Professors unable to travel, students unwilling. Civilization might well return to the Stone Age.

The Stone Age.

Baynes thought about that for a moment as the chanting beat out like thunder from the skies. The Stone Age, he thought. Everything gone. Could it happen? Maybe.

He knew what to do. He would have to buy up some good cave property as a hedge. In the meantime, all was right with his world, and he opened his lungs to shout, "Kill for the love of Kali." And his children joined him this time.

And then, suddenly, the ashram fell silent. All eyes turned to the door in the back as a young man raced forward, down the aisle, his eyes glittering with excitement. "She has provided," he shouted. "She has provided." In his hand he held a large pile of airline tickets. "I found them on the street outside," he said. "She has provided."

The other followers nodded. Some mumbled. "She always provides. We love Kali."

A moment later, Ban Sar Din ran out into the ashram from his holy office in the back, dumped out a batch of yellow handkerchiefs, and ran back to his office. The floor of the ashram shuddered with the slam of a steel-reinforced door.

# Ten

Holly Rodan finished making her five hundredth tissue-paper carnation and attached it to the garland draped around the statue's neck.

"Oh, Kali," she purred. "You are even more beautiful with these. When he comes, he will not be able to resist you."

She sang a little song as she wound the paper flowers around the statue, as if it were a maypole. One of the flowers must have fallen from the garland and gotten underfoot, because suddenly her foot slipped out from under her and she fell forward on her face with a crash.

"Clumsy me," she giggled, and applied a blob of spittle to her skinned knee.

She had just barely started on the 501st carnation when she fell again with a loud thump. This time she slid almost to the edge of the raised platform on which the statue stood. She tried to get up and fell again, this time careening completely off the platform with a hard thump.

"Noise! Noise!" Ban Sar Din screeched, waddling out of his office. On his way out, he slammed into a computer console that had been delivered that morning for A. H. Baynes.

"First the crazy American installs two private telephone lines in my sacred office, and now this," he snapped. He kicked the computer. "What does he want of me? Oh, I live the life of a pig."

Holly thumped loudly to the floor again, this time near the empty chairs of the faithful.

"What is the matter with you, noisome child? In my land, women do not crash on the floor, even when they bend to kiss the feet of their husbands. Do you not think I have headaches enough with this Baynes pirate taking over my inner sanctum? Boom, boom, thump, thump. Even in Calcutta it is not so noisy."

"A thousand thousand pardons, Holy One and respected of Kali," Holly said. "I just can't seem to get a grip on my . . ." With that, she slid halfway across the floor and banged her head on the incense table. "I've got it," she suddenly cried, sitting up. "I know why I'm stumbling and falling all over the place."

"Ah, drugs. It is the curse of our age. What are you on?" he said.

"It's Kali," Holly said, beaming. "Don't you see, Holy One? She's pushing me out the door. She wants me to leave on a mission. Alone. And somehow I knew She would. That is why when the others left on their trips, I chose to stay behind to decorate the statue."

"If you say so," Ban Sar Din said.

"The goddess has spoken to me," Holly rhapsodized. "Me, Holly Rodan. She has chosen me especially to serve Her." She stood up with dignity, crashed to the floor again, then crawled on her hands and knees toward the statue. "O Holy One," she shouted. "I can *smell* her."

"Fine, fine," Ban Sar Din said, smiling and nodding agreeably. Inwardly, he made a mental note not to let Holly go on any more flights. The young woman had obviously gone over the edge. A planeful of closet killers was risky enough, but a genuine loudmouthed loony-tune like Holly among them was sure to attract attention.

"The scent, the scent," Holly chanted, whipping her long blond hair back and forth across the base of the statue. "She wants me to carry her scent with her. Smell for Kali," she intoned. "Smell, smell, SMELL. O Holy One, I will never wash again," she said.

"Very Indian," Bar Sar Din said. The telephone rang.

"Smell for Kali. Kill for Kali," Holly was chanting.

"It's for you," Ban Sar Din said. "I think it's your mother."

Holly made a disgusted face as she disentangled her hair from the goddess's feet.

"Oh, Mother, what is it now?" she said into the phone. "Yeah. Yeah. So what? Huh? Well, I don't know. God . . . that's it. *She* made it happen. What? I'll explain later."

She hung up and looked at Ban Sar Din with an unalloyed expression of pleasure. "Holy One. My father's been killed in a car wreck," she said breathlessly.

"Poor child. My sympathies—"

"No, no, no. Don't you see? Kali did it."

Ban Sar Din looked dubiously at the statue for which he had paid forty-three dollars. "Kali killed your father? Is he around here somewhere?"

"No. He's in Denver. Or what's left of him is in Denver. See. That's where Kali wants me to go. The call from my mother was a sign. My mission is to go to Denver. Maybe there's someone special I'm supposed to kill there."

"Now, don't be rash, Holly," Ban Sar Din said, wondering what would happen if she got picked up for murder alone, without another member of the ashram around to kill her before she could spill the beans to the police. "Perhaps you should be accompanied . . ."

"I must go alone," Holly said fervently. "I must go where Kali sends me."

"And Kali is sending you to Denver?" Bar Sar Din said. He realized he no longer had any plane tickets to Denver.

"Denver," Holly said, her voice almost lyrical. "Kali is sending me to Denver."

"Fly tourist," Ban Sar Din said. "I don't have a free ticket to Denver."

Holly Rodan chanted "Kill for Kali" under her breath during the taxi ride on the way to the airport. She chanted while she waited for her plane in the Just Folks terminal. It was now the most crowded terminal in the airport. Banners everywhere with Just Folks's red-white-and-blue logo announced it as "the Friendly, SAFE Airline." In the waiting area, loudspeakers droned constantly, giving the safety statistics of Just Folks compared with International Mid-America Airlines.

The loudspeakers annoyed Holly. It was hard to chant with words blaring at her, but she kept trying. "Kill for Kali," she said softly, trying to concentrate. "Kill for the love of Kali."

"Hey, baby," rumbled a voice in her ear. The owner of the voice was a middle-aged man wearing a raincoat.

Holly looked up at him, blinking. Was he the reason for her journey? Had Kali sent this man for her to kill? "Maybe you're the one," she said.

"You bet I am," the man answered. He pulled open his raincoat to expose a flabby naked body underneath.

Then he ran away, but the experience left Holly shaken. "It's a test," she told herself. "I *am* supposed to go to Denver. Kali has decreed it. And She knows all."

On the plane, she sidled up to an elderly woman and asked if she could help her with anything. The lady punched her in the stomach. Then as the passengers were leaving the plane in Denver, Holly flashed a bright smile at a good-looking young man and offered him a ride to his hotel.

"The games and ploys of aggressive heterosexual females is something I find particularly disgusting," he said.

"Oh, I'm sorry."

"You'll do anything you can to get a man, won't you?"

"I was only offering—"

"Yes, I can see that you're very generous with your offers. Well, you can take that hairless perfumed carcass of yours and parade it around some singles bar. Some of us happen to prefer the pure beauty of our own gender."

"Faggot," Holly said, walking away.

"Breeder," he called after her. "And you smell bad, too."

In the Denver terminal, a teenager with red-and-blue streaked hair began to walk alongside her.

"Are you the one?" she asked in despair.

"The one and only," he answered. "Superman, doing it through the night, a whole lot of loving just waiting for you, and I work hard for the money. I am the One."

Her worries disappeared. "Thank Kali," she said. "Can I be your friend?"

"Sure," he said. "Give me all your money and I'll be your friend forever." He snapped open a switchblade, pressed it against her throat, and herded her into a narrow dark corridor. "Let's see some friendly greenbacks."

Holly shambled into Denver broke and disappointed. She had failed in her mission. Kali had selected her to serve in a unique and special way, and Holly had blown the opportunity. "Maybe I'll never be worth anything as a killer," she said in despair. As she walked into her parents' split-level suburban home, her mother saw Holly's tears and ran to comfort her.

"Poor baby," Mrs. Rodan said. "I know this is a crying time for both of us."

"Oh, get lost, Mother. Where's Father?"

"He's dead. Remember?"

"Oh, yeah. It's about time."

"Would you like some tuna-noodle casserole?" her mother asked.

"I'd rather eat barf."

"Yes, dear. The funeral's in an hour. I've had your good black dress cleaned."

"I'm not going to any funeral," Holly said.

"But, dear, it's your father."

"I didn't come here for any stupid funeral. I've got important things on my mind."

"Of course, dear. I understand," said Mrs. Rodan.

Holly wandered aimlessly around the streets of Denver, pondering her obscure mission for Kali. If the statue had wanted her to leave the ashram, she reasoned, it must have been for a purpose, a serious purpose. But no one seemed to be available for killing. She had tried to be a faithful executioner, but things kept going wrong.

"A sign," she said aloud. "What I need is a sign."

The sign came from the Mountaineer National Savings and Loan Association, which was inaugurating its first nighttime hours and having them commemorated by a bank robbery. The armed robber came fleeing through the doors of the bank with pistols blazing. He killed a policeman nonchalantly, fired into a crowd of onlookers, and dashed toward a tan Lincoln Continental parked half a block away. Holly was

standing directly in front of the door on the driver'
side of the car when he reached it. With a curse, h
shoved Holly aside, tossing her into the line of traffic
and flung open the door.

As he got into the car, almost as an afterthought, h
turned and pointed his pistol at Holly to kill her.

Then a peculiar thing happened. A thin young mar
with thick wrists stepped between the two of them
Holly watched as the door on the driver's side of the ca
ceased to exist. Then the steering wheel magically spur
off its column and embedded itself in the bank robber'
stomach.

The young man then turned and appeared to stop
an oncoming automobile five inches away from Holl
Rodan's head by placing the heel of his shoe agains
the car's bumper.

The bank robber, hopelessly pinned in the car
watched, feeling his insides turn to mush. Then he fel
himself being lifted from the seat by the thin man
moved so quickly he felt like a blur. He felt the air
whoosh around him as he sailed through the air, back
toward the Mountaineer National S. & L. He landed ir
a lump in the midst of a crowd of onrushing police
men, who pinned him to the ground. The last thing
the bank robber saw was a reflection in a plate-glass
window of the man who had stopped him.

Holly huddled on the street, her long hair strewr
about her face like golden seaweed.

"Are you all right?" Remo asked as he bent over her

She looked up and gaped at him. "You're the one,'
she said.

"Oh, no." Remo stood up and skittered away from
her. His back moved against a telephone pole. He
couldn't breathe. A ghastly fear shook him to the pit of
his stomach.

"Get away," he whispered as Holly Rodan rose and
came toward him.

"No." Holly's voice was triumphant. "I finally understand. You're the reason She sent me here. I wasn't sent to kill. I was sent to bring you back. For Her. For Kali."

"Go away. I don't know what you're talking about. And besides, you smell like a steer."

"It's the scent of Kali. It's on my hair," Holly said. "Come, smell it."

"Go fumigate the county jail with your hair," Remo said. He edged farther away from her.

"Don't be afraid," Holly said, smiling sweetly. "I know about you. I know who you are."

"You do?" Remo said. Maybe now, maybe this time he could kill her. Maybe if the reason was strong enough, he could do it. Maybe if she knew too much, if she was a danger to CURE, to the country. Maybe then he could kill her.

"Who am I?" he said.

"You're Kali's lover. She selected you and She sent me here to bring you to Her," Holly said. She moved closer and wrapped her arms around Remo's neck. The scent of her hair disgusted and excited him. He felt a loathsome stirring in his loins.

"Go away," he said hoarsely. "Go away."

She rubbed her hand on his thigh and Remo felt his resistance drain away. Her hair was so close to his face, the smell so pungent. It was a smell of far away and long ago.

"Maybe you don't understand," she whispered into his ear, "but I do. I know your destiny. You must come with me. Follow me to Kali." She pulled him off the street and into a narrow twisting alley between two tall buildings. He felt powerless to resist.

"What are you called, Lover of Kali?" she asked.

"Remo," he said numbly.

"Remo." She savored the word. "I am Kali's messenger, Remo. Come to me. I will give you a taste of what She will give you." She kissed him. The sickening, perverted smell crawled into his nostrils and set fire to his blood.

"Take me," Holly said, her eyes glazed in a trance. "Take what Kali gives you." She pulled him down to the slimy bricks of the alley, littered with rotted cabbage leaves and coffee grounds and bird droppings. "Take me here, in the filth, for it is as She wishes." She opened her legs to Remo and then gasped as she felt his flesh burn inside her.

When it was over, Remo turned his face to the wall of the building. He felt ashamed and dirty. Holly took his hand, but he brushed it away as if it were a maggot.

"I don't always do this on the first date," she said.

"Go away."

"It really wasn't my idea," Holly said. "It's something that came over me."

"Just get out of here, all right?"

"Look, I've heard of postcoital tristesse, but isn't this a bit much?"

Remo stumbled to his feet and staggered back from the young woman, who still lay on the ground amid the dirt of the alley. He barely had the strength to move. The smell of her was as a drug in his nostrils; his limbs felt leaden.

"You can try to leave," Holly said. Her voice broke into brittle sharp laughter. "You can try, but you will follow me all the same. Kali wants you. She will bring you to Her. You'll see. You will come to Kali."

Her voice grew small in the distance as he stumbled away. But even when Remo could no longer hear her, the scent of her still followed him like an invisible, teasing demon, and he knew that the girl was right. He *would* follow her, and somehow he knew the path would lead to death.

He had been wrong in trying to solve things alone. He needed help.

He needed Chiun.

# Eleven

It was dark in the hotel room. The only illumination came from the stars that shone brightly in the clear Rocky Mountain night.

Remo lay on a mat on the floor in the middle of the room, his hands folded across his stomach as Chiun had placed them. The old Korean sat in a lotus position on the floor near Remo's head.

"And now you will speak," Chiun said.

"I don't know what's wrong with me, Little Father. I thought I could shake it, but I can't."

"Speak of it," Chiun said gently.

"I think it was a girl," Remo said.

"Just a girl?" Chiun said.

"No one special," Remo said. "Belonged to some crazy cult. I followed her when we took that Just Folks flight into North Carolina and two of her friends tried to kill me."

"Did you kill them?"

"The friends. But not her," Remo said. He shivered from the memory, but then his body grew calm as Chiun, sensing Remo's pain even in the darkness, reached out a hand and touched his shoulder.

"I couldn't kill her. I wanted to. But she wanted to die. She wanted me to kill her. And she was chanting, they were all chanting, and it made me crazy and I had to get out of there. That's when I went to the mountains to think."

Chiun was silent.

"Anyway, I saw her again tonight and I thought I could kill her this time. She had something to do with the deaths on the planes, and I thought I could do my job and kill her. But I couldn't. It was her smell."

"What kind of smell?" Chiun said.

"It was a smell . . . but not really a smell," Remo said into the darkness of the room. "More like a feeling."

"A feeling of what?"

Remo tried to find the words but could not. He just shook his head. "I don't know, Little Father. Something big. Frightening. More frightening than death. A terrible thing . . . God, I *am* going crazy." He rubbed his hands together nervously, but Chiun took them in his own hands and replaced them over Remo's solar plexus.

"You said they chanted," Chiun prompted. "What kind of chanting?" he asked softly.

"What? Oh. Crazy stuff. I don't know. 'Long live death. Long live pain. *She* loves it.' I tell you, they love death, even their own. And it was that way tonight too. She told me I would have to follow her, and I knew, Chiun, I knew that even if I had killed her, she would have been saying, 'Kill me, kill me, kill me, because it is right.' I couldn't kill her; I let her go."

"Why must you follow her?" Chiun asked.

"Because I'm supposed to be somebody's lover. Somebody wants me."

"Who is this person who wants you?" Chiun asked.

"A name. A funny name. I think it's a woman's name," Remo said. "The name was . . ." He paused, trying to remember.

"Kali?" Chiun asked. His voice was hardly more than a breath in the blackened room.

"That's it. Kali. How did you know?"

Remo heard Chiun sigh, and then the old Korean's voice was brisk again.

"Remo, I must arrange to meet Emperor Smith at once."

"What for?" Remo asked. "What's he got to do with it?"

"He must help me prepare for my journey," Chiun said.

Remo looked at him, puzzled. Even in the darkness of the room, his eyes were able to gather enough light to see clearly. The look on Chiun's face was one of pained resignation.

"I must go to Sinanju," Chiun said.

"What for? Why now?"

"To save your life," Chiun said. "If it is not already too late."

## Twelve

Harold W. Smith walked briskly into the Denver motel room.

"What is it? What was so important that you couldn't tell me over the telephone?"

"Don't look at me," Remo said. He was leafing through a magazine and did not bother to look up from its pages.

Chiun sat in a corner of the room on a straw mat. As Smith turned to him, the old man raised his head slowly. His face looked older than Smith had ever seen it before.

"Leave us, Remo," Chiun said softly.

Remo slapped the magazine down into his lap. "Come on, Chiun. Isn't this a little much? Even for you?"

"I said, leave us," the old man snapped. His face reddening, Remo threw the magazine onto the floor and strode out the door, slamming it behind him.

"Is something wrong?" Smith asked Chiun.

"Not yet," the old man said impassively.

"Oh," Smith said. Chiun did not speak, and Smith felt uncomfortable in the silence. "Er, is there something I can do for you, Chiun?" He looked at his watch.

"My needs are small, Emperor," Chiun said, and Smith thought he recognized the opening of a new salary negotiation. Every time Chiun said that he needed nothing, it turned out that only more gold would save him from an eternity of disgrace in the eyes of his ancestors.

Smith felt an unaccustomed small surge of anger. The pressure was mounting on CURE from the White House to end the airline killings. International Mid-America Airlines had just about gone belly-up, and who knew how many airlines would follow. The news media were putting people in an afraid-to-travel panic. Civilization, which in the long run meant the free flow of goods and ideas, was in danger. And Chiun was going to try to beat him out of more money.

"You remember, Master, you said the matter with Remo would be straightened out." He watched Chiun's face, but it revealed nothing. "Yet I come here, and instead of working, he is reading a magazine. Remember your promise? For four extra gold bars, if you remember. It was our last conversation, Chiun. Do you remember?"

He had tried to keep the irritation out of his voice, but he had not been too successful.

"It was not fair," Chiun whispered softly.

"I beg your pardon?"

"It was not fair," Chiun repeated.

"It most certainly was," Smith snapped, making no attempt now to conceal his annoyance. "You agreed that for a nine-weight payment to Sinanju, you would get Remo to work again. If he has refused—"

"It was not you who were unfair," Chiun said. "Not you, O gracious Emperor. It was I." He lowered his eyes in shame.

"I see. You mean Remo refuses to work, even with the additional tribute."

"He does not refuse to work. He has been unable to work."

"Why?" Smith asked. "Is he ill?"

"He is afraid."

Smith felt himself flushing with anger. Afraid. Smith, too, had been afraid many times during his life. Many times he had faced death. He had never been blessed with Remo's natural skills or his training, but all the same, when the crunch came, Harold Smith had overcome his fear and gone on about his work. Fear was no excuse. In the rocky New Hampshire soil where Smith had grown up, there was an old saying that he had somehow absorbed into his rock-hard soul: "Do it afraid if you have to, but just do it."

"He'll just have to get over being afraid," Smith told Chiun tersely.

"I have said it incorrectly, Emperor. It is not the fear that will stop Remo. He will find the source of the airplane killings, because he will not be able to stop himself. And he will fight whoever is at that source."

"Then what's the problem?"

Chiun sighed. "Remo will not survive the fight."

Smith took off his hat and turned the brim around in his hands. "How can you know that?"

"I know. I can explain no more. You are not of Sinanju and you would not believe." He lapsed back into silence as Smith twirled the brim of his hat.

"Are you saying this is the end?" Smith said at last. "The end of Remo? The end of our working together?"

"Perhaps," Chiun said.

"I'm not going to pretend I understand anything you are saying," Smith said. "And I don't know what I could do about it even if I did."

He looked toward the door, and Chiun said, "Do not go, Emperor. I have thought of a way to protect him."

Smith's lips tightened. The usual, he thought. Just done with a little more dramatic flair this time.

"More tribute, I suppose," he said sarcastically. "Chiun, I'm a busy man. There was absolutely no reason to call me away from my office for this. If what you wanted was more gold, you could have told me over the telephone. I want you to know I don't appreciate this. Not one bit." He turned to leave.

"I do not want gold," Chiun said.

Smith's hand was on the doorknob. It froze there. "Then what?"

"I must go to Sinanju immediately," Chiun said.

"Out of the question. Things like that take time to set up."

"It is the only way," Chiun said.

"No."

"There is something in my village that can save Remo," Chiun said.

"And you just happen to get a free vacation at the same time," Smith said. "You're cried wolf once too often, Chiun." Smith opened the door.

"Hold!" Chiun's voice was like electricity cracking. He rose to his feet in one smooth movement that seemed like a puff of colored smoke rising, walked over, and pushed the door shut. "I rescind my request," he said.

"Pardon?"

"For the additional tribute. The extra four-weight of gold was not Remo's wish, in truth. It was my own for the welfare of my village. I hereby offer it back to you in exchange for my passage to Sinanju and back. Immediately."

Smith studied the old man's face. It was the first time he had ever heard Chiun give up an opportunity to amass gold. "This is serious, isn't it? It means that much to you?"

"Yes, Emperor."

"You honestly think it will help Remo?"

"I do not know. I can only try," Chiun said.

"Maybe if you'd tell me . . ."

"It is no dishonor to you, Emperor, that you would not understand. There are things in this world that none understand but me. This is because I am reigning Master of Sinanju and the history of scores of centuries rests with me. I must go. Now."

The two men looked into each other's eyes for a long time. Smith realized how small and old and frail Chiun was. Finally the American nodded. "Done. You'll go back to Folcroft with me. I'll arrange for jets and a submarine."

"Thank you, Emperor. Before I leave, I must see Remo."

"I'll send him in," Smith said.

"I'm glad you two had such a nice chat," Remo said as he plopped down on a chair.

"Our conversation had nothing to do with you. Nothing really," Chiun said.

"Oh, bulldookey. You think I was born yesterday? You think I don't know about your little arrangement to have me bumped off in case something goes wrong? Like if I can't work anymore?"

"That was an old agreement that I made with Emperor Smith. Long before I knew who you were and what you would become," Chiun said. "This did not concern that."

Remo stared at Chiun for a moment, then buried his head in his hands. "Maybe it should have," he said. "I'm . . . I'm just . . . nothing left. It's getting stronger, Chiun. The smell, the feeling. It's with me all the time now, and I can't shake it."

"And you will not be able to shake it, as you say," Chiun said.

"I'm losing my mind. That's all there is to it. Maybe you ought to go back to that old agreement and get it over with and send me to never-never land. Sometime when I'm not looking. No. Do it when I'm looking. I want to make sure you keep your elbow straight."

He smiled at the private joke between them. For ten

years he had learned at Chiun's feet and absorbed all
that the Master had given him of the disciplines of
Sinanju. But praise was not Chiun's way to teach, and
when Remo did something perfectly, without flaw,
Chiun's final defense against having to praise him was
to complain that Remo's elbow was bent and no one
with a bent elbow had ever amounted to anything.

But Chiun was not smiling. "I am not going to
remove you, no matter what my contract says with the
Emperor," he said.

Remo was silent, and Chiun went on. "Instead, I will
tell you a story."

Remo's face fell. "Maybe it'd be better if you just
killed me."

"Silence, you pale piece of pig's ear. I have little
time. This story concerns Master Lu the Disgraced."

"You gave me all that one before. He cleared the
muggers off the roads of Rome and then went to work
in a circus. Lu the Disgraced. Tsk, tsk."

"And I told you there was more to his story," Chiun
said. "And now the rest. And don't you go telling anybody this, because the last years of Lu's life are a story
so secret that knowledge of them is restricted always to
the reigning Master. I am violating tradition by telling
you."

"He must have done something really bad," Remo
said. "What was it? It must have had something to do
with money. The worst thing that all those old Masters
ever did was forget to get paid. Master Lu the Unpaid.
No wonder he was disgraced."

Chiun ignored him. He closed his eyes and spoke in
Korean, his singsong voice taking on the cadences of
ancient poetry as he unfolded the rest of the story of
the disgraced Master Lu, who, after his shame in the
arenas of Rome, fled that decadent city to wander
through the uncharted regions of Asia.

The Master's wanderings, as Chiun related the story,

gave Lu no peace in his heart until one day, after all
the moons of the year had passed and come and passed
again, he ventured into a small village high in the
mountains of central Ceylon. The village was an iso-
lated place, far smaller than Sinanju, and the people in
it showed the effects of a population closed to outsiders. They were a beautiful people, unlike any the
Master had ever seen. Neither white, nor black, nor
red, nor yellow, the people of Bathasgata, as the village
was known, resembled all the races of the world and
yet none.

No one in Bathasgata knew the origins of the
humans who lived there, but they were grateful for
their land and their village and the companionship of
one another.

As a token of their gratitude, the people created a
statue out of the clay of their village. They fashioned
the statue in the form of a woman more beautiful than
any ever made of living flesh and worshiped her by the
name of Kali.

But something happened after the statue was completed. The once peaceful villagers began to abandon
their fields and flocks to devote all their time to the
adoration of Kali. They claimed that although their
love pleased the goddess, Kali wanted more than gar-
lands of flowers and prayers written on paper, folded
into the likenesses of animals.

She wanted blood. With blood, the devotees
claimed, Kali would love them back. But none in the
village was willing to sacrifice himself or a loved one to
the statue.

It was then that Lu appeared in Bathasgata.

"It is a sign," the worshipers of Kali shouted. "The
stranger has come just in time to serve as Kali's sacrifice."

And so the four strongest men of the village fell upon
the traveler and sought to kill him. But Lu was Master

of Sinanju, and greatest assassin on all the earth, and soon after their assault on him, Lu's attackers lay dead upon the ground.

"They seem only to be asleep," one of the village women said. "There is no blood."

Then the oldest of the village spoke. He said that the arrival of Lu the Master was indeed a sign from the goddess Kali. But the stranger was not to be the sacrifice, rather the instrument of sacrifice. Then the Old One instructed the others to take the bodies of the four dead men to Kali to see if their unshed blood, encased in death, pleased her.

They placed the four bodies at the base of the statue at the time of the setting of the sun, prayed, then returned to their homes.

With the break of the new day, they saw the result of their sacrifices. The statue had grown a new arm.

"A miracle," the villages exclaimed.

"A sign from Kali."

"Death pleases Her."

"She loves it."

"Kill for Kali."

"Kill for Kali."

"Kill."

"Kill."

"Kill."

With respect, they brought Lu forward to face the statue, and the Old One again spoke to the goddess. "Most revered Kali," he said, "this traveler has killed these men in Your service. He has shed no blood so that they might be delivered whole into Your embrace."

The growing of the new arm was the First Miracle of Kali, and now the Second Miracle of Kali happened. Although the statue was as hard as stone, Her eyes looked directly into those of the man standing before Her and the corners of Her lips curved up into a smile.

Astonished, the villagers knelt in obeisance to the goddess and to Lu, the man She had taken to Her heart, and the Third Miracle of Kali occurred.

A strange smell emanated from the statue. It permeated the small village square. Master Lu thrust his hand into his kimono and pulled forth a yellow cloth with which he tried to seal off his face from the aroma, but it was too powerful and finally he dropped to his knees and kissed the statue's feet and looked up at its face with the eyes of love.

"She has taken him for Her own," the old one said. "Kali has consummated the union of love."

Lu was frightened of the strange power which the stone statue had over him. At first, he said nothing to dissuade the villagers of Bathasgata from believing that he was of special importance to their homemade goddess, because he feared reprisal for killing four of their people. Then, during the second month of his stay, the Fourth Miracle of Kali occurred and caused him to fear for more than his life.

The remains of the first four sacrifices had long since rotted and been buried when the goddess again hungered for the taste of blood.

"She wants more," the Old One said, but Lu refused to kill senselessly for the appeasement of a piece of clay.

"She will make you kill again for Her," the Old One prophesied.

"No one can force the hand of a Master of Sinanju," Lu said, and walked to the center of the village to stand before the statue of Kali. "You have no power over me," he told the stone goddess with all the conviction of his soul.

But it was not enough. Once again, the statue emitted the woman-scent of the goddess and the aroma insinuated itself into Lu's senses and he fell into a fierce and uncontrollable lust.

"He is ready to kill again," the Old One said.

The villagers talked excitedly. "Whom will he choose?"

"He will not choose," said the Old One. "Kali will choose."

"How?"

"We will know. We will have a sign," the Old One said.

And in the Fourth Miracle, the sign appeared. On the forehead of the Old One appeared a faint dot of blue. As the villagers gaped in wonder, the dot grew darker.

"It is the Old One she has chosen," the villagers shouted.

"No!" Lu struggled to pull away from the statue and the terrible power that filled him. "I will not . . . kill . . ."

But the Old One knew that the goddess he and his people had created would be satisfied only with his death, so he bowed before the Master Lu and exposed his throat.

Lu cried out in anguish, but the knowledge of right and wrong could not stop the goddess's wrath that coursed through his blood and directed his powerful hands. He took again the yellow cloth from inside his robe and wrapped it around the man's neck, and with one powerful wrench, the Old One lay dead at the feet of the statue.

Lu collapsed on the earth, a wail of defeat issuing from his now corrupt soul.

And the statue smiled again.

"C'mon, Chiun," Remo said in disgust. "A statue? Sticks and stones may break my bones, but statues you can shove."

"Some things are real even before they take form," Chiun said. "Look. I will show you." He lifted the small

ooden chair from the writing desk of the hotel suite.
This, you say, is a chair. Correct?"

"Right. Chair," Remo said.

Chiun leaned over the desk, and with a pen and a
iece of hotel stationery quickly executed a sketch of
ie same wooden chair.

"And this too is a chair?"

"Yeah. I guess so," Remo said cautiously.

Chiun folded his hands into his sleeves. "And there,
Remo, is the failure of your thinking. For neither these
ieces of wood nor this piece of paper decorated with
nk is a chair. They only appear as chairs because you
hoose to believe that they are."

"Huh?"

"The true chair is in your mind, my son. And that
oo is a mere imitation. The original chair was an idea
n the mind of someone long forgotten. But the idea is
vhat is real. The solid object is no more than a house
or the idea."

"That's too heavy for me," Remo said. "I'm not sup-
osed to be a philosopher. I'm just supposed to kill
eople."

"No. You are supposed to be an assassin. It is just
our ineptitude that reduces it to 'killing people.' But
hat is what Master Lu became at the bidding of the
oddess Kali. No longer an assassin, he became a killer
f people. Under the power of the *real* goddess, the
ormless force which had been encased in clay. But the
orce was before the clay."

"Why are you telling me this?" Remo asked.

Chiun's face was anxious. "I want you to under-
tand, Remo. Because I believe that you are now
acing the same power that Master Lu faced."

"I don't plan to visit Ceylon before Christmas,"
Remo said.

Chiun sighed. "If you feel Kali's presence here, then
he is not in Ceylon," he said patiently.

"Who says I feel anybody's presence? I *smell* some
thing. There's nothing supernatural about that
Maybe I just ought to change deodorants."

"Silence your face while I resume the tale," Chiun
said.

"All right. I just don't see what any of this has to do
with me."

"You will. Later. You will understand later, but first
you will listen."

Lu continued to kill for the goddess, and with each
death, more of his strength and skill diminished. Each
time, as the bodies with their blue-marked forehead
lay still warm at his feet, Lu fell weeping to the ground
spent as if he had copulated with the stone image and
delivered his seed into it. Each morning, after the kills
the goddess grew a new arm, while Lu was taken to res
in a bed of flowers. He slept for days on end, so drained
was he of his powers. He belonged to Kali now, and al
the discipline of Sinanju which Lu had spent a lifetime
learning was used only to serve his mistress.

After two years, nearly the entire village of Bathas
gata had been sacrificed to the goddess, and Lu found
himself a sick, weak man, old before his time.

One who had watched his degeneration was a gir
who lived in service to Kali. She was young and beauti
ful and loved the goddess she served, but the sight of
the once powerful stranger reduced to a mass of skin
and bones who left his bed only to kill at the statue's
bidding saddened her. Although the others of the
village feared Master Lu and did not come into his
presence except on occasions of celebration, this young
girl ventured at night into Lu's house of straw and
flowers and began to nurse him back to health.

She could not much improve his physical condition,
but the companionship of the young woman gladdened
Lu's broken heart.

"Do you not fear me?" he asked.

"Why? Because you will kill me?"

"I will never kill you," Lu promised.

But the girl knew better. "You will surely kill me," he said, "as you will kill all of us. Kali is stronger than he will of a man, even a man such as you. But death omes to all who live, and if I were to fear death, I ould also fear life. No, I do not fear you, Master Lu."

And then Lu wept, for even in the depth of his egradation, when he had betrayed all the teachings of is life, the gods of Sinanju had seen fit to bring love to im.

"I must leave this place," he told the girl. "Will you elp me?"

"I will go with you," she answered.

"But Kali?"

"Kali has brought only death and sadness to us. She our god, but I will leave Her. We will go to your omeland, where men like you may walk in peace."

Lu took the young woman in his arms and embraced er. She opened herself to him, and there, in the ilence of Lu's sickroom, he gave her his true seed. Not he wretched parts of his strength that Kali took, but he inviolate essence of his own clean soul.

They left that night, in the darkness, and journeyed or moon upon moon toward Sinanju. Sometimes the ever of Kali would come upon Lu and he would cry ut to his wife to tie him with weighted ropes until the errible feeling passed and until the scent had left his ostrils.

She obeyed, glad that Lu trusted her. The seed in er belly had swollen and she was soon to deliver a child to him.

"Your son," she said when she presented Lu with heir child. Lu had never been happier in his life. He vanted to cry out the news, but he was still a stranger vho knew no one in this new land to which they had ourneyed. He walked for miles, reveling in his good fortune at finding a woman who loved him enough to take him away from the evil goddess, a woman who had given him a son.

The countryside he walked through grew more familiar with each step. Sinanju? he wondered. But it did not look like the place of his birth. It was lush while Sananju was cold and harsh. It was not anything like Sinanju. It was . . .

He screamed when he reached the crest of the hill he was climbing. For below, in a shallow mountain valley was the village of Bathasgata.

"Kali has brought me back," Lu whispered. His hopes shattered. There was no escape from Kali.

He went back to the crude camp where his wife had delivered their son to tell her the horrible news. When he saw her, he began to tremble like a palsied man.

There was a blue dot on her forehead.

"Not her," Lu screamed.

"Lu . . . Lu . . ." His good wife tried to raise herself to find the ropes to tie him down, but she was weak from birthing and moved clumsily. She implored him to be strong, but his strength was as nothing compared with the power of Kali. He tried to cut off his own arm to prevent what he knew would happen, but Kali would not allow it. Slowly he pulled the yellow cloth from his kimono and wound it around the neck of his beloved, and then inexorably tightened it and squeezed the life from her body.

When it was done and Lu lay close to death beside the body of the beautiful woman who had loved him, he knew what he must do. He took a ring from the finger of the woman he had loved and killed, then buried her by the light of the moon. After saying a prayer to the old gods of Sinanju, he took his infant son in his arms and walked into the village. At the first house, he delivered the baby to the occupants. "Raise him as your own," he said, "for I will not live to see the sun rise."

Then he went alone to stand before the statue of Kali. The statue was smiling.

"You have destroyed me," Lu said.

And in the quiet of the still night, the statue answered him from a place deep within his own mind: "You tried to betray me. It was a just punishment."

"I am prepared to die." He touched his wife's ring and felt it give him strength.

"You will die when I command it," Kali said.

"No," Lu said, and for a moment the old power returned to him, and he said, "I am the Master of Sinanju. *You* will die when *I* command it. And I command it now."

With those words, he put his arms around the statue and uprooted it from the ground. Kali burned him with Her stone flesh, and Her many arms reached out to gouge his eyes, but Lu would not stop. He carried the statue down the mountain to the sea and with each step he was mutilated by the terrible force of the goddess. And with each step did he remember the love that had given him life, the love he had killed with his own hands, and he walked onward.

When he reached the cliffs overlooking the sea, the goddess spoke to him again.

"You cannot destroy me, fool. I will come back."

"It will be too late. I will be dead with you," Lu said.

"I will not come back for you, but for your son. Your descendant. One who follows your line will be mine, and I will exact my revenge on him, though it take many thousands of moons. He will be my instrument of revenge and my wrath will be mighty through him."

With the last of his strength, Lu cast the statue over the cliff. It sank into the blue water without a ripple.

Then, as dawn sent out its first rays of light, the

Master Lu wrote his story with his own blood on reeds that grew along the cliff's edge. With his final breath he wound the reeds through the ring which had belonged to his wife, and there he died.

"The Brothers Grimmsville," Remo said. "A fairy tale."

"We have the reeds," Chiun said.

"How? If Lu died in this mythical spot in Ceylon, how'd you get them back to Korea?"

"Fate works in strange ways," the old Oriental said. "Lu's body was found by a merchant who spoke many tongues. He delivered the reeds to Sinanju."

"I bet it was great for the merchant," Remo said. "Knowing your village, I suppose they slit his throat."

"He was not killed. He lived a long life of wealth and luxury with many wives and concubines."

"But he was never allowed to leave town, right?" Remo said.

Chiun shrugged. "Who would want to leave Sinanju?"

Far below, a horn sounded in the street and Remo parted the curtains and looked out. "It's Smitty. I recognize the Rent-a-Wreck. I thought he left an hour ago."

"He wishes for me to travel with him," Chiun said.

"Where are you going?"

"I told you. I must journey to Sinanju."

"I'll wait here until you get back," Remo promised.

Chiun smiled sadly. "Would that were true, my son. When you leave, leave a mark for me so that I may follow."

"Why should I leave? I can go nuts in Denver just as well as anywhere else."

"You will leave," Chiun said. "Just do not forget the story of Lu."

The old man gathered his kimono about him and

glided toward the door. "Promise? You will not forget, Remo?"

"I don't know what any of this is about," Remo said. "I'm not Lu's descendant. I'm from New Jersey."

"You are the next Master of Sinanju. An unbroken line of thousands of years connects you with Lu the Disgraced."

"You're wasting your time on this trip," Remo said.

"Remember Lu. And try not to do anything stupid while I am gone," Chiun said.

# Thirteen

If Ban Sar Din had learned one thing during his reign as head of an Indian religion, it was never to trust anybody who believed in an Indian religion.

So he had his doubts about A. H. Baynes, but the problem was that he could not figure out why. Because —going against the tradition of centuries of his family and telling the truth—Ban Sar Din had to admit that Kali had no more loyal follower than the airline executive.

Baynes had taken to sleeping inside the ashram each night now, huddled on the floor at the foot of the statue, just "so no crazies come in and try to harm Our Lady." And all his waking hours, too, were spent in the ashram, and when Ban Sar Din asked him if he didn't have an airline to run, Baynes had just smiled and said:

"It's running itself. We're the safe airline. No deaths. We don't even have to advertise anymore. The people are waiting in line for tickets on Just Folks."

But was that all Baynes wanted? Ban Sar Din wondered. So the American had struck a deal with Ban Sar Din and now there were no more killings aboard Just Folks. But Baynes could have had more. He could have had a cut of the proceeds. He could have used the killers as instruments of revenge on people who had offended him.

But he seemed to want none of those things. He said he wanted only to serve Kali. "I've served Mammon, big business, all these years," Baynes told him, and clapped a big hand on the small round Indian's shoulder. "It's time I served something I believed in. Something bigger than myself."

He had sounded sure of himself when he said that, and this morning, he was even more convinced. He had come running into the small yet luxurious apartment Ban Sar Din had built inside a garage across the alley, waving a fistful of tickets.

"She provided. She provided," Baynes was shouting.

"She provided what?" asked Ban Sar Din. "And who's She?"

"O blessed Kali," Baynes said. There were tears of joy streaming down his cheeks. "I slept all night under the statue. No one else was there. And when I woke up this morning, these were in Her hand." He waved the tickets. "A miracle," he said. "She blessed us with a miracle."

Ban Sar Din checked the tickets. They were all on Air Europa, all round trips, enough for an entire plane. A telephone call to the airline confirmed that they had all been paid for, in cash, but no one remembered who had purchased them. Ban Sar Din was nervous. God was one thing, but miracles, real miracles, were something else.

"Isn't it wonderful?" Baynes said.

"Well, it saves us some money anyway," Ban Sar Din said. "We'll give them out tonight. Along with a lot of rumals."

"A lot of rumals out," Baynes said. "A lot of cash coming back. And all through the grace of Kali. O Kali be praised." And he had left Ban Sar Din's apartment to go back to the burgeoning office he had set up in the small room behind the ashram where Ban Sar Din had been living.

Later in the day, when Bar Sar Din went into the office, Baynes had a finger stuck in his ear and was shouting into the telephone.

"Sure thing, Herb, old buddy," he yelled. He was yelling because the chanting in the outer room would have registered on a seismograph.

"No," Baynes shouted. "I can't go. I've got my religious work. But I thought it would be good for Evelyn and the kids to get away for a while, and they get along so well with you and Emmie."

"Kill for Kali," came the chant from the outer room. "Kill, kill, kill."

Baynes hung up the phone, and when Ban Sar Din's eyes questioned him, he explained: "That was my next-door neighbor, Herb Palmer. I'm sending the wife and kids and him and his wife on vacation to Paris. I don't think Kali wants us only to work and . . . well, these tickets came into our hands . . . so why not?"

"Why not indeed?" Ban Sar Din said. This was something he understood. Petty theft. Baynes was taking five of the ashram's tickets for personal use. It was worth it, just to know that the man was human after all.

"Unless you think I shouldn't?" Baynes said. "Unless you think there's something wrong?"

"No, no," Ban Sar Din singsonged back. "Nothing wrong. A vacation will do your family good."

He was brushed aside by Baynes's two children, who marched into the office, followed by Mrs. Baynes.

"Kill for Kali," Joshua Baynes intoned in his most serious voice. He picked up a bottle of ink and upended it on Baynes' desk.

"Isn't he cute?" Mrs. Baynes said.

"Kill, kill, kill." Joshua made a paper airplane out of Baynes' computer printout.

"He sounds so darned grown-up already," Mrs. Baynes said, her eyes moistening.

The Baynes girl belched.

"They've lost so many of their inhibitions since they got here," Mrs. Baynes said, blowing kisses to her youngsters. "All this killing talk is keeping them off the streets, A. H. I am absolutely positive that Joshua has no desire to drink hard liquor or to experiment with girls."

"Kill," Joshua chanted.

"Isn't that sweet?" said Mrs. Baynes.

"Warms my heart," Baynes said.

"And you haven't noticed," the woman said accusingly.

"Noticed what?"

"My sari." She twirled in the center of the office. "You see, I've adapted to my new life-style, A.H. I don't need designer clothes or charity balls or a live-in maid. That motel down the block is fine for me. I've followed my husband to enjoy the spiritual fruits of a simpler life. Aren't you proud of me, dear?"

The chanting from the outside room was so loud now that Ban Sar Din went out to ask them to quiet down before someone called the police. His request resulted in an incense pot being thrown in his general direction, and he went back into the office, just as Baynes was telling his wife: "And Herb Palmer and Emmie are going too. I thought it would be a nice break for you and the kids."

"I want to stay here and kill for Kali," Joshua said sullenly.

"Me too," said the daughter.

"How they go on," Mrs. Baynes said with a smile.

"Don't worry," Baynes said. "I'll convince them." He ushered his wife out of the office and looked at Ban Sar Din, who said, "They don't even listen to me anymore. Someone's going to call the police."

"Maybe they'll listen to me," Baynes said. "They know I'm one of them."

"Why should they listen to you?" said Ban Sar Din. "You're not even holy."

"Then make me holy," Baynes said.

The Indian shook his head. "You come in here, a walk-in, you take over my office with your computers, you encourage other walk-ins at our services. I don't think you're ready to be a Holy One."

"Maybe I should ask the people outside?" Baynes said. He started for the door.

"Welcome to the ranks of the holy, O Chief Phansigar," Ban Sar Din said, then sullenly traipsed out of the office to go back to his apartment across the alley. He saw Baynes put a big arm around the shoulders of his two children and pull them to him, just before he closed the office door.


A. H. Baynes stood on the raised platform next to the statue of Kali and looked out over the crowd in the ashram. It seemed as if every square foot of floor space was filled. The goddess was attracting new followers every day, and he felt proud of himself for the part he had played.

"Brothers and sisters in Kali," he intoned, "I am your new chief phansigar."

"Kill for Kali," someone murmured softly.

"That's right," Baynes said. "And She has provided us the means."

He waved the sheaf of airline tickets over his head. "This is a whole planeful of tickets for Air Europa, going to Paris," he said. "A whole planeful. Kali provided."

"She always provides," said Holly Rodan.

"She loves it," someone else said.

"This is how we're going to use them," Baynes said. "Europa's got two planes leaving for Paris, just an hour apart. These tickets are for the first plane. All of you are going to fill up that plane and go over there, and then when the second plane lands, you're each going to latch on to somebody from that plane and do Kali's work. I don't want anybody who was on that second plane to be coming back to the United States," Baynes said. "Not one. That was what She meant when She gave us a full planeload of tickets."

"She is wise," murmured someone in the front row.

"So is our chief phansigar," someone else said, and for a moment they all chanted, "Hail our chief phansigar," until Baynes blushed and stopped them with a wave of his hand.

"We only reflect Her glory," he said, and then bowed his head as the wave upon wave of chants filled the room.

"Kill for Kali."

"Kill for Kali."

"Kill for Kali."

"Sing it out, brothers and sisters," Baynes said.

"Kill for Kali."

When the excitement had reached a fever pitch, Baynes tossed the batch of plane tickets out among the faithful, and a jubilant roar rushed from the throats of the disciples.

Baynes picked out his son among the crowd. The boy was standing with his arms folded, his Europa ticket held between thumb and forefinger. Baynes winked and the boy responded with a knowing nod.

# Fourteen

The devotees had gone and the ashram's door was locked. Outside on the street, horns blared and people were singing. It was ten o'clock in the morning and drunks were already shouting to one another in the street.

"Sardine! Sardine!" bellowed A. H. Baynes. "You get your fat ass in here."

Ban Sar Din stepped into his former office from his current home in the garage.

"What the hell is that racket out there?" Baynes demanded.

"It is Saturday. People in this city celebrate many strange things. Today they celebrate Saturday."

"How the hell do they expect a man to get any work done?" Baynes said.

They stopped talking as they heard an insistent rapping at the front door.

"Why don't you go answer that?" Baynes said, and Ban Sar Din returned a few minutes later holding a brown envelope.

"Messenger," he said. "It is for me. It is addressed to the leader of the ashram."

"Hand it over," Baynes said. He tore the envelope from the Indian's hand.

"Why are you so belligerent today, Mr. Baynes?" asked Ban Sar Din.

"Because I'm wondering about you," Baynes said. "I just don't know how devoted you are to Kali, and I think maybe you're just in this for the money."

"It is not so," Ban Sar Din said stiffly. "I will have you know that I was worshiping Kali when you were decorating Christmas trees in your home."

"We'll see," Baynes said. "We'll see."

When Ban Sar Din left the office, Baynes opened the envelope and found a typewritten message:

> Meet me at the Orleans Café at three o'clock. You will recognize me. The meeting will benefit you greatly.

The note was not signed, and Baynes said, "Usual nut," and tossed the paper away. He kept working all morning, but he was unable to totally forget the note. Something kept pulling his mind back to it, something subtle yet powerful. Several hours later he picked it out of the wastebasket and studied it.

The paper was of high quality, densely woven and difficult to tear, and its edges were lined with gold. But Baynes realized that that was not what had attracted him. It was something else.

Experimentally he held the letter to his nose. A sickly-sweet aroma, faint but compelling, held him suspended out of time for a moment. He clutched the letter tightly and ran into the empty sanctuary and pressed his face against the statue of Kali. It was there too. The same smell. He checked his watch. It was 2:51.


The streets of New Orleans looked like a dress rehearsal for Mardi Gras, and the Orleans Café was crowded with people in garish costumes. *You will recognize me,* the message had read. Baynes searched the clientele, which seemed made up mostly of large hairy men dressed as women.

He noticed a lean young transvestite wearing Dracula makeup eyeing him steadily.

"Do you know me?" Baynes asked.

"Depends," the creature said. "You into getting your tongue tattooed?"

Baynes slipped away and had almost reached the door when he saw someone sitting alone near a window. The someone was covered from head to foot in a costume of stone gray. Its head was adorned by a cap of rhinestones. Its face was a garish painted mask. It had eight arms.

"Of course," Baynes said. "Kali."

The person at the table nodded to him, and one of the hands, covered by thick gray gloves, beckoned to him. He sat down across from the uncanny replica of the statue.

"I knew it would be you who came," the person in the costume whispered. There was no hint of gender in the voice, no characteristics to mark it as male or female.

"How did you know?" Baynes asked. He had to lean forward to hear the answer.

"Because you are the true leader of the cult of the Thuggees. You control the members. You may do as you wish."

Baynes sat back and asked, "What do you want?"

"Kali," the statue whispered.

"Sorry. The statue's not for sale." He began to rise.

"One million dollars."

He sat back down. "Why so much?"

"That is my offer."

"How do I know I can trust you? I haven't even seen your face. I don't know if you're a man or a woman."

"You will learn in time. And to trust me, you need only test me."

"Test you? How?"

The statue took a pen and wrote a telephone number on a cocktail napkin. "Memorize this," it whispered. As Baynes looked at the number, the person said, "Call anytime. One favor. Anything. It is yours." Then the statue burned the napkin over a candle on the table, stood up, and left.

# Fifteen

**Numbers 129 and 130.**

Mr. Dirk Johnson of Alameda, Illinois, squeezed his wife's hand as they stepped off the Europa L-1011 jetliner into the futuristic grandeur of Charles de Gaulle Airport.

"This'll make up for the honeymoon we never had," he said, smiling proudly. "I bet your daddy would never have believed we'd be standing here in Paris, France, one day," Johnson said.

"I always knew you better than he did," Mrs. Johnson said, pecking him on the cheek. "Isn't the hotel supposed to send a bus to pick us up or something?"

"Excuse me," a bright-eyed young woman interrupted. "If you need a ride, my friends and I are going right into the city. Can we give you a lift?"

"Now, isn't that nice, Dirk?" Mrs. Johnson said. "You know, well, it's really nice." She wanted to say a lot of things about there being so many nice young people today who contradicted the rebel-teenager stereotype, but she thought she might sound gushy.

"We'd be obliged, miss," Johnson said. "I don't see the hotel bus anywhere."

"Believe me, it'll be our pleasure," the young woman said brightly. "Here's our car."

Mrs. Johnson noticed the twisted yellow handkerchiefs around the necks of the clean, good-looking young folks. "Don't you look nice," she said. "Are you students?"

"More like a club," the young woman said as the automatic door locks clicked the car's doors shut. "These rumals are our insignia."

"Isn't that sweet? Kind of like the Scouts."

"We'd like you both to have one," the girl said.

"Oh, no. We couldn't—"

"Please. It'll make our day. Here, just slip it around your neck. You, too. . . ."

## Number 131, 132, and 133.

Samantha Hall and Roderick Van Cleef explained to the chauffeur that if he couldn't do his job, he could find another.

"But the car was running perfectly just minutes ago," the French driver said, with a touch of that French arrogance that wonders what it is doing even talking to lesser people, much less apologizing to them.

"Well, that obviously isn't the case now," Samantha drawled, spinning her Oscar de la Renta cape dramatically about her shoulders.

"What a bore," Roderick said with a sigh.

"It's all your fault, Roddy. If we had flown the Concorde . . ."

"What's that got to do with this? Besides, the Concorde's as uncomfortable as ballet shoes."

"We could have chartered a plane, then," Samantha said.

"For a bloody weekend?"

"My last lover did," Samantha said.

"Your last lover was too fat to fit into the seat of a commercial jet."

"She was not," Samantha said. "And anyway—"

"Pardon me, but I see you're having some car trouble," said a young man with a yellow handkerchief in his pocket. "May I give you a lift?"

"Roddy, have this person arrested," Samantha snapped.

"Why? He's offering us a ride."

"In a Chevrolet," Samantha hissed. "And he's wearing polyester. You don't want me seen with someone in a polyester jacket, do you?"

"Frankly, I wouldn't give a damn if he were wearing fig leaves. Look at the taxi line."

"Actually, the car's quite comfortable," the eager young man said with an engaging grin.

Samantha heaved a great sigh. "All right. My weekend's already ruined anyway. I might as well turn it into a total fiasco. Bring on the Chevrolet."

She stepped haughtily toward the blue American sedan. Another young man smiled at her from the front seat. He was holding a yellow handkerchief in his hands.

"You can come too," the young man told the French chauffeur.

"I will not ride with a paid laborer," Samantha screeched.

"It'll be all right," the young man said soothingly. "He can ride in the front seat with us. And the trip will be over in no time at all."


Number 134.

Miles Patterson sat in the airport bar sipping a martini, his well-worn leather bag at his feet. He had been flying internationally for twenty-five years and he had found that a couple of stiff drinks immediately after a long flight helped eliminate jet lag. Let others scurry through corridors dragging their bundles and bags and kiddies and then wait interminably at the baggage claim and then again for a cab ride. Miles

Patterson prefered to blot up two martinis in silent ecstasy, until Paris looked like a warm and friendly place.

"Do you mind if I sit next to you?" a young pretty girl asked as Miles was nearing the end of his second martini. She was less than twenty years old and had Brooke Shields's hair and melon breasts. Paris had never before seemed so warm and friendly.

He shook his head and the girl asked shyly, "Are you visiting?"

Miles stared, stupefied for a moment, before dragging himself back to reality. "Uh, no. Business. I'm a jewelry merchant. I make this trip six, eight times a year."

"Goodness," the girl said, looking down at the leather bag. "If those are your samples, you'd better be really careful."

"No, no," Patterson said, smiling. "The samples are on me. Big security risk, you know. I have a hell of a time getting through customs."

The girl laughed as if he'd said the funniest words ever uttered. "It's so nice to meet another American," she gushed. "Sometimes I get so . . . I don't know, hungry . . . for men like you."

"Hungry?" Miles Patterson said, feeling the olives from the martinis tumbling around inside his stomach.

"Um," the girl said. She licked her lips.

"Where are you staying?" he asked quickly.

The girl leaned close and whispered. "Very near here," she said. "We can walk there. Right through a field of deep grass." Her chest rose and fell.

"What a coincidence," he said. "I've just been thinking that what I need most right now is a good brisk walk." He tried to laugh. She brushed her breasts against him as she stood up. A yellow handkerchief dangled from her belt.

"You lead the way," he said.

"Oh, I will," the girl said. "I will." As they left the airport, she took the handkerchief from her belt and stretched it taut between her hands.

Mrs. Evelyn Baynes was not wearing a sari. Not today. Not in Paris. She was wearing the latest Karl Lagerfeld walking suit in mauve and her hair had been done by Cinandre in New York. She was wearing the most uncomfortable Charles Jourdan shoes that money could buy and she felt terrific for the first time in weeks.

"Hurry up," she said, prodding her two children toward the portly couple waiting at the baggage claim area. "Joshua, take Kimberly's hand. And smile. This is the first time we've been out of that pit in God knows how long."

"The ashram is not a pit," Joshua said hotly.

"And I don't like Mrs. Palmer," Kimberly balked. "She always tries to kiss me. Can I kill her, Joshua?"

"Sure, kid," the boy said. "Just wait for me to give you the signal."

Evelyn Baynes beamed. "That's using psychology, Joshua," she said. "You'll be a fine leader someday."

"Someday I will be chief phansigar," the boy said.

"Now, I don't want to hear another word about that god-awful place. We've got a whole week in Paris to be civilized again." She squealed as she embraced Mrs. Palmer. "My, Emmie, the extra weight agrees with you," she said.

"You've simply withered away to nothing, dear," Mrs. Palmer cooed back. "Have you been ill? Oh, no. That's right. You've been living with some religious cultists or something, haven't you?"

"Now, Emmie," Herb Palmer broke in.

"Well, it *is* the talk of the neighborhood, dear. The Madisons have already moved out."

"Emmie . . ."

"It's all right," Mrs. Baynes said, flushing violently. "Actually, the ashram's the latest. All the rage among the 'in' Europeans."

"You called it a pit, Mommy," Kimberly Baynes said.

"Where's the car?" shouted Mrs. Baynes.

"Coming around the corner."

The black driver smiled and touched his fingers to his cap as they climbed into the car. Joshua helped Mrs. Palmer and his mother and sister inside. He started to get in, then hesitated. "I have to go to the bathroom," he said.

"Oh, *Joshua.* Not now. It's not far to the city," his mother said.

"I said I have to go. Now."

Mrs. Baynes sighed. "All right. I'll go with you."

"I want *him* to take me." He pointed to the black driver.

"No problem," Herb Palmer said. "Go ahead. I'll just drive around the block and wait for you both."

When he had circumnavigated the block twice, Joshua was waiting at the curb alone. "Your driver quit," he said as he got into the car.

"What?"

"He met some woman inside the airport. They told me to get lost and then they went away together. They said they'd never be back."

"Well, I never . . ." Mrs. Palmer said.

"We'll see what the company has to say about that," Palmer said through clenched teeth.

"You poor brave little boy," Mrs. Baynes said, clutching Joshua to her breast.

They drove away before the body of the black man was discovered in the men's room and the screaming began. Number 135.

*    *    *

**Numbers 136, 137, and 138.**

"We want to go to the Bois de Boulogne, Mother," Joshua said.

"Don't be silly, dear. We're going straight to the Georges Cinq."

"But it's special," chimed in Kimberly.

"Yes. Special. We read about a special place in a book. Kimmy and I wrote a special poem to recite to you there. The three of you. It has to be now."

"Hey, why not?" Herb Palmer said. "We're all on vacation. Forget schedules."

"Such sweet children, Evelyn," said Mrs. Palmer.

They stopped by a swamp on the northern end of a swan lake.

"But don't you think it's nicer over there, children?" Mrs. Baynes suggested. "Near the birds, where the people are?"

"No. It has to be here," Joshua said stubbornly.

"Oh, very well. Let's hear your poem, darlings."

"Outside," Herb Palmer said. "Poetry needs sun and sky and water and fresh air."

The adults all moved out and sat on the bank that ran down to the brackish water and looked out at the swans far away.

"The poem," Herb Palmer said. "Let's hear the poem."

Joshua smiled. Kimberly smiled. They pulled yellow handkerchiefs from their pockets.

Mrs. Baynes said, "Those look familiar. Did you bring them from that . . . that place?"

"Yes, Mother," Kimberly said. "You all three have to wear them."

"No," Mr. Palmer said laughingly. "The poem first."

"For luck," Joshua insisted.

"Please," Kimberly pleaded. "Josh even has an extra one for you, Mother."

The children slipped the kerchiefs around the necks of the three adults.

"And now the poem," Joshua announced to the backs of the three adults.

"Is that the signal?" Kimberly whispered to him.

"That's the signal."

She jumped up behind Mr. Palmer, and as they chanted, "Kill for Kali, Kill for Kali," they pulled the yellow rumals around the Palmers' necks.

"Kill for Kali. She loves it. Kill, kill, kill."

Mrs. Baynes was watching the swans. Without turning, she said, "That's a strange poem. It doesn't even rhyme. Is that what they call free verse? Or blank verse?"

"Kill, kill, kill."

The Palmers' eyes bulged. Mrs. Palmer's tongue lolled out of her mouth, violet and swollen. Herb Palmer struggled to free himself but the metal clasp on the rumal around his fleshy neck held tight.

"I don't think the Palmers are enjoying your poem, children," Mrs. Baynes said acidly, still without turning.

"Kill, kill, kill."

When Herb Palmer's arms finally stopped twitching, the two children released the rumals.

Mrs. Baynes turned and saw the other two adults sprawled on the grass.

"Very funny," she said. "I suppose the four of you have staged this little farce to shock me. Well, believe you me, I'm not easily shocked. Remember that I changed both your diapers? At least Kimberly's. Once. It was in December, I think. The nursemaid was sick. Herb? Emmie?"

The Palmers did not move from their strange positions, faces bloated, eyes bulging from their sockets, staring directly up at the blue sky. Mrs. Palmer's tongue was blackening and hugely distended.

"Emmie," Evelyn Baynes said, shaking her. "I want you to know you don't look at all attractive. A stout woman should never let her tongue hang out, it makes her look retarded." She looked at her children. "Why don't they move? Are they . . . ? I believe . . . they are . . . they're dead."

"Really, Mother?" Joshua Baynes slid behind her.

"But it can't be—you were just playing, weren't you? You weren't trying to . . ."

"She loves it," Joshua Baynes said softly, tightening the yellow rumal around his mother's neck. "Kali loves it."

"Josh . . . Jo . . . J—"

Evelyn Baynes's dying prayer was that her children would at least have the courtesy to put her tongue back in her face after she was dead.

They didn't.

# Sixteen

Harold W. Smith was alone in the basement of Folcroft Sanitarium. He walked past the immaculately clean pipes, hearing his own footsteps clacking on the concrete floor.

He walked past the rows of unused and obsolete hospital equipment, past the sealed boxes containing files from decades past, to a small door with a keyhole so small that no one could see through it, and also six feet off the ground for good measure.

He inserted a special key that had no duplicate and walked into a small cubicle of a room. It was made entirely of wood, and beneath the wooden wall panels were layers of highly flammable plastic. The room had been designed to burn in case of fire.

Immediately above it was Smith's office. Unlike this room, its walls were covered with fireproof asbestos. But its floor was wood and would burn.

Smith checked his casket. It wasn't really a casket but more like a straw cot built on highly flammable materials. It resembled a Viking funeral pyre, but Smith's mind was not imaginative enough to think up any name for it but "casket." It was where his body would lie in death, and so it was as much a casket as anything else.

Inside the stuffing of the casket was a sealed bottle of

cyanide. Smith held it up to the light and made sure that it had not leaked any of its contents.

The poison capsule he carried with him was un certain. He might lose it, or he might have to use it or someone else. But the cyanide in the casket was always there.

If CURE should be compromised and its existence become known, a fire in Smith's office would first destroy the computers, the four enormous monoliths that had been adapted and improved for more than twenty years, the computers that held the secrets of almost everyone in the world.

Meanwhile Smith would come downstairs to his basement room and open the vial of cyanide. It would smell like almonds if he was among the fifty percent of human beings who were able to detect the scent in a lethal dose of the drug. It would be painful but merci fully quick. A wrenching agony, a convulsion, and then death. Just moments before the fire burned through the floor of his office and down into this room that had been designed to be a tinderbox.

Everything was in place and Smith felt a small touch of satisfaction. He clasped his hands together, as if holding on to himself for support. When he noticed the gesture, he stopped, but he could still see the white bands formed by the grip of his fingers on his skin. He pinched a piece of flesh from the back of his hand. It took several seconds for the skin to fall back into place.

His were old hands, he realized, dry and brittle. The elasticity of their skin had vanished, sometime between his youth, when the wrongs of the world had enraged him and filled him with righteous commitment to correct them, and now, when the sign of an unbroken bottle of poison, designed to give him death, could genuinely set his mind at ease. How small we become, he thought, walking upstairs. In what infinitesimal ways do we take our pleasures.

The red phone rang only moments after he entered his office.

"Yes, Mr. President."

"I've just been told that an entire flight of passengers on Air Europa has been wiped out. They were all found strangled in Paris."

"I know, sir," Smith said.

"First it was the International Mid-America disaster a week or so ago. Now Europa. The killers are spreading out."

"It appears that way."

"This isn't good," the President said. "The press is blaming us."

"That isn't unusual, Mr. President," Smith said.

"Dammit, man, we've got to give them something. What has your special person found out?"

"Still working on it, sir."

"That's what you said the last time," the President said.

"It is still a correct status report," Smith said.

"All right," the voice on the other end said with forced patience. "I'm not going to meddle in your methods. But I want you to understand the kind of crisis we're in. If the airways can't be kept safe, there really isn't a lot of reason for any of us to be here."

"I understand, sir," Smith said.

There was a click on the other end and Smith replaced the receiver quietly. It was all going downhill. What the President had meant was that there wasn't a reason for CURE to be kept in existence.

He plucked the skin on the back of his hand. Maybe it was his age. Maybe a younger man could have done something, maybe even the Smith of a few years ago could have stopped things before they got out of control.

Today, he didn't even know if Remo was working. And Chiun was somewhere in the Pacific Ocean with a notion that some sort of talisman was going to save America from slipping back into the Stone Age.

Smith shook his head. It all seemed so ludicrous.

He took a pen from a plastic coffee cup on his desk and began to compose a letter to his wife.

"Dear Irma," he began. But after that, his mind went blank. He was never much good at writing personal letters. Still, he couldn't very well die knowing his body would be reduced to just a thin layer of black ash, without at least trying something.

He turned on his office radio. Perhaps some music would help set the mood for the letter to his wife.

He listened to the last few bars of "Boogie Woogie Bugle Boy" and decided it didn't offer the mood he needed. He was about to change the station when the announcer began reciting stock quotations.

"On the Big Board today," the smooth voice said, "stocks were mixed in active trading. But the big story continued to be in the airlines industry. On the heels of the murder tragedy in Paris, Europa Airlines dropped seventeen points in the first hour today and is now trading at ten dollars a share. International Mid-America Airlines, which ran into problems with passenger deaths last week, dropped another two points and is now trading at thirty-seven and a half cents a share, and inside talk along Wall Street is that the firm will declare bankruptcy this week. Bucking the trend continues to be Just Folks Airlines. Its stocks opened today at sixty-seven, up two from yesterday's close, and an increase of more than forty-one points since the company began its new campaign of promoting itself as 'Just Folks, the Friendly, SAFE Airline.' In other stock activity, U.S. Steel—"

Smith switched off the radio. He felt his breathing speed up. Impatiently he crumpled the unfinished letter to his wife and tossed it into the wastebasket. He turned on the computer console at his desk and went to work.

He had been at the business of learning people's secrets for most of his life, and one of the things he had learned was that at the core of most mysteries was money. If you found something unusual going on, and if you stayed at it long enough and you dug into it deeply enough, sooner or later you would find somebody with a monetary interest behind it all.

When the airline deaths had affected only Just Folks Airlines, he had been inclined to think it might have been the work of cultists or lunatics, attracted by the airline's low fares and willing to settle for the few dollars they might get from economy-minded passengers.

But suddenly Just Folks had been moved off the passenger kill list and International Mid-America and Air Europa had been savaged, and in a different way. The Just Folks killings had been small, one at a time, small family groups. But the two other airlines had been hit in such a way as to maximize the impact of the killings on the airlines' reputations and stability.

Money was involved somehow. Smith knew it.

He had the computers roll up an ultrarapid scan of all U.S. airline ticket sales during the past month, and concurrently had the machines check for any sizable cash withdrawals from any airline official with IMAA or Air Europa. As an afterthought, he included Just Folks.

Then he sat back and let the computers permute for all they were worth.

It was the great beauty of the computers—which he called the Folcroft Four and which he had personally designed—that their exteriors looked like oversize scrap heaps, obsolete in their technology, and excessively dependent on exotic maintenance systems. But inside, each one was a masterwork, with much of the technology invented by Smith himself when he could not find it available through commercial channels.

And for years, into the four computers had gone the information gathered by a network of people who reported all the bland and mediocre details of their jobs. For this work, they got a small stipend from Smith. Of course, none of them had ever heard of Smith or CURE and did not know who was sending them money. They just assumed it was the FBI or the CIA and didn't really care who it was as long as the small monthly checks kept coming.

These reports were organized by Smith's computers, indexed and cross-indexed, cataloged and cross-cataloged, so that they were able to answer within minutes almost any kind of question about any kind of activity in the United States.

And now they answered his questions, and from the answers Smith extracted one glaring, blinding detail:

A. H. BAYNES, PRESIDENT OF JUST FOLKS AIRLINES, REMOVED FIVE THOUSAND DOLLARS FROM PERSONAL ACCOUNT 7/14. On 7/15 TWENTY-ONE TICKETS ABOARD INTERNATIONAL MID-AMERICA AIRLINES PURCHASED BY UNKNOWN BUYER FOR $4,927 CASH. A. H. BAYNES SOLD STOCKS WORTH $61,000 7/23. On 7/24, 120 TICKETS ABOARD EUROPA FLIGHT TO PARIS PURCHASED FOR $60,000. PROBABILITY OF CONNECTION, 93.67 PERCENT.

Smith felt like whooping for joy. Instead he pressed the intercom button on his desk and said in his usual dry, lemony voice, "Hold my calls for a while, Mrs. Mikulka."

Then he called Just Folks Airlines and got a cheerful recording saying that if he really wanted to talk to someone, he should hold. He waited through three long selections of Muzak, made even longer because it was the music of Barry Manilow, before a female voice broke through with a crackle.

"Just Folks, the friendly, SAFE airline," she said.

"I'd like to speak to Mr. A. H. Baynes, please," Smith said.

"I'm sorry, but Mr. Baynes is unavailable."

"Is this his office?"

"No, this is the reservations desk at the airport."

"Then how do you know he's unavailable?"

"Do you think a millionaire like A. H. Baynes would be standing here getting varicose veins and hawking tickets for poverty wages?"

"Would you please connect me with his office?" Smith said.

"Mr. Baynes's office," another female said. Her voice had the steel edge of the executive secretary.

"Mr. Baynes, please. This is the Securities and Exchange Commission calling."

"I'm sorry, Mr. Baynes isn't in."

"Where can I reach him? This is an urgent matter."

"I'm afraid I can't tell you," she said, the flinty voice mellowing with a kind of desperation. "He's away on personal business."

"Now? With the crisis in air travel?" Smith said.

"At Just Folks, there is no crisis," the secretary said levelly.

"Does he call in for messages?"

"Occasionally. Do you want to leave one?"

"No," Smith said, and hung up.

He realized he was alone. No Remo. No Chiun. And the clock was ticking away on CURE. But he knew Baynes had something to do with the airline killings. He knew it.

He would have to find Baynes. And he would have to do it alone.

## Seventeen

Remo sat on the edge of the bed in the New Orleans motel room, his elbows braced on his knees, his hands covering his face. Why was he in New Orleans?

He didn't know. He had come on his own, walking, hitchhiking, following road by road, following something he could not explain or understand.

*Where was Chiun?* Chiun would understand. He knew about the Kali business. It had seemed to Remo like a fairy tale when he had first heard it—the hopeless fantasy of an old man who believed too strongly in legends—but Remo wasn't sure anymore. *Something* had brought him to this shabby room on this dark street. *Something* had pulled him all the miles from Denver to here.

The worst of it was that he could feel its influence growing inside him. There was something dark and alien and frightening right under his skin. That something that had compelled him to shame himself with that blond girl in a public alley. A normal man, burning up the way Remo was, might run amok and kill someone. But what of someone with Remo's strength and killing techniques? How many would *he* kill? How much damage could *he* do?

It was a nightmare and there was no way Remo could wake from it. Little by little, he had given in.

From his first tentative steps outside the hotel room in Denver, he had convinced himself that he was only going for a walk around the city streets. He had told himself, very calmly and logically, that he couldn't very well wait inside a closed room for the days or even weeks that it might take Chiun to return.

Reason was on his side and Chiun's story about Master Lu and the talking stone goddess was unreasonable. He would have been a fool to hide out for fear of a silly legend. So he walked out of his hotel room in Denver, and his reason told him that it was a perfectly reasonable thing to do. But something in the back of his mind knew better.

In the old days, before he knew of Harold Smith or CURE, when he was just a foot cop walking a beat in Newark, New Jersey, Remo had tried to quit smoking. The ritual occurred every year: he would stop cold, filled with righteous willpower and a sense of mastery over his own impulses. Then, generally after a week, he would allow himself one cigarette. It was nothing, one cigarette. His reason told him so. He didn't even enjoy the one cigarette. But it always marked the end of his good intentions, and even though his reason told him that one single cigarette was harmless, his inner mind knew the truth: that he was a smoker once again.

And so when he left the hotel room in Denver, he wrote the Korean characters for "going" in yellow chalk on the outside of the hotel building. He had marked it on two other places in Denver and sporadically throughout his journey, throwing out crumbs of bread for Chiun to follow.

Because he knew in the back of his mind that he was already lost.

*Chiun, come find me.* He clenched his hands into two fists and held them in front of him, shaking.

The lust was growing within him. *It,* the thing, Kali, whatever. *It* wanted him to move. His destination was near. He had known it when he reached the dark street in New Orleans. The force inside him had grown so great that it had taken all his effort to fight it and duck into this seedy hotel with no bedspread, a battered television set strewn with wires, and only a thin yellow hand towel in the bathroom.

There was a telephone too. If he'd had a friend, he would have called just to listen to a voice. A voice might keep him sane. But assassins had no friends. Only victims.

He stood up. He was bathed in sweat and his breath was labored and rasping.

He had to get out. He had to breathe. It was only reasonable.

"What's happening to me?" he shouted aloud. The sound reverberated through the silent room. *It* wanted him out. *It* wanted him to come. *It*, with its sickly-sweet smell and arms of death.

He smashed his fist through the mirror. His image splintered into a thousand pieces and flew in all directions. With a sob, he sat down.

"Get it together. Calm down." He spoke the words softly, gently. He smoothed his hands together until their violent trembling stilled. He turned on the battered television.

"The victims of the most recent wave of airline killings which struck Air Europa earlier this week are still turning up in Paris," the announcer said.

Remo moaned and listened.

"The bodies of three prominent Denver-area residents were found early this morning in a public park near Neuilly, France, a suburb of Paris. They were identified as Mr. and Mrs. Herbert Palmer and Mrs. A. H. Baynes, wife of the president of Just Folks Airlines. Apparently she was traveling with her two children, Joshua and Kimberly Baynes, whose whereabouts are still unknown."

"Oh, God," Remo said. It had been his job to stop the airline killings. *His* job.

How long had it been since he had given a thought to his job, to his responsibilities, to his country? He felt sick. He knew what to do now. He had to go back to work. He had to forget this force that was pulling him away.

He reached for the telephone and began to dial the complex routing code that would eventually connect him with Harold Smith.

The connections were slow. His hand strayed to replace the receiver, but he forced himself to hold on, knowing that *It* wanted him to hang up. *It* wanted him alone. For herself.

When Smith pulled into the driveway of his home, he thought about the letter he had meant to write to his wife. Like all the other letters he had planned to write her, it had not been written. And perhaps he would never have the chance again.

He was no fool. The President's phone call had been his last warning to CURE. Unless Smith could do something about the air deaths, the next communication from the White House would be to disband. And with Remo gone, with Chiun gone, Smith had no illusions. He might return empty-handed, and that would be the end of CURE, and of Harold W. Smith.

He owned Irma a good-bye.

As he got out of the car, he saw two neighbors sitting in their front yard and he realized that he had been living in the same house with Irma for twenty years and he did not know the names of any of his neighbors.

Irma, of course, knew everyone's name. She was like that. She was in, and of, the neighborhood. Her flower garden had won first prize in the neighborhood gardening contest for fourteen years in a row, until she had decided that delphiniums weren't worth the effort.

But each June, until then, a bright blue ribbon had hung proudly from the Smiths' door. Most years, it was the only acknowledgment Irma made that she had won, and Smith realized that he had never told her that the garden looked nice.

As he walked up the drive, he could see Irma, through the bay window, tearing off her apron and patting her hair in place in preparation for his arrival. It made him smile one of his infrequent smiles. His plump wife, her hair now a bluish ghastly silver, always treated him like a beau coming to call on their first date. If she was awake. Most nights, he would come home too late and she would already be asleep. But a plate of food, always awful, always covered with some kind of tomato-soup goo, would be waiting for him. But there were never any accusations, never any recriminations for keeping the hours he did. As far as Irma was concerned, anything was an improvement over the old days when Smith worked in the wartime OSS and then the CIA and was gone without a word for months at a time. During the whole of World War II, she had seen Smith twice. During the five tensest years of the Cold War, she had seen him only once, and had received two telegrams from him, each exactly ten words in length.

"You're just in time for supper," she said, pretending as she always did, not to be excited about seeing him.

"I'm not hungry. Please sit down."

"Oh, dear." She sat, her forehead wrinkled. "Is it very bad?" She picked up her knitting.

"No. Nothing of the sort." There was a long, awkward silence.

"Will you take off your jacket, dear?" Irma asked.

"No. I have to be going."

"Busy at the office, I expect."

"No. Everything's fine. I have to go out of town. Maybe for some time."

Mrs. Smith nodded and managed a smile. She had always smiled. Even when Smith had left for Europe at the start of the war, after they had been married only three weeks, she hadn't cried. She had only smiled. Smith looked at her and wondered: How do you tell a woman like that that you may have to commit suicide very soon?

She clasped his hands. "Go do what you have to do, dear," she said gently.

He stared at her for a moment. It had never occurred to him that Irma might know that he did secret work, that he had more of a job than just head of Folcroft Sanitarium. But maybe she did. No. She couldn't know. He had never discussed his work with her. Really, he thought with some shame, he had never discussed much of anything with her. And yet she had always made things easy for him. Even now, she was making it easy for him to leave, as if she sensed that it was somehow very important.

"Right." He cleared his throat, nodded, and left the table. Halfway out the door, he turned around.

"Irma, I have to tell you something."

"Yes, dear?"

"I . . . er, you . . . that is, I . . ." He exhaled noisily. "The garden is lovely."

She smiled. "Thank you, dear."

A. H. Baynes's home was in a suburb of Denver where there were more trees, more schools, more parks, and more money than anywhere else in the area. All the houses were on large tracts of manicured lawn, with garages the size of most single-family dwellings in the city.

There was no answer at the home of Baynes or at the

home of the late Mr. and Mrs. Herbert Palmer. The neighbors on the other side of Baynes's house were named Cunningham, and when Smith rang the bell, a stylish middle-aged woman in expensive tweeds answered.

"Mrs. Cunningham?"

She shook her head. "I'm the housekeeper. May I help you?"

"I'd rather speak with Mrs. Cunningham, if you don't mind." He took a Treasury Department ID card from his wallet. "It's rather urgent," he said.

"Mrs. Cunningham's in her studio. I'll announce you."

She led him through a house furnished with all the latest trends, from mauve furniture in the living room to a green-and-white kitchen adorned with butcher-block floor tiles, to a sparkling chrome gym in the rear of the house. Puffing on an exercise bicycle was a short woman, agonizingly underweight, wearing a trendy V-neck leotard and trendier, high-cut green sneakers.

"Mr. Harold Smith from the Treasury Department, ma'am," the housekeeper announced.

"Oh, all right. Bring in my breakfast, Hilary." She turned her attention to Smith, obviously appraising his unstylish suit. "You'll have to forgive me, but I won't be able to talk with you until I've eaten."

Hilary brought in an old Worcester china plate that held a single slab of raw tuna fish. Mrs. Cunningham picked it up with her fingers and popped it in her mouth. Smith closed his eyes and thought of the flag.

"There," she said with satisfaction. "Oh, I'm sorry. Would you care for some sushi?"

"No, thank you," said Smith, swallowing hard.

"Very low in calories."

"I'm sure," he said.

"Hilary won't work for anyone who eats meat."

"The housekeeper?"

"Isn't she a dream?" Mrs. Cunningham rhapsodized. "So Waspy. Nothing ethnic about her at all. Of course, she doesn't do much work. It would ruin her clothes."

"Mrs. Cunningham, I'm looking for A. H. Baynes," Smith said.

She rolled her eyes. "Please don't mention that name around here."

"Why not?"

"As acting chairperson of the Neighborhood Betterment Committee, I have forbidden it."

"You mean, because Mrs. Baynes is deceased?" Smith asked.

"Gawd, no. Dying was the first decent thing Evelyn's done in months. Too bad she had to take the Palmers with her. They were a good element."

"What about Mrs. Baynes?" Smith persisted.

"Dead in Paris."

"Before Paris," Smith said.

"Well, there was that awful business that ruined them in the neighborhood," she said.

"What was that? It's for the good of the country."

"In that case . . ." she said. She leaned forward. "They went to live in some religious commune." She stood back, eyes gleaming, hands on hips. "Can you believe it? I mean, it's not like throwing a party for revolutionaries. That's a *statement*. What sort of statement can religion make? They're not even doing that in Southern California."

"Was this commune in the neighborhood?" Smith asked.

"I should hope not. Episcopalians don't have communes. My church doesn't even have services. But that's what it was all about. The Byneses were talking about communes in the neighborhood. Well, the last thing we wanted was some hairy old thing from China or someplace having religious sex orgies on our lawn. So we told the Bayneses we didn't approve."

"Have you seen Mr. Baynes recently?"

"Not a glimpse. Not even at the funeral. But then, he was always a strange one. He didn't even like racquetball."

"Do you know where this commune is that they joined?"

"No, I don't," she said. "And if you find out, don't bother to tell me. I want to think only beautiful thoughts."

Smith was sitting in his chair, pondering his next move, when a buzzing sound came from inside the attaché case on the front seat. He opened the case and lifted the miniature telephone built into it.

"Yes," he said.

"It's . . . Remo."

"Where are you?" said Smith. Remo sounded strange, hurt.

"New Orleans . . . don't know the street . . . a motel. . . ."

"Remo." The voice was a command. "Stay on the line."

"*It* wants me. I can't stay," Remo said.

"Pull yourself together."

"Too late. . . . I have to go . . . have to—"

There was a sound as Remo dropped the telephone. Smith heard the receiver banging against the wall as it hung on its cord.

He called Remo's name several times, then punched a message into a secondary unit in the attaché case, directing the Folcroft computers to trace the call on his telephone.

Remo started for the door of the room. He tried to

stop, and at the last minute darted into the bathroom and slammed the door shut.

But he could still smell the scent. *It* wanted him. He tried to block out the smell. He took the yellow towel from the sink and tried to jam it under the door, but the smell persisted, filling his nostrils and his mind. He held the towel over his face, but it didn't stop the smell.

When he could resist no more, he stood and jammed the yellow towel into his pocket, pulled open the door, and walked toward the door to the hall.

A terrible sadness whistled through him like wind in a storm as he opened the grimy door to the room.

From his pocket he pulled the piece of yellow chalk that he had used to mark his way from Denver. He would not need it anymore.

*It* was near, and his next stop would be with *It*.

He tossed the chalk to the floor. On the other side of the room, the telephone swung rhythmically from its cord.

# Eighteen

Across the alleyway, Ban Sar Din could hear the ashram filling up. He rose from his brocade-covered water bed and stretched.

This was the day.

It was the first gathering of the Thuggees since A. H. Baynes had sent them all off to Paris aboard Air Europa, and he, Ban Sar Din, was now ready to speak to them.

He would tell them that their ways were in error. He would tell them that it was wrong to permit outsiders in the ashram. He would tell them that the true nourishment of the soul depended upon a true spiritual leader and that their leader should be treated with courtesy and respect. He would tell them that belief in Kali was the key to eternal happiness.

Ban Sar Din would tell them all that. He would speak and the faithful would listen, and then he would again take his rightful place as the head of the cult of Kali.

He walked across the alley, past his Porsche, through the heavy steel-reinforced door, and strode deliberately into the ashram. The roar of the devotees resounded in his ears.

He paused and saw at the foot of the statue four large woven baskets. Around the baskets were scores of yellow rumals, each of them twisted and soiled with use.

"Kill," the devotees shouted when they saw him.

"Kill for the love of Kali."

Ban Sar Din stepped onto the dais in front of the statue and held his arms up high. "Listen, listen!" he shouted. But the crowd was still in a frenzy.

"I want to tell you, as your Holy One, that it is wrong what you do." His voice cracked from the strain and he looked around the room, waiting for an incense pot to come flying toward his skull. When he was not assaulted, he went on: "Kali does not wish you to kill so much. Kali does not want numbers of deaths; Kali wants the right deaths. Especially since the deaths make the front pages of the newspapers full every day. Soon the wrath of the authorities will be upon us."

The crowd was still chanting. Some of the members stepped forward, and Ban Sar Din flinched, but they merely went to the large baskets in front of the statue and removed the covers.

"I am your Holy One," Ban Sar Din shouted, "and you must listen to me."

The crowd quieted.

Ban Sar Din's eye caught a glimmer of blue-white coming from the baskets. They were filled with jewels. The jewels were lying on beds of green American cash.

"Yes, Holy One," Holly Rodan said. "We listen to your wisdom."

"Well, uh . . ." Ban Sar Din picked up a diamond pendant. Five carats total weight, he estimated.

"Speak, O Holy One." The room reverberated with the chant.

There were about a half-dozen good sapphires.

"I . . . um . . ." Rubies, he thought, digging into the baskets. The price of rubies was skyrocketing. A two-carat ruby was often worth more than a two-carat diamond.

"I . . . um . . ."

"I think I can speak for the Holy One," said A. H. Baynes, stepping forward from behind the partition that separated the public part of the ashram from his office. His thumbs were hooked into his suspenders and he was grinning broadly, his teeth showing. It was his sincere grin.

"What old Sardine means is, golly, you're a swell bunch of kids."

The throng cheered.

"And don't think the little lady with the arms doesn't appreciate it."

"Hail, Chief Phansigar."

"Kill for Kali."

"Why, just the other day, I was telling Old Sardine here—" A. H. Baynes began, but he was interrupted.

Holly Rodan screamed. Every face turned toward her.

"He's here. He has come."

Ban Sar Din pocketed a half-dozen of the biggest jewels in case someone bad had come. "Who?" he shouted. "Where?"

"There," Holly shouted. "He has come. Kali's lover. He has come."

"Oh, him," said Ban Sar Din, but he looked to the back of the ashram, even as he filled his other pocket with more jewels and cash.

In the doorway stood a tall thin young man wearing a black T-shirt. His wrists were large. His face was haggard and his eyes held a look of helpless despair. If someone had asked him who he was, he would have answered that his name used to be Remo Williams.

"Hail, Lover of Kali," the Thuggees chanted, falling to their knees before him.

Woodenly Remo walked forward.

"He is carrying the rumal," people shouted, for

Remo was nervously twisting the thin yellow hand towel he had taken from the motel bathroom.

In the crowd, leaning against a pillar, was A. H. Baynes. It was a face that Remo remembered, but it meant nothing to him now. He passed on.

The pull on him was irresistible. It felt as if the statue had him by a rope and was pulling him toward her. He saw the statue on the raised platform. It was hideous, a different creature from a different world, but still he walked toward it. The stone face was impassive, but behind it, suddenly another face seemed to stir to life. It was a beautiful face, full of sorrow. Remo blinked, but the face lingered for a moment, then disappeared, again replaced by the pitted graven image of the statue.

"Who is he?" someone whispered.

Remo heard the answer. "He is Kali's lover. The one for whom She has waited."

A lover? He was not even a man, Remo thought. He was a puppet and his time was short. With each step, he felt something inside him weaken. By the time he reached the dais and stood face to face with the statue of Kali, he could barely move. The yellow towel slipped from his fingers and dropped onto the floor.

The scent pierced him, ancient and malevolent. It coursed through him like an evil, burning serpent, twisting its way through his bloodstream.

*It is too late,* he thought. *Too late.*

And even as the thought formed, he saw the lips of Kali curl into a smile.

# Nineteen

"Bring me death."

The words echoed inside his head, and Remo jolted awake. He was in a small room on a narrow cot. Two large cubes of incense burned in a porcelain plate at the foot of his bed.

His skin was prickly white gooseflesh. He looked around, and his first reaction was one of relief that the ghoulish vision of the many-armed statue smiling slyly at him had been only a nightmare. But the faint smell of the goddess still hung in his nostrils, and he knew that the real nightmare was only beginning.

"Baynes," he said shortly. A. H. Baynes had been the face he recognized in the crowd. And Baynes, for better or for worse, was *real.* He had to concentrate on Baynes.

The smell was stronger now, and again he heard the words inside his mind: "Bring me death."

Quickly, noiselessly, still feeling a jittery fear at the base of his spine, Remo slid out of bed and moved toward the door to the room. It opened silently and he looked out at the ashram, where the mindless, chanting cultists slept on the hard wooden floor. He moved like a cat among them, but Baynes was not there. He turned and saw the statue of Kali. Its eight arms seemed to be waving to him, and the sight sickened him and filled him with fear. He ran toward the door in the back of the room.

He was in an alley. A large black Porsche was parked there, and beyond it, Remo heard humming coming from a garage. He went toward it.

Ban Sar Din ceased his tuneless rendition of "When the Saints Go Marching In" when he saw the haggard stranger in the doorway. He rose from his water bed where he had been busying himself, jotting down the telephone numbers of dating services that promised, in magazine advertisements, that *Beautiful Scandinavian Blondes Want to Meet You.*

"Shoo," he said to Remo. "Shoo, shoo, shoo. You are not allowed in the Holy One's quarters."

"I'm looking for Baynes," Remo said thickly. The smell was less strong here. He felt as if his head were starting to clear.

"Now I recognize you," Ban Sar Din said. "You are the lover."

"Lover?" Remo repeated.

"The one Kali has chosen to be Her husband."

"Scratch that," Remo said. "I'm a confirmed bachelor. I want to know what Baynes has to do with this place."

Ban Sar Din snorted. "Why don't you ask him?"

"I couldn't find him," Remo said. "And I wasn't feeling too good in there."

"Maybe you're not eating well enough," Ban Sar Din said. "You're too thin. I know this great French restaurant—"

"It's not the food. It's the statue," Remo said.

"It is only a harmless stone figure," Ban Sar Din said.

Remo shook his head.

Ban Sar Din pinched his nose. "All right. Maybe there is something unusual about it. I don't like it, but they do." He jerked his head toward the ashram.

"What is it, anyway?" Remo said. "What does it do?"

"It grows arms."

"Come on," Remo said in disgust.

"It's true. I don't know how. I just know some mornings I go in there and it's got more arms than it did when I went to sleep. It makes them crazy in the ashram."

"Crazy enough to kill people?" Remo asked.

Ban Sar Din swallowed as a long shadow hovered over Remo. "Whoa, there, pard," A. H. Baynes said, grinning his most sincere toothy smile. "Did I hear my name?" He reached out his hand to shake Remo's. "Let's press the flesh."

Remo kept his hand stubbornly at his side. "Keep your flesh to yourself," he said. He looked Baynes over. The airline president was wearing a checkered cowboy shirt and white pants tucked into intricately worked white cowboy boots. Around his bare throat hung a knit black string tie.

"That your concession to your wife's death?" Remo asked, touching the tie.

"I'd say that's my business, mister."

"How about the yellow handkerchiefs all over the floor of this place? Is that your business too?"

Baynes moved to the side so that Remo's body shielded him from the view of Ban Sar Din, and he pursed his lips and squinted, motioning Remo to be silent.

"Come on in the office and we'll talk," he said. Loudly, over Remo's shoulder, he said, "You can go back to sleep, Sardine. I'll take care of our guest."

"Good," the Indian said. "I was just in the middle of some very important paperwork."

Remo followed Baynes out of the garage, and as the airline man led him back across the alley to the ashram, he whispered, "I couldn't say anything in front of the old fraud, but I'm here for a reason, you know."

"I bet the reason has something to do with murder," Remo said.

"Damn right. I've been weeks tracing down these bugbirds. They're behind the killings on the airplanes," Baynes said.

"Odd you didn't think about going to the police or the FBI," Remo said. They were in Baynes's steel-walled office.

"Don't tell me, pal," Baynes said. He sat heavily in a chair and dropped his head into his hands. "I wanted to get proof, and I waited too long. Now my wife is dead and my kids are missing." He looked up at Remo and there were tears in his eyes. "I swear to you, mister, I'm going to get these bastards. Every last one of them."

"I'm sorry, Baynes," Remo said. "What do you know about the statue? Is it true, all that magic stuff?"

Baynes shook his head, a sly insider's smile on his mouth. "Hah. I'll show you how true it is," he hissed. "Come on."

He opened the door to the ashram, and the scent curled in, attacking Remo's nostrils, and he hung back. But in a sudden movement, A. H. Baynes grabbed his wrist and yanked him out into the ashram. Remo could not resist. The strength was gone from his body and he felt like a rag doll.

Baynes, with no more effort than he would have used to steer a child around the aisles of a department store, tossed Remo onto the platform at the foot of the statue, leaned over close, and whispered, "It is true. It's true," he said. His eyes glistened with excitement. "She *is* Kali and She loves death."

A small helpless cry escaped from Remo's lips. He could feel Her, close to him. She was suffocating him. "Baynes . . . Chiun . . . yellow cloth . . ." Remo mumbled, trying to preserve a part of his mind from the stupefying influence of the stone statue, but Her scent was filling his body, blocking out everything except a wild maniacal lust he felt swelling inside him.

The room swirled. Nothing existed for him except the statue. She was the goddess Kali and She owned him.

"Bring me death." He heard the voice again, but this time it did not seem to come from inside his own mind, but from the lips of the statue. And this time he knew he would obey Her.

A. H. Baynes watched Remo move like a zombie toward the door to the street and then go outside. He waited. Then he took the miniature camera from inside his shirt pocket, extracted the tiny roll of film, and put it into his pocket.

Inside his office, he made a telephone call. It was the first time he had ever used the number. The receiver on the other end was picked up but there was no greeting.

"Hello? Hello?" Baynes said.

"One favor you are allowed," the androgynous whisper said. "Then the statue is mine."

"A deal," Baynes said. "I've got a man here. He's a fed and he's got to go."

"I understand."

"I don't care how you do it," Baynes said.

"I will tell you how."

A half-hour later, Baynes met his contact at the site of a condemned building. The person was swathed in cloaks and wore gloves. Baynes passed over the roll of film.

"His name's Remo," he said to the invisible stranger. "This is what he looks like."

The figure nodded.

"I guess that's it, then," Baynes said.

"Prepare the statue."

"What if you fail?"

"I will not fail."

Baynes started to leave, then hesitated. "Will I see you again?"

"Do you want to?"

Baynes gulped and said, "Maybe not. Tell me, though. Why do you want that statue so badly? It's not worth a million dollars."

"I want many things . . . including you." The figure's hands went to its cloaks and began to open them.

## Twenty

Remo careened crazily down the darkened street. The only sound he heard from the sleeping city was the insistent thrum of his heartbeat, and it seemed to be speaking to him, saying, "Kill for me, kill for me, kill for me."

His hands hung rigid at his sides. He staggered up the street like a man dancing with death, insensate, drunk with a lust he did not understand. *Don't listen,* a smaller voice inside him said, but it was too faint to hear now. And then it was stilled.

A pigeon startled him as it flew off its perch on a telephone line and fluttered to the ground in front of him. It walked in jerky circles, unused to the night.

*Bring me death,* Kali's unspoken voice called to him.

The pigeon stopped and cocked its head to one side, then the other.

*Bring me death.*

Remo closed his eyes and said, "Yes."

The pigeon, only amused by the sound, looked at him quizzically as Remo crouched. Then, seeming to sense the power of the human who moved without sound, who could hold a position as still as a stone, the pigeon panicked and flapped its wings to soar upward.

Remo sprang then, leaping into a perfect spiral in the manner he had learned from Chiun, a way to cut through the air without creating countercurrents that pressed back against one's body, forcing it downward. It was pure Sinanju, the effortless bound, the muscles pulling in flawless synchronization as the body turned in the air, the hands reaching up to halt the pigeon in flight, the sharp snap that broke the tiny creature's neck.

Remo held the limp, still-warm body in his hands, and the sound of his heartbeat seemed to explode in his ears.

"Oh, God, why?" he whispered, and fell to his knees on the oil-slick street. A car blared its horn as it swerved past him, setting his ears to ringing from the shock of the sound. Then it settled and his heartbeat slowed. The night was silent again and he still held the dead bird softly in his hands.

*Run,* he thought. He could run away again as he had before.

But he had come back before, and he knew he would again.

Kali was too strong.

He stood up, his knees weak, and walked back to the ashram. With each step, he realized he had disgraced Sinanju, had trivialized it by using its techniques to snuff out the life of a poor harmless creature whose only sin was getting in his way. Chiun had called him Master of Sinanju, the avatar of the god Shiva. But he was nothing. He was less than nothing. He belonged to Kali.

Inside the ashram, which still hissed with the sounds of the sleeping members, he placed his offering at the foot of the statue.

She smiled at him. She seemed to caress him, sending out unseen tendrils of passion to this man who gave Her his strength and had brought Her the bloodless death She craved.

He moved closer to the statue, and Her scent, like the fragrance of evil flowers, filled him with a blinding desire. For a moment the other face he had seen before hovered behind the statue's. Who was she? A crying woman, a real woman, and yet, the image of the weeping woman was not real. But somehow it made him ache in pain and loss. And the statue itself reached out toward him with Her strangling hand, and on his lips he felt Her cold kiss and he heard Her voice say, "My husband," and he was weakening, suffocating, giving in. . . .

With a violent wrench he pulled his arm back and struck one of the statue's arms. As it fell to the floor with a shattering clatter, a horrible pain welled up inside him. He doubled over, sinking to his knees. The statue's hand leapt upward and fastened itself around his throat. He yanked it loose and turned, running toward the door of the ashram.

The devotees had been awakened by the noise, but he was out onto the street before they could react.

By instinct, he ran blindly across the street to the shabby motel. It was only when he was in his room, safely behind a locked door, that he realized he still held the hand of the statue. In revulsion he threw it across the room. He heard it hit and skitter along the floor. And then the room was still.

He should do something, but he didn't know what. Maybe he should call Smith, but he couldn't remember why. Maybe he should find Chiun, but it would do no good. He should do many things; instead, he collapsed on the bed and slept.

He was asleep in seconds, but his sleep was not peaceful. He dreamed of the beautiful face he had seen behind the statue's face, the weeping woman whose mouth had parted to kiss him. But before they touched, the face vanished and there was Kali's garish face and Her words, Her voice, saying: "Bring me death."

He turned in his sleep. He imagined someone entering and leaving his room. He tried not to dream, but always there was Kali's face, and suddenly he sat bolt upright in bed, his body drenched with sweat, his heart pounding.

He couldn't allow himself to sleep again. He had to

leave this place now. *Go anywhere,* he told himself, sitting up, holding his throbbing head. *If* It catches you again, you're lost. Go.

He stumbled toward the door and stopped short. He turned and saw the hand of the statue on the floor, but there was something in its fingers.

Frightened, Remo went to it and cautiously plucked the piece of paper from the shattered hand. In the hallway he looked at it.

It was an airline ticket. To Seoul, Korea.

Korea. That's where he would find Chiun. He knew he must go.

"It doesn't matter if it's a trick," he said. He had to get to Chiun. No one else could help.

Once more he walked out into the darkness. This time he could breathe.

Inside the ashram office, A. H. Baynes lit a cigar. The smoke burned his eyes and tasted good.

It was almost time to pack it in, he told himself. He had accomplished everything he'd set out to do, and then some.

All he had to do now was to wait for the final report on the thick-wristed federal agent, and then get rid of the statue.

Maybe someday in the future he would do the whole operation all over again. But not just now, not just yet.

There was a faint tapping at the door, and he said, "Enter."

Holly Rodan stepped inside.

"Chief Phansigar," she said, and bowed.

"What is it?"

"Your children have arrived back safely." She stepped aside, and Joshua and Kimberly Baynes walked into the office.

"Nice to see you home, kids," Baynes said.

They smiled at him.

# Twenty-one

The face was what stopped him.

Remo was at the airport, standing among the crowd ready to board the flight for Seoul, when he saw her. And as soon as he did, he knew he had not made a mistake by planning to go to Korea to find Chiun.

She was tall and slim, dressed in a white linen suit. Her dark hair was pulled under a small hat with a veil that partially covered her face, but nothing could hide her beauty. Her skin was pale and translucent, like the petals of a flower. She had full lips that looked as if they were unaccustomed to smiling; a narrow, high-bridged nose; and eyes like a deer's, wide-set and soft.

She looked like no other human being Remo had ever seen. There were no traces of any racial ancestry in that face. She looked as if she had been created, apart from the evolution of the planet earth.

Without realizing it, Remo was moving out of the throng of passengers waiting to board and was working his way through the press of people around her.

"Excuse me . . . Miss . . . Miss . . ."

She looked up, registering mild alarm. "Yes?"

Remo swallowed, unable to speak.

"Did you call me?"

He nodded, and she nodded back.

He tried to think of something to say to her, but his mind had voided all the words in his vocabulary. Looking at her, all he could think of was the sound of a choir singing in church on Christmas Eve.

"I'm sorry," he said lamely. "I guess I just wanted to look at you."

She picked up her suitcase and turned away.

"No," he said. He took her arm, and her eyes widened in fright. "No. Don't be scared," he said. "Honest, I'm not a nut. My name's Remo and—"

She wrenched herself free of him and scurried into the crowd. Remo sat back against a railing, ashamed of himself. Whatever had possessed him to approach a perfect stranger while a wave of killings was frightening airline passengers all over the world? And then he had behaved like some lunatic wand-waver. He was lucky she hadn't called the police.

Maybe there was something wrong with him. Maybe Sinanju started to play tricks on you after a while. Nothing like this had ever happened to Chiun, but Chiun was Korean. Maybe the old man had been right when he had said, all those thousands of times, that the knowledge of Sinanju was not meant for white men. Maybe there was something in Western genes that couldn't tolerate the training and caused insanity.

*Oh, Chiun,* he thought. *Be there when I come.*

The woman had been right to run away from him. He shouldn't even be permitted to walk among normal people. If he ever saw her again, he resolved, he would ignore her. It was a good thing he would never see her again. Damned good, because he would cut her dead. Besides, she probably wasn't as beautiful as he had thought. He would ignore her. Too bad he would never get the chance again, because he would ignore her to the point of insult.

She was on the plane, and Remo bodily ejected the man who was seated next to her.

"You're the most beautiful thing I've ever seen," Remo said.

The woman reached for the stewardess call button.

"No. Don't do that," Remo said. "Please. I won't say another word to you for the entire flight. I'll just look."

She stared at him blankly for several moments, and finally said, "Is that all?"

Remo nodded, unwilling to break his promise so quickly by saying even a single word.

"In that case, my name is Ivory." She extended a small white hand, manicured and sporting a large diamond ring on its index finger. She smiled and Remo wanted to curl up inside that smile like a cat.

He smiled back. "Can I talk now?"

"Try. I will let you know when to stop," she said.

"Where are you from?"

"Sri Lanka," she said.

"I don't even know where that is," he said.

"It is an old, small country with a new, large name," she said.

"Is that where you're going now?"

"In a roundabout way. Mostly I'm going to travel the Orient, shopping."

"Tough life," Remo said.

"At times," she said. "It's my job, you see, not my hobby. I buy antiquities for collectors. Some might call me a glorified errand boy."

Remo thought that no one would ever call her any kind of boy, but he simply asked, "Antiquities? Are they like antiques?"

She nodded. "Only older. My clients want Greek wall friezes, lintels from Egyptian temples, things like that."

"Like old statues," Remo said softly, thinking of something else.

"Sometimes. As a matter of fact, I was looking for one in America and traced it all the way to New

Orleans. But I lost it. The one who owned it sold it, then died, and no one knows who bought it."

"Was it valuable?"

"Very old, worth perhaps a quarter of a million dollars," Ivory said. "The owner's landlady said he sold it for forty dollars."

"Must be a beautiful statue to be worth that much," Remo said.

She shrugged. "I've never seen it myself, but I've seen replicas. A stone goddess with several arms. The exact number differs in the catalogs."

"Kali," Remo said, closing his eyes.

"I beg your pardon."

"Nothing. Never mind. Maybe you weren't meant to find it. Maybe it would have been bad luck or something."

"If I worried about curses or luck," she said, "I'd probably never buy anything more than a week old. But this statue might have been special."

Remo grunted. He didn't want to be reminded of the statue. It made him nervous. He imagined he could smell the scent of Kali on the airplane. But it would be gone soon. And perhaps Chiun could rid him of it forever.

He caught her staring at him. For a moment their eyes locked and a terrible sadness came over him.

"You look so familiar," he said, his voice almost a whisper.

"I was just thinking the same thing about you."

As the engines began to rev up, he kissed her. He couldn't explain why, but he saw the haunting, longing look in Ivory's eyes and knew if he couldn't touch her, couldn't have her, his heart might as well be torn out of him. As his mouth touched hers, she accepted him with a hungry urgency. Time vanished. In the woman's embrace, he no longer felt like Remo Williams, assassin, running away from his fear. Instead, he was only The Man and Ivory was The Woman and they were in a place far removed from the noise of a twentieth-century jet engine.

"Oh, no," she said, pulling away abruptly.

"What's wrong?"

"My gifts." She rose hurriedly, squeezing past Remo's knees. Her face was suddenly lined with worry. "I bought some presents and left them at the check-in counter. I'll be right back."

"Hurry," he said.

Ivory argued for a few seconds with the stewardesses at the front of the plane before they let her leave. When she rushed down the steps, the two attendants looked at each other and shrugged. One of them picked up a microphone.

"Ladies and gentlemen, we are ready for departure. Please take your seats and observe the seat-belt sign."

Remo looked at the small bag Ivory had left behind in front of her seat. He strained to see through the tinted glass of the airport. A woman's figure was running, stopping, fidgeting with something, running back.

The plane began to move.

"Hey, stop this," Remo yelled. "A passenger's coming."

Several of the other passengers looked over at him, but the stewardesses pointedly ignored him and went to the front of the plane. Remo pushed all the lights and buzzers he could find as he saw Ivory step out of the airport building. "Hey. Stop the plane. The lady wants to get on."

"I'm sorry, sir. No passengers are permitted to embark at this time," the frazzled stewardess said, turning off the fifteen call buttons Remo had activated.

"She doesn't want to embark," Remo said. "She wants to get on."

But the plane was moving away from the terminal. Through the window, Remo saw Ivory stopped by a maintenance man wearing headphones. She looked up at the taxiing plane in despair, then set down the boxes and bags in her arms and waved at the plane. It was a good-humored gesture, the resignation of a victim to one of life's little screw-ups.

Remo felt worse, hurt and cheated. He had barely known the woman named Ivory, but still he felt that he had known her forever, and now, as quickly as she had entered, she was gone from his life.

As the plane roared into takeoff, Remo picked up the soft fabric overnight bag Ivory had left under the seat. Perhaps there was some identification in it, he thought. But inside were only a couple of nightgowns, all lace and silk—like her, he thought—and a small bag filled with toiletries that carried the same soft scent he remembered from the brief moment he had held her.

It was a strange scent, not flowery like most perfumes, but deeper, somehow intoxicating. And for a moment he didn't know if he really liked it, but then he remembered her face, and decided he did.

But there was no identification in the bag, and sadly he put it back under the seat.

The plane was up now, barely a hundred feet in the air, but instantly turning west away from Lake Pontchartrain. Remo heard a deep rumbling from beneath the craft, as if it were a large flying bird noisily digesting its dinner. Within a half-second the sound had exploded into a deafening roar. In another second the whole front of the plane had ripped off and shattered into fragments before his eyes. A stewardess screamed, blood pouring from her mouth and ears, then fell backward toward the gaping hole, hit a ragged metal edge, then flew into space, leaving a severed arm behind. Everything loose in the plane fell through the opening. Some seat belts snapped under the strain and gave up their passengers to the gaping maw in the front of the craft.

The plane was tumbling toward the water.

Remo heard someone whimper, "Oh, my God."

And he wondered if even God could help them all now.

# Twenty-two

It was late and Smith was bone-tired when he reached the ratty Seagull Motel on Penbury Street.

As he started to enter the building, he heard chanting coming from a nondescript structure almost directly across the street from the motel.

Chanting?

Across the street from where Remo had stayed?

Smith's fatigue disappeared. His heart racing, he walked across the street, pushed open the door, and stepped inside. The big room was dark. Immediately he was assaulted by the acrid sting of burning incense and the overpowering heat from too many human bodies in an enclosed space.

The people were young, some of them barely into adolescence, and they were chanting at the top of their voices. The object of their attention was a statue set in a prominent position on a small platform at the front of the room. The chanters bowed frequently to the statue, raised their arms, and whirled around in improvisational ecstasy. It seemed to Harold Smith that every activity the group embraced was singularly useless and undignified.

He scanned the room thoroughly, then sighed and backed toward the doorway. His weariness returned. A. H. Baynes was not there, and neither was Remo. It had been an idea worth exploring, he told himself, even though it had led, like all his other ideas in this case, to a dead end.

He was at the door when a strange little Indian man shouted to him. "You. What do you want here?"

None of the chanters paid any attention to them, and Smith said dryly, "I doubt very much if I want anything here."

"Then why are you here? You just walk in?"

"The door was open. I did just walk in."

"Why did you walk in?" the Indian asked irascibly. "Are you looking for religion?"

"I'm looking for a man named A. H. Baynes. My name is Smith."

The Indian took a sharp, startled breath of air. "Baynes?" he squeaked. "No Baynes here. Sorry." He pushed Smith firmly to the door. "You find yourself another church, okay?"

"There's another man I'm looking for," Smith said. "Tall, with dark hair. He has thick wrists—"

The Indian pushed him out the door and Smith heard it lock behind him.

On the other side, Ban Sar Din leaned against the door sweating. Then he pushed his way through the crowd of faithful and went into A. H. Baynes's office in the rear of the ashram.

"A federal agent was here," he said.

Baynes looked up, bemused, from behind the desk. "But he's not here anymore, is he?"

"He was here. Just a few minutes ago, looking for you. Oh, unfortunate star that I was born under . . ."

"How did you know he was a fed?" asked Baynes, suddenly more interested. "Did he tell you that?"

"I knew," the Indian said. The veins in his neck throbbed visibly. "He is of the middle age, with tight lips. He wears steel eyeglasses and he has a briefcase and he says his name is Smith. Of course he is a federal agent."

Baynes rubbed his chin. "I don't know. It could be anybody."

"But he was looking for you. And when I told him you weren't here, he wanted the other one."

"What other one?"

"The one that the crazies said is supposed to be Kali's lover."

Baynes stiffened, then relaxed with a smile. "He'll have a hard time finding him," he said.

"It doesn't matter," Ban Sar Din said, his voice now rising near the panic level. "He'll come back. Maybe next time with the immigration people. I can be deported. And if they find out about you . . ."

"If they find out what about me?" Baynes asked threateningly.

Ban Sar Din flinched at the hint of violence in the man's eyes. It had been growing, a deep malice that had swelled as he had extended his power over the devotees of Kali. Ban Sar Din could not answer. Instead he just shook his head.

"Damn right, Sardine," Baynes said. "There's nothing for anybody to know about me. Nothing at all. All I do is go to church a lot, and don't you forget it. Now, get out of my way. I've got to go talk to the troops."

"I'm looking for a man named Remo. Tall, dark hair," Smith told the clerk at the Seagull Motel.

"Big wrists?" the clerk said.

Smith nodded.

"You're too late. He went out a few hours ago. Tossed some money on the counter and left."

"Did he say where he was going?" Smith asked.

"No."

"Is his room still empty?"

"Sure. This isn't that kind of place. We rent rooms by the night, not by the hour," the clerk said.

"I'll take his room," Smith said.

"It hasn't even been cleaned yet. I got some other rooms."

"I want his room."

"All right. Twenty dollars for the night. Payable now."

Smith paid him, took the key, and went up to the room. The bed had been slept on, not in, but there was nothing to give him a hint of where Remo had gone.

He sat heavily on the bed, removed his steel-rimmed spectacles, and rubbed his eyes. Just a few hours' sleep. That's all he wanted. Just a couple of hours' sleep. He lay back on the bed in the dingy room, his hands folded across the attaché case which he held on his stomach, and the case buzzed.

Smith dialed the combination which freed the two locks, opened the case, and lifted the telephone.

When he received a series of four electronic signals, he put the telephone receiver into a specially designed saddle bracket inside the case. Seconds later, the instrument noiselessly began printing a message which emerged on a long narrow sheet of thermal paper from a slot inside the case.

There was another sequence of four beeps which indicated the message was over, and Smith replaced the receiver, tore off the paper, and read the message that had come from his computer at Folcroft:

ADDITIONAL INFORMATION ON A. H. BAYNES. TWO DAYS BEFORE FIRST DEATH REPORTED ON INTERNATIONAL MID-AMERICA AIRLINES, BAYNES SOLD SHORT 100,000 SHARES OF IMAA AT $48 PER SHARE. AFTER DEATHS ON IMAA, STOCK DROPPED TO ONE DOLLAR PER SHARE AND BAYNES COVERED HIS SHORT

POSITION. PROFIT TO BAYNES, $4.7 MILLION. DAY
BEFORE AIR EUROPA KILLINGS, BAYNES PURCHASED
THROUGH BLIND STOCK FUND SIMILAR NUMBER OF
SHARES OF AIR EUROPA AND AFTER DEATHS COVERED
SHORT POSITION. PROFIT REALIZED, $2.1 MILLION.
BAYNES HAS REINVESTED MOST OF PROFITS INTO PUR-
CHASING STOCKS OF BOTH COMPANIES AND NOW HOLDS
CONTROLLING INTEREST IN BOTH AIRLINES AS WELL
AS MAINTAINING CASH PROFIT OF $1.9 MILLION. END
MESSAGE.

Smith reread the message before he touched a match
to it and watched the chemically treated paper flash
instantly into a small pile of ash.

So there it was. Baynes not only improved Just Folks
Airlines' stock performance when the killings stopped
there, but also moved into position to make a fortune
and take over the two other airlines.

It was enough motive for murder, Smith thought,
even for mass murder.

It was Baynes.

He swung his legs off the bed and sat up again.
There was no time for rest now.

Then he saw something he had not seen before. He
walked across the room and fished the object out of a
corner. It was a hand, the hand of a statue, made of
some kind of fired clay. As Smith turned it around in
his own hand, he realized where he had seen that kind
of hand before. It was on the statue in the little storefront temple across the street. So Remo *had* been
there. And probably so had Baynes. His Denver
neighbor had said he had joined a religious cult, and it
would be too much of a coincidence for that ashram
not to be Baynes's new headquarters.

He sighed, readjusted the locks on his attaché case,
and left the room.

When he got to the storefront church, the door was

locked. From inside, he could hear voices, but they were muffled and indistinct. He backed off to the curb, looked the building over, but saw no way to enter it from a higher floor. So he walked to the corner and into an alley to see if he could find a back entrance.

A. H. Baynes thought that politics had lost a star performer when he had decided to become a businessman. But there was still time. He was still young and now he owned three airlines, and when he stopped the killings aboard Air Europa and International Mid-America and merged them with Just Folks, his stock interests would be worth a quarter of a billion dollars. Not too shabby, and a pretty good campaign fund with which to launch a political career.

It made pleasant thinking, but first he had the crazies to deal with.

He stood alongside the statue of Kali on the raised platform and looked out at the expectant young faces.

"*She* loves you," he said.

And they cheered.

"And I, your chief phansigar, love you too."

"Hail the phansigar," they shouted back.

"The European operation was a total success and Kali is pleased. And I am pleased that my children have returned to this country safe and sound." He tried a warm smile as he nodded to his son, Joshua, standing nearby. "Of course, it's a little late for my daughter to be up, so she's staying with friends. But Joshua is here to be with you other sons and daughters of Kali. Isn't that right, Joshua?"

"Kill for Kali," Joshua said in a dull monotone. "Kill."

The others picked up the word and soon the room throbbed with the chanting. "Kill. Kill for the love of Kali. Kill. Kill."

Baynes raised his hands for silence, but it took several minutes to quiet down the crowd.

"Soon there will be another trip that you will take for Kali," Baynes said. Just then, Baynes saw in a mirror near the door the reflection of a man in steel-rimmed spectacles. He must have come in the rear door because he was standing in the small hallway that led to Baynes's office.

The federal man, he thought.

He turned back to the crowd. "Our path has not been easy, and tonight it grows even more difficult," he said.

The faces of the young people looked up at him questioningly.

"At this moment there is a stranger in our midst. A stranger who seeks to do us harm with lies and hatred for Kali."

Smith heard the words and felt a tightening in his throat. The crowd, unaware of his presence, murmured among themselves. He started to back away. They had not seen him yet; he might still escape.

A hand reached out and grabbed his wrist. He turned and saw the pudgy little Indian man.

"Psst. In here," Ban Sar Din said. He pulled Smith into Baynes's office and locked the steel door behind them.

"He is going to kill you," Ban Sar Din said.

"I gathered that was his intention," Smith said.

"I'm not going to let him kill a federal agent," Ban Sar Din said.

"I never said I was a federal agent," Smith said.

Ban Sar Din slapped his forehead in despair. "Okay, look. I won't argue. Let's just get out of here." Suddenly there was a thumping on the door of the office, and then the thumping took on the rhythm of the chanting voices and the chant was: "Kill for Kali. Kill for Kali. Kill for Kali."

"Maybe withdrawal would be reasonable," Smith said.

"And you'll put in a good word for me with your immigration people?" Ban Sar Din asked. "Remember. I killed no one."

"We'll see," Smith said noncommittally.

The wood around the steel-reinforced door began to squeak ominously under the thudding of many fists.

"You got a deal," Ban Sar Din said desperately. He went to the far wall, pressed a button, and a steel panel slid back, opening the room to the back alley. "Quick," he said. He reached the passenger door of the parked Porsche and got in. Smith got in beside him and the Indian started the motor, then peeled away down the alley toward the street.

"Whew," Ban Sar Din said. "That was close."

Smith didn't want to hear small talk. "Before, I asked you about the other American. The dark-haired one with thick wrists. Where is he?"

Ban Sar Din turned to glance at Smith. "He's dead," he said.

Smith winced involuntarily. "Dead? Are you sure?"

"I heard Baynes talking," Ban Sar Din said. "That man, Remo?"

"Yes, Remo."

"He was on a plane that took off from the airport a couple of hours ago. It crashed into the lake. I think Baynes put a bomb on it."

Numbly Smith said, "There's no end to his killing, is there?"

"He's crazy," Ban Sar Din said. "He makes the airlines go broke with the murders, and then he buys them. But he doesn't want just money. He wants power, but now the power is too great. He doesn't understand the source of the power."

"The source?" Smith said. "Isn't the source killing?"

"The source is Kali," said Ban Sar Din.

They were two blocks away from the ashram, and Ban Sar Din stopped for a red light. "I don't understand it myself," he said. "The statue was just a piece of junk I bought. But it has power, some kind of power, and I don't—"

They came out of the bushes. They came from behind trees, from beneath the manhole covers in the street. Before the Indian could slam his foot on the accelerator, the Porsche was surrounded by people, dozens of them, male and female, every one of them carrying a yellow rumal.

"Good God," Smith said as they started beating on the car.

They got Ban Sar Din first, smashing through the windows with sticks and rocks, then dragging the little Indian through the splintered glass and beating him until he screamed with the pain.

They beat him repeatedly with bloody rocks and stubs of branches until their faces glistened and their eyes shone wild and hungry, and then Ban Sar Din screamed no more.

Then they came back for Smith.

They opened the door and pulled him out. *My attaché case,* he thought. The lunatics were going to kill him and take the case too. They couldn't do anything with it, of course. The technology of the computer-hookup telephone was probably too sophisticated for any of them. But even if the executive offices at Folcroft Sanitarium caught fire, as they should if Smith failed to make contact within twelve hours, the case would still exist and it might be traced back to Folcroft. And there was a chance, a slim chance, that someone might find out what CURE had once been and the government of the United States would surely topple.

"The case," he called out as the first blow from a stick staggered him.

There were rocks and fists and clumps of hard dirt

too, before someone finally said, "What about the case?"

It was the young boy, the one Smith had seen in the ashram. He picked up the attaché case off the street. "Hold it, hold it," he said softly to the attackers as he walked through the crowd. "Let's just see what's going on." He extended the case to Smith as if to give it to him. "Here's your case. What's in it?"

But as Smith reached for it, the young boy yanked it back and kicked Smith in the shoulder.

"Important papers, maybe? Or just a little black book with hookers' names in it?" The boy laughed.

"Don't open it. Please," Smith pleaded. *Open it, you little bastard.*

"Why not?" the boy said. He stood over Smith with his legs apart. His expression bore the unmistakable mark of someone who enjoyed looking down at people. In that instant Smith knew that the boy was A. H. Baynes's son.

"Please don't. Don't," Smith said. "Don't open it."

He closed his eyes and tried not to think of it.

Joshua Baynes propped the case against the over-turned Porsche, just as Smith knew he would. He manipulated the clasps in the usual way, just as Smith knew he would, and the explosives set into the hinges of the case went off with their predictable fireballs. Afterward, the boy lay on the street with black formless stumps where his head and hands had been and the case was gone, an unrecognizable lump of melted plastic and metal.

The body of the car had shielded Smith from the blast, but now he felt a yellow kerchief looped around his neck. He barely minded it. *Now I can die*, he thought. *CURE will die too, but the United States will live.*

On his right lay Ban Sar Din's body, little more than a mound of exposed flesh awash in blood. A stone smashed against one of Smith's legs and he flinched. It would be a hard death, as hard as the Indian's had been. Maybe all deaths were hard, he thought. But his was long overdue and his only regret was that he had not been able to report in that A. H. Baynes and this crazed cult were behind the airline murders. But someone else would find out; someone else would stop them. It wouldn't be Remo; Remo was dead, as Smith soon would be. And without Remo, there would be no reason for Chiun to stay in the country. He would return to America, find that his disciple had been killed in a plane crash, and return to his life in his Korean village. Maybe, Smith thought, maybe someday there would be another CURE. Maybe someday, when things got bad enough and America's back was pressed against the wall hard enough, some President would stand up and say: Dammit, we're fighting back. The thought gave him some comfort as, with shaking fingers, he tried to breathe deepy and evenly to control the pain that coursed through his body.

It was time. He reached for the white capsule in his vest pocket, the pill that promised a death fragrant with almonds. He rolled over onto his stomach and popped the pill into his mouth, just as the rumal tightened around his neck.

Then there was a scream. Just one. Before Smith could register the fact that the beating on his body had suddenly stopped, he was being jerked to his feet. He choked, and the poison capsule lodged in his throat. Then he felt himself sailing in free flight. He landed belly-first in an empty lot and spat out the cyanide capsule whole. He lay there staring at the white plastic cylinder for a moment, until his senses awakened again and he turned to see what had happened to his attackers.

There were bodies strewn all over the street, and while a dozen still stood, something seemed to be whirling in their midst, something turquoise that moved so fast there did not appear to be any substance behind the movement.

One by one the young killers dropped, until only one was left, a woman, and she fled. There, on the street, surrounded by bodies, stood Chiun. He folded his hands inside his turquoise brocade robe and walked slowly toward Smith.

"Chiun," acknowledged Smith.

"I am really disappointed in you, Emperor," Chiun said. His voice sounded like bacon sizzling.

"Why?" Smith asked in honest puzzlement.

Chiun raised his heel and ground the cyanide capsule under his foot. "Do you think I will have it said of me by future generations that an emperor under my protection was forced to take poison? Oh, the shame of it."

"Sorry," said Smith. It was the only thing he could think of to say. He tried to rise, but his legs were wobbly under him, and then he felt himself being lifted into Chiun's arms as if he were a baby.

At the Seagull Motel, Chiun told the clerk, "We do not wish to be disturbed."

"Just a minute, there. You got to register like everybody else," the clerk said.

Holding Smith in one hand, Chiun used his other hand to rip the stairway railing from the banister. He tossed it onto the desk of the clerk.

"On the other hand," the clerk said, "you can register in the morning."

Inside the room, Chiun placed Smith on the bed and then began probing his body with his long-nailed fingers. After several minutes, he stood and nodded.

"There is no serious injury, Emperor," he said. "With rest, your body will return to the same despicable condition which is its normal state."

Chiun looked around the room, distaste evident on his parchment-like face, and suddenly Smith realized that Chiun did not know about Remo. How could he tell him? He reached deep down into his reserves of rock-hard New England character and said, "Master of Sinanju, Remo is dead."

For a moment Chiun did not move. Then he turned to face Smith. His hazel eyes flashed in the glare from the bare overhead light. "How did this happen?" the old Oriental said slowly.

"In a plane crash. Someone at the ashram over there . . ." He tried to point across the street but was unable to move his arm because of the pain. " . . . over there told me," he said.

Chiun went to the window and looked out. "That slum is a temple?" he said calmly.

"Yes," Smith said. "Kali, I think."

"Is the statue there?" Chiun asked.

"It was a half-hour ago," Smith answered.

"Then Remo is not dead," Chiun said.

"But I was told . . . The crash . . ."

Chiun shook his head slowly from side to side. "Remo must yet face death," he said. "That is why I went to my village."

"Why?" Smith said. "I don't understand."

"I went for this." Chiun reached into the sleeves of his robe and pulled forth a tarnished silver ring.

"For that?" Smith said.

"For this."

Smith reddened. It had cost untold thousands of dollars and threatened all kinds of security to send Chiun to North Korea, and he had gone there to bring back a silver ring worth twenty dollars at a generous pawnbroker's.

"For just a ring?" he said.

"Not just a ring, Emperor. The last time it was worn,

it gave a man like Remo the strength to do something he had not the courage to do before. Remo needs that courage because he faces that same adversary."

"A. H. Baynes?" Smith asked.

"No. Kali," Chiun said.

"Chiun, why do you think that Remo's alive?"

"I *know* he is alive, Emperor."

"How do you know?"

"You do not believe the legends of Sinanju, Emperor. No matter how many times you have seen them come true, you believe only in those ugly metal cabinets you have in your office. I could tell you, but you would not understand."

"Try me, Chiun. Please," Smith said.

"Very well. Remo came to me a dead man after you brought him into the organization. Did you ever wonder why I deigned to train a white when it is well-known that whites are incapable of learning anything important?"

"No," Smith said. "Actually, it never occurred to me to wonder about that."

Chiun disregarded the answer. "I did it because Remo fulfilled one of the oldest prophecies of Sinanju. That someday there would be a dead man that would be brought back to life. He would be trained and would become the greatest Master of Sinanju, and someday it would be said of him that he was not just a man, but the rebirth of Shiva, the Destroyer god."

"And that is Remo?" Smith said.

"Such is the legend," Chiun said.

"If Remo is this Shiva god, why doesn't he just arm-wrestle with Kali and beat her?"

"You scoff," Chiun snapped, "because you choose not to understand, but I will answer anyway. Remo is still just a child in the way of Sinanju. The power of Kali now is greater than his power. That is why I brought this ring. I believe it will make him strong,

strong enough to win and to live. And someday he will be Sinanju's greatest Master. Until that day, I continue to teach him."

"Because of that, you know he's not dead?" Smith said.

There was utter disgust on Chiun's face, the countenance of someone trying to teach calculus to a stone.

"Because of that," he said simply, and turned away.

It was too much for Smith. Sadly, he felt that Chiun was deluding himself, holding on to the slim hope of some legend because he refused to face the hard fact that his disciple, Remo, was dead. But all things die. Didn't the old man know that?

"I have to call the police," Smith said. "I have to get them to round up everybody at that ashram."

"No," Chiun said.

Smith walked to the telephone, but Chiun took his arm and led him back to the bed.

"We will wait for Remo," Chiun said coldly. "This battle belongs to him, not to the police."

Harold Smith decided to wait.

# Twenty-three

Remo held Ivory's hand as they drove from the airport back toward downtown New Orleans. For him, the miracle was not that he had survived the explosion on the plane, but that he had found Ivory after it was all over.

During the panic-stricken seconds right after the blast, the scene in the Air Asia plane was a horrible vision. Remo had felt his seat belt come undone and his body being tossed into a group of hysterical passengers who were trying, illogically, to undo their seat belts to free themselves.

Remo had scurried to the big yawning hole where the cockpit had once been, and stationed himself there to stop people from tumbling out into the nighttime sky.

The lake below was racing up toward them. Those who survived the impact had a chance to live if they all kept calm. Every nerve, every muscle fiber in Remo's body was pulled violin-string-tight. He had no time for horror and none for rage, even though he knew this had not been an accident.

The muffled thunder he had heard had come from the belly of the plane, not its engine. As soon as he had heard it, he knew it was a bomb. Some lunatic had somehow managed to plant an explosive inside the plane.

Some lunatic, he thought, as a piece of the plane hurtled down the last few dozen feet toward the lake. Why hadn't he thought of it before? It had been set up so simply. Someone had wanted him dead, someone careless enough about human life to be willing to sacrifice a hundred innocents just to kill him.

Who else but A. H. Baynes? He caught an old woman who was sliding down the aisle toward the ripped-open front of the craft and held her in his arms. He glanced behind him. Twelve feet. Six. Impact.

The plane hit with the flat slap of an egg dropped onto a tilted kitchen floor. As soon as he felt the first pressure of contact under his feet, he put the old lady into a seat and unstrapped a stewardess who was still buckled in.

"Are you all right?" he asked her.

She looked at him, in shock, as if unable to comprehend what had happened. Remo reached behind her head and pressed a hard index finger into a cluster of nerves at the back of her neck.

Suddenly her eyes cleared and she nodded decisively.

In the rest of the plane, people were screaming, breaking from their seat belts, starting to claw their way to the front of the plane to get out.

"All right," Remo said. "You help these people. Make sure they've got floats or whatever they need. Get all the uninjured ones off. Give me room to work."

She got to her feet.

"We're going to die. We're going to die. We're drowning." Voices came down the aisle of the plane.

Remo's voice barked above all the others. "Shut up and listen. You're not going to die and you're not going to drown. One by one, you're going to leave this plane and get away from it before it sinks. Just do what this lady says."

"What are you going to do?" the stewardess asked.

"I've got to see if anybody's alive in the forward section. If I can find it."

Remo turned and dived out into the cold black water of the lake. As he surfaced, he heard the stewardess's calm voice behind him, telling the passengers to remove their seat cushions and use them as .loats and then slide out into the water.

Through the darkness, he saw a faint bump in the water fifty yards away and moved to it, not slapping his way through the water like a high-speed competition swimmer, but sliding through it like a fish, in movements so smooth that someone might look at the lake and see, not a human swimmer, but just one ripple among many.

When he was closer, he saw that the small bump he had seen was the hump atop the cockpit. The front half of the plane was settling, sinking down into the waters of Lake Pontchartrain. Another minute or so and it would be totally submerged.

He dived down under the water and into the forward section of the plane, past the twisted ripped metal that showed where the bomb had exploded.

The pilot and copilot were still in their seats. Peering like a fish under the inky water, Remo could see that their eyes and mouths were open. They were beyond help, and he only hoped that their deaths had been swift. They hadn't deserved this.

He felt the rage he had been controlling starting to rise in his throat. The plane had been snapped apart just slightly behind the pilot's cabin. All the passengers were in the section that Remo had left behind, and he swam through the forward section of the plane for a few moments, but there were no other bodies. He felt the pressure as the plane began to slip under the water, and he swam out and surfaced.

On the shoreline of the lake, he could see the revolving lights of emergency vehicles, and his ears picked up the onrushing whirring of a helicopter.

Good. Help was coming. He looked quickly around him, but he saw no bodies floating, no one who needed help.

As he swam back to the other section of the plane, he was able to see the stewardess moving people out in a rapid line, one after another, into the water.

But the section of the plane had begun to tilt forward, and soon it would knife its way under the lake.

Remo slipped back to it and pulled himself into the cabin section.

"How we doing?" he asked the stewardess.

"I lost one," she said. Tears streamed down her face. "A little boy. He dropped his float and then went out. And I couldn't reach him. He went under." She was sobbing even as she was continuing to help people into the water.

"We'll see what we can do," Remo said. He let the air from his body and dropped like a stone under the waters of the lake. As he dropped, he rotated his body in the Sinanju spiral so that he commanded a full 360-degree view. The Sinanju spiral, he thought. This is how it should be used. For people's good. The last time he had used it, it was to kill a pigeon.

He saw a dark shape floating aimlessly in the water a dozen feet away. It was the young boy, and Remo wrapped him in his arms and shot back to the surface like a bubble.

He hoisted the boy's body into the cabin and put him on a seat.

"Oh. You got him. Oh . . ." The stewardess could

barely talk. The plane had now been emptied except for six people who lolled unconscious in their seats. The others bobbed like cork chips in the water, away from the plane.

"Will he be all right?" she asked.

"Get yourself a float and get out of here," Remo said as he pressed his fingers into the boy's solar plexus. He had stopped breathing, but it had only been a minute or so. There was still time. With his fingertips, Remo grasped a small clump of tissue and twisted it.

"He's dead, isn't he?" the stewardess said. "He's dead."

The boy's mouth opened and then a flood of water and bile came pouring out. The boy gasped and sucked up a huge mouthful of air.

"Not anymore," Remo answered her. "He'll be all right. Take him with you."

He handed the boy to the stewardess, who wrapped her arms about him, then took a seat-cushion between her hands and slid out smoothly into the water.

She was a good one, Remo thought, moving toward the back of the plane. She deserved a medal.

The water now was above his waist and he knew that in only a few minutes this section of the fuselage would go under the lake waters.

The six people still in their seats were unconscious, and a mere glance told Remo that their injuries were more serious than he was able to deal with.

He couldn't let them drown.

He remembered the emergency kits he often saw in the rear of plane compartments, and he went under the water to the very tail of the plane, where he found a large metal container. It was closed and locked, but he ripped off the metal top and felt vinyl under his hands. As he brought it closer to his face, he could see that it was an inflatable raft.

He surfaced again.

The water in the cabin had risen another foot.

He pulled the control on the raft and it began to hiss and expand. Remo moved it toward the jagged opening of the fuselage and pushed it out into the waters of the lake. Then one at a time he came back for the passengers and carried them out and placed them in the raft. He had just gotten the last one on the bright yellow float when he turned and saw the silver section of the plane tip once, as if making a final bow, and then slide down under the water.

He heard the sound of boat motors racing across the water toward them. Fifty feet away he saw the stewardess, still clinging grimly to her life preserver and to the young boy, and he pushed the raft over to her.

When he tried to take the boy from her, she tightened her grip around his body until Remo said, "It's me. It's all right." She recognized him and released the boy, and Remo put him in the raft.

"You're a helluva lady," Remo said, and then he let himself slide under the water and propelled himself toward the shoreline. He didn't want to be "rescued," and he didn't want to be interviewed, and he didn't want to be seen. Perhaps it would serve his purposes best if A. H. Baynes was allowed to think that Remo had died as planned.

He swam away from the large cluster of people standing on the shore, manning emergency lights and playing them on the faces of the survivors a few hundred yards out into the lake. When he was sure that no one could see him and he was out of the ring of lights, he walked slowly onto dry ground.

And couldn't believe his eyes.

There stood Ivory. Her white suit was rumpled and her face looked tense and anxious. "Oh, Remo," she said, and ran into his arms. "Somehow I knew," she said.

He kissed her and immediately felt a rush of triumph

flood over him. *This is why I'm alive,* he thought. And all the guilt and self-recriminations about the people who had died because of him retreated to a remote area of his mind. *He* was alive and Ivory had come back for him. "How did you know?" he asked.

"I didn't. I just hoped, and then there was the crash and I came running here and somehow I knew that this would be the spot."

"That's one plane I'm glad you missed," Remo said, holding her close to him. "Come on, let's get out of here before the crowds arrive."

"You're wringing wet," she said. "You'll freeze."

"Don't worry about it," he said.

He took the first car he found in the parking lot. The driver had left the keys under the front seat, and as he drove from the airport, slowly, past the police emergency lines that had been set up to control sight-seer traffic, he turned to her and said, "I have to tell you something about the statue."

"Statue?" Her expression was bewildered.

"The statue you were looking for in New Orleans. I know where it is."

"What? Why didn't . . . ?"

"Too long a story for now," he said. "But I'm going back there, and when I'm done, well, then you can have the statue."

"Doesn't the owner have something to say about this?"

Remo wanted to tell her that no one could own Kali, but he stopped himself. Ivory had a hard enough time believing that he had somehow survived the plane crash. Anything more might drive her away in fright. Instead, he just reached over and touched her knee.

"I don't understand it," she said, and he knew what she meant.

"Neither do I," he said. "I hardly know you, but . . ." He couldn't finish.

"Maybe we knew each other in a previous life," she said with a smile.

"Don't tell me you grew up in Newark too," Remo said.

"No. I grew up in Sri Lanka. An old family. But I studied in Switzerland and Paris. Did you . . .?"

Remo shook his head. "I don't think our backgrounds have much in common. Time out. Where's Sri Lanka, anyway?"

"It's near India. It used to be called Ceylon."

"Ceylon?" He stared at her so long that he nearly veered off the road.

"You have been in my country?" she asked.

"No. I've just got the jitters, that's all. Ivory, about that statue."

"Yes?"

"Every time I looked at it, I saw another face over the statue's. I'm sure it was your face. But it was sad and it was crying."

"Is this flattery? Telling me I look like a two-thousand-year-old statue?"

"It wasn't the statue," Remo said. "That's what I'm saying. There was another face behind it, or over it, just hovering there. Your face. I . . . Oh, forget it."

She smoothed his hand. "Are you all right, Remo?"

"Fine. Just forget I mentioned the statue and the face, okay?"

"Okay," she whispered, and kissed him softly on the cheek.

But he could not forget it. The face hovering behind Kali's stone visage had been Ivory's, absolutely, unmistakably.

She was the Weeping Woman.

# Twenty-four

A five-foot-tall box sat in the corner of A. H. Baynes's office, but Holly Rodan did not even glance at it as she dragged herself into the ashram. Tears streamed down her cheeks and her voice caught and broke. "He got away," she gasped.

"Ban Sar Din?"

"No. He's dead. The one that Kali wanted us to kill, the one with the briefcase. He got away."

A. H. Baynes looked up as she said, "And all our people are dead."

"Josh too?" Baynes asked. "My son?"

"I'm sorry," she said. "All of them. I'm the only one who escaped. It was terrible. That awful man had help. This Oriental creature jumped in to save him and it was just brutal and vicious what he did to our people."

Baynes was holding a pencil as he sat behind his desk. The pencil had not moved since Holly had told him of his son's death, but now he tossed it onto the desk blotter and stood up.

"It's time to move on then," he said. "We can't stay here anymore."

"But where will we go?" she asked tearfully.

"Kali has provided," he said. "I have a bunch of Air

Asia tickets. What would you think about a place like, say, Hong Kong?"

Her eyes twinkled through her tears. "Hong Kong? Really?"

"Why not. You use those tickets and we'll set up a new temple, a bigger one, in Hong Kong. And we'll start all over again."

"Will we kill some more?" she asked hesitantly.

"Of course," Baynes said.

"That will please Kali," Holly said.

"And what pleases Kali pleases me," he said.

"I know that, Phansigar." She frowned. "But you can't be chief phansigar anymore."

"Why not?"

"Because Ban Sar Din, the Holy One, is dead. That makes you the new Holy One."

"Good. Then you'll be the new chief phansigar," he said, and checked the cash in his wallet.

"Me? A female phansigar? I—"

"Why not? Kali understands. She was the very first feminist," he said, and he had to hold back the laughter when Holly Rodan nodded sincerely in agreement.

"What about you?" she asked.

"I'll meet you in Hong Kong. I have to prepare myself for my responsibilities as Holy One. I think I'm going into the mountains to meditate."

"I'm from Denver," Holly said. "If you need a place—"

"No. I've got a place of my own in the mountains near there. Nothing like a little Colorado mountain air to prepare a man for his lifelong calling." He put an arm around her and said, "You round up whoever's left, get the van, and go to the airport."

"What about Kali? Should I prepare her for the journey?"

"No," he said, his eyes as hard as steel. "I'll wrap the statue."

"But—"

"We don't have any time to waste," he said. "We are surrounded by unbelievers. We must move quickly."

"I'll get everybody right now."

Five minutes later, he heard a horn beep in front of the ashram. He swore to himself. The stupid little broad didn't even have enough sense to park in the alley behind the building.

He struggled outside, carrying a large object wrapped loosely in cloth.

There were only six Thuggees left, besides Holly, and they were crammed into the silver-striped van like creamed herring in a jar. They were chanting and the van reverberated with their noise.

"Quiet down," Baynes snapped as he opened the van's rear door. "Do you want the cops to catch you before you make it to the airport?"

"We care nothing for police. We kill for Kali."

"Kill. Kill."

Baynes slugged the nearest chanter in the face.

"Well, I care, you assholes. They're swarming all over the place, so let's get a move on."

He hauled the heavy object to the front of the van and placed it on the front seat. Holly Rodan was behind the wheel and he handed her a sheaf of Air Asia tickets.

"Guard this carefully," he told her, pointing to the object. "It is Kali."

"With our lives, Chief Phansigar," she said zealously.

"No. You are chief phansigar. Now I am the Holy One."

Shyly she nodded. "Go with Kali, Holy One."

"Enjoy your trip, Chief Phansigar," Baynes said.

\* \* \*

Smith turned from the window and bolted to the door of the motel room. "They're getting away," he said.

"Remo is not yet here," Chiun said.

"We'll save the statue for Remo," Smith said. "But I'll be damned if I let those killers get away."

He was out in the hallway and heading down the stairs, when Chiun decided to follow him. Smith was still suffering from the injuries he had received earlier. He might need Chiun nearby.

On the street, Smith flagged a taxi. "Follow that van ahead of us," he said as Chiun entered the cab behind him, his bright turquoise robe flowing.

"Come on, mister. Mardi Gras ain't for another six months or so."

A yellow hand reached out and twisted the cabbie's head around with a pain more excruciating than any the driver had ever known.

"The emperor requests that you follow this vehicle in front of us. Do you agree to perform this service?"

"Sure thing, Emperor," the cabbie squeaked.

"Then do it with eyes open and lips closed," Chiun ordered.

"Now, keep your heads down and keep quiet," Holly commanded through the window that led to the back of the van. She liked being chief phansigar. She decided that giving orders was basically what she liked doing best in the world.

"We're going to the airport," she yelled, "and take Kali to Hong Kong."

"What'll we live on?"

"There'll be other passengers on the plane," she said. "Somehow Kali will provide, from them."

Feeling good about flexing her authoritative muscles, she pulled over at the next red light and ordered one the Thuggees to come up from the rear and take the wheel.

"It's the chief phansigar's job to protect Kali," she said, sliding in on the passenger's side of the front seat and twining her arm around the cloth-covered figure. "Hey, what's this?"

Something was protruding from Kali's stomach.

"Maybe She's growing another arm," Holly said, loosening the cloth that encased the statue. "If it's another arm, then it's a sign that She approves of this move to Hong Kong. She is giving us a sign."

Excitedly she peeled the cloth away, then stared at the statue in bewilderment.

"Is it an arm?" The Thuggees in the back of the van strained against the small window opening to see.

"No. It's . . . it's a clock." Holly touched her finger to the numbered disk embedded in the statue's belly.

"What's a clock doing in Kali's stomach?" one of the Thuggees asked.

Holly didn't want to admit surprise. Officiously she said, "The Holy One consulted with me about it. He said that it would make it possible to get the statue past customs."

"Good thinking," a Thuggee said.

"Hail the Holy One," several chanted.

"Hail the chief phansigar," Holly shouted, when no one else did.

Why was there a clock in Kali's stomach? she wondered. She looked at it carefully. In the rear of the van, they were still praising A. H. Baynes and somehow it annoyed her. "The foolish Holy One," she said. "He didn't even set the time correctly."

"It's nine-oh-four," a Thuggee said.

"Thanks," she said, moving the hands on the clock to the correct time. Nine-oh-two, nine-oh-three, nine-oh—

When the statue exploded, a piece of it jammed into the driver's brain and killed him instantly. A secondary blast from the van's engine blew the vehicle apart in a cloud of flame and smoke. Holly Rodan was blasted through the windshield into the shrubbery of someone's front lawn. This she took as a sign that Kali did not want to go to Hong Kong.

Holly felt herself dying in the smooth dirt behind a row of hedges. And suddenly she knew why she was dying and who had caused it. She tried to speak, but when she opened her mouth, only blood came out. With an effort, she tried to feel her fingers, to see if they were still attached to her body. They moved. Alongside her face, she began to scrawl a message in the dirt.

"C . . ." she began. Just moving her finger enough to form the letter exhausted her. She wrote an O. She traced an L.

It was all she could do. In her last moments, Holly Rodan was too tired even to chant "Kill for Kali." But she smiled anyway, because she knew that above all else, Kali loved to see Her own die.

The explosion was so powerful that the taxicab following the van spun about in the middle of the street.

Smith gasped as he saw the bodies fly out of the flaming vehicle like pieces of popcorn over a high flame. Chiun was already out of the cab, and the moment Smith's reflexes could work again, he followed the Oriental toward the wreckage.

They pulled five injured young men from the flaming van. House lights came on along the street and a police siren screamed in the distance, growing louder.

The young men were dying, but still chanted.

"Kill."

"Kill for Kali."

"We die and She loves it."

". . . loves it."

Smith looked at Chiun, who pronounced the five

young men's death sentences by slowly shaking his head. They would not live.

"Emperor—" he started.

"Not now, Chiun. Wait," Smith snapped. He leaned over one of the cultists and pointed a fountain pen at him. "Who is your leader?" he asked.

"The Holy One. Ban Sar Din."

"No," a youth lying next to him said. "Ban Sar Din has fallen in disgrace. The new Holy One is our leader."

"What's his name?" Smith asked.

"Baynes," the Thuggee said proudly. "He has given all to Kali. And we follow his bidding."

Smith rummaged in the man's pocket and brought out the Air Asia ticket.

As the police and ambulance sirens wailed to a stop, Smith led Chiun back to the throng of bystanders who had gathered on the sidewalk around the wreck.

"Forgive me, Emperor," Chiun said. "I did not mean to interrupt you while you were threatening these cretins with your writing tool—"

"It's a microphone," Smith said, nervously watching as the police moved the injured into ambulances.

"Whatever it is," Chiun said, "I thought you would like to know who is arriving."

"Who?" Smith squinted to see in the direction that Chiun was pointing. Past the blockade of police cars, two figures ran toward them. One of them was Remo.

Remo strolled up, surveyed the accident, and said, "I go away for just a few minutes, and look at the mess you two make."

"Maybe if you had been around tending to business—" Smith began.

"Take a hike. I was busy being blown out of the sky," Remo said. "Anyway, I hope this teaches you a lesson."

"What kind of lesson?" Smith asked.

"Sign Chiun's petition. If you have amateur assassins, you're going to have mess after mess, just like this."

"I have one here," Chiun said, reaching a long-nailed hand into his kimono.

"No, no, no," Smith said. "Please, Master of Sinanju. Put it away. You and I will discuss that another day."

"Maybe these people standing around would like to sign," Chiun said hopefully. "They must be disgusted by all this noise and waste."

He looked around, but then stopped as Smith suddenly wobbled a little on his feet and began to sink toward the sidewalk. Remo caught him and held him in his arms.

"What happened, Chiun?" he asked.

"The Emperor was assaulted tonight by these creatures. He will be all right."

"I'm okay now," Smith said, pulling himself away from Remo, obviously embarrassed at his momentary display of human weakness. "Let's just collect A. H. Baynes and put him away, and I'll feel fine."

"I figured Baynes," Remo said. "I think he planted a ticket on me while I was sleeping and then rigged a bomb on the plane to try to kill me."

Ivory caught up with them, slightly breathless and wobbling on her high-heeled shoes. She looked around at the accident victims, then placed her hand on Remo's and said, "Is there anything we can do?"

Smith eyed her coldly, then called Remo away from the woman. "Who is she?" he demanded.

"Somebody I met."

"How can you bring a stranger in on the middle of a case like this?" Smith hissed. His anger was visible.

"She doesn't how anything."

"She better not," Smith said. "As it is, she's seen the three of us and—"

"Remo," Ivory called. She was standing behind some shrubs and her face was ashen. He walked over and she pointed down to the body of Holly Rodan. Smith and Chiun came over also.

"She's dead," Remo said, feeling for a pulse.

"There is dirt beneath the fingernails of her right forefinger," Chiun said. "She was trying to write a message in the earth." He looked up at Ivory. "Right where you are standing, madam."

Ivory gasped and moved backward. Just above Holly's finger was the smeared footprint of a high-heeled shoe.

"I'm . . . so sorry," Ivory whispered.

"It's all right," Remo said gently. He put his arm around her. His eyes were on Smith and in those eyes was a challenge.

Chiun dropped to the ground beside Holly and looked carefully at the earth. "She had written a C," he said. "But that is all I can discern."

"I don't know if it means anything," Ivory said, "but I called you over because of that." She pointed to Holly's left hand. In it was clutched a fragment that looked like stone.

Chiun removed it and held it up. The fragment was in the shape of a small hand.

"The statue?" Remo said.

"Not the statue," Ivory sighed. "It can't be. I've got to see if there are other pieces around." She darted away from Remo into the crowd.

"It is apparently the hand of a statue," Chiun said.

Smith looked at the fragment carefully. "What's this all about?"

"The statue, Emperor," said Chiun. "The one of which we spoke. Of Kali."

"Well, thank God we'll have no more talk of magical statues," Smith said. "Now all we've got left to do is get Baynes."

He handed the statue fragment to Remo, who said casually, "There's one other problem."

"What's that?"

Remo held the piece of statuary up to his nose. "It's the wrong statue," he said.

"What?" asked Smith.

"I don't feel anything. Baynes switched statues. This isn't Kali."

There was a long silence. Finally Chiun said softly, "There is another problem, Remo."

"Huh? What?"

"The woman."

"Ivory?" Remo looked around, but Ivory was nowhere in sight. He combed through the crowd, even slipping past the police to look into the wreckage of the van, but the woman was gone.

He stood in the middle of the street and yelled, "Ivory."

But there was no answer.

The three men returned to the ashram. Remo hoped that Ivory had gone there looking for the statue. But there was no sign of the statue, of Ivory, of A. H. Baynes. All had vanished.

# Twenty-five

"Ivory," A. H. Baynes whispered to the beautiful woman who lay next to him in bed.

Outside, the sun was rising in the Rockies beyond the glass wall of the chalet. The tips of tall pines glistened with dew in the valley below the cliff where Baynes's mountain house stood, surrounded by early-morning fog.

It was a perfect sunrise, and with Ivory's creamy body rubbing against his, Baynes was glad she had awakened him to see it.

"How did you know I'd be here?" he asked, stroking the inside of her white thighs.

"The girl. The stupid one with the blond hair."

"Holly? She told you?"

"Of course not. She was dead. She wrote C-O-L in the dirt. I assumed it meant you had a place in Colorado."

"Dead? What are you talking about?"

"You can stop the pretense, darling. I'm the one who wears disguises, remember? Anyway, I erased the message with my foot. No one knows we're here."

"All right," Baynes said. "She was getting to be a pain in the ass anyway. All of them with that chanting crap. I got a lot out of them anyway. Two new airlines to add to Just Folks. *If* the feds aren't after me."

Ivory rose languidly and walked over to a cream-colored suitcase. She opened it. "And if they are," she said, "this will set you up all over again somewhere else." She tilted the suitcase to show neat rows of used hundred-dollar bills.

"I have something for you too," he said.

"I was hoping you'd say that."

Baynes hauled a large box from behind the sofa in the living room. He tore open the box and set the statue of Kali on a low table in front of the glass wall overlooking the cliff. Against the background of peaked mountains and clouds, the statue looked for a moment like a real goddess to him, serene and inscrutable, floating in the sky.

"She's magnificent," Ivory said in hushed tones.

"A hell of a lot of trouble for a hunk of stone," he said. "I can tell you I'm glad to get it off my hands."

Ivory went back inside the bedroom to dress. She emerged wearing a pair of slacks and a heavy sweater.

"Planning on going out?" he asked.

"No, just a little chilly," she said.

"Well, sit down and have a drink." He poured bourbon for both of them. "You are a marvelous-looking woman," he said, handing her a glass. "I'll never get over my surprise when I met you at that abandoned building. I thought you were a man, for Christ's sake."

"I was wearing cloaks."

"With nothing underneath. I've never been seduced like that before," he said.

"You never owned the statue of Kali before," she said.

His pride felt perforated and he said, "Damn that hunk of rock. Who's willing to pay so much money for it, anyway?"

"No one. Kali is for me. My people.'"

Baynes guffawed. "*Your* people? Where are *your* people from? Scarsdale?"

She looked at him levelly. "I am from a mountainous region in central Ceylon. My ancestors created the statue. It belongs to their descendants."

"This piece of junk?"

"I would advise you not to refer to Kali as junk," she said.

"Hell, you believe it too. I used to have those ninnies at the ashram running around in circles, making believe that the airline tickets grew magically out of Her fingers every night. And all I did was stick them there."

"And the arms the statue grew?" she asked.

"That was Sardine's con. I never did figure out how he did it, but it worked. It kept the crazies in line pretty well."

"The Indian had nothing to do with it," she said.

"You really believe it," he said, making no attempt to hide his astonishment. "Growing arms, needing a lover, wanting deaths and all that shit. You believe it."

"How little you really know," she said. "I have spent six years tracking this statue."

"Well, if you think there's anything special about it, you ought to be disillusioned now. Look at it. It's junk, and it's ugly junk to boot."

She walked behind him slowly, caressing his shoulders. "Perhaps you weren't worthy enough to see its beauty," she said, and pulled from her pants pocket a yellow silk rumal. "You see, Kali only intervenes for those She loves. You were only a small link in the chain, Mr. Baynes. I doubt if She will intervene in your behalf."

She slid the rumal around his neck.

**Number 221.**

# Twenty-six

The oxygen-thin mountain air filled Remo's lungs with cold and he adjusted his breathing to allow his body to absorb more oxygen.

"What a godforsaken dump," he said.

"I thought white people were always enamored by the mountains and the snow," Chiun said. "That as they succumbed to frostbite and starvation, they always shouted 'back to nature.'"

"Not this white person," Remo said. "I hope Smitty's right about this."

"Those four piles of mechanical junk in his office—"

"His computers," Remo said.

"Correct. Those four piles of mechanical junk determined that this house is secretly owned by A. H. Baynes," Chiun said.

"Yeah. He owns it," Remo said, "and he's probably in Puerto Rico, sunning himself on a beach."

They bounded silently up the craggy cliff. Above them, on a rock overhang, stood the modernistic chalet with its glass walls overlooking the cliff.

Neither man had spoken the thought that was most on their minds. If Baynes was here, so was the statue of Kali.

As they approached the turnoff to the house's driveway, Chiun said, "Hold, Remo. There is something I must give you." He reached under his robe. "You have not asked me about my visit to Sinanju."

Remo felt his nerves tighten. "I don't want to think about that now, Little Father. I just want Baynes, and then I want to get out of here."

"And the statue?"

"Maybe he doesn't have it. He might have sent it somewhere," Remo said.

"Do you believe that?" Chiun asked softly.

"No." Remo leaned against a tree. "You were right about the statue having some kind of power," he told Chiun. "I couldn't destroy it, and every time I was near it, something happened inside me." He closed his eyes tightly.

"What causes you such pain?" Chiun asked.

"It was a bird," Remo said. "Just a bird, and I killed it. It could just as easily have been a person. I killed it and I brought the body back for Kali. It was for Her."

"That was then. This is now," Chiun said.

"And it's going to be different? Chiun, I ran away from that place. I was trying to get to Korea so I could hide behind you." He laughed mirthlessly. "The history of Sinanju thinks Lu was bad for fighting tigers in the circus. I couldn't even face a statue, Chiun. That's what I'm really made of."

"Time and history will judge what you are made of, Remo," Chiun said. "I have brought you a gift." From his sleeve he brought out a band of silver and handed it to the white man. "It was the ring Lu wore when he thrust the statue of Kali into the sea. Take it."

"Is that why you went to Sinanju?" Remo asked. "To help me?" Suddenly he felt very small.

"That is the duty of a teacher," Chiun said. He proferred the ring again.

Remo took it, but it did not fit any of his fingers. "I'll keep it in my pocket." He smiled gently. The old man really believed that a silver ring might just make a man out of a coward, and Remo loved him for that.

"You are no weaker than Lu," Chiun said. "Remember that you are both Masters of Sinanju."

Remo wanted to tell him that he was not a Master, that he would never be a Master, and that all the times Chiun had called him an untrainable, unruly pale piece of pig's ear, he had been dead right. Remo Williams was a nobody from Newark, New Jersey, and that was all he would ever be. He thought those things, and to Chiun he said, "Right. Let's get on with it."

They moved from beneath the tree and broke into the chalet silently, through the garage. They heard no one, and it was not until they reached the large, airy living room on the upper level that they found A. H. Baynes sprawled across a sofa, his head bent backward in an unnatural position, his eyes bulging, tongue black and swollen, a red ring around his neck. His flesh was still warm.

"He's dead," Remo said. Suddenly he began to pant and he could not breathe. His legs weakened and he felt dizzy. Above all, the scent that filled the room seemed to clutch at his insides and paralyze his thoughts.

"It's here," he whispered. "The statue."

"Where?" said Chiun.

Without bothering to look, Remo pointed to a corner of the room, where a cardboard box had been heavily taped for shipping.

But as if the spirit inside the box had seen him, the cardboard sides split from the middle outward. The torn edges singed and smoke poured from the corners of the box. The stiff cardboard melted away to black ash, and in the middle of the container's charred remains stood the statue of Kali. As Remo turned to look, its mouth appeared to smile.

Remo fell to his knees. Only Chiun turned when the sound of footsteps came from the bedroom.

"We have a visitor, Remo," he said.

Remo whirled around, then rose to his feet shakily. In front of him stood the woman named Ivory. There was a gun in her hand, but her face was not that of a killer. Her eyes were full of pain and sadness.

"Why did it have to be you?" Remo asked, feeling his heart break.

"I asked myself the same," she answered quietly.

"You don't have to lie now, Ivory. I may be stupid but sometimes I can see things. Like how your foot just happened to rub out that dead girl's message."

"I didn't want you to come here. I didn't want to have to kill you."

"That didn't seem to stop you from trying on the plane," he said. "You checked a bomb with your baggage and you knew it would go off right after take-off."

"I had to have the statue," she said. "I did not know you then, Remo. If I had, I could not have killed you."

"But now you can," he said, nodding toward the gun in her hand.

"Not now. Not if I don't need to. Remo, the statue of Kali belongs to the people of Bathasgata. It is a danger anywhere else. Kali is not a kind goddess."

"The statue is a danger wherever it is," Chiun said. "It must be destroyed."

"And will that destroy the goddess within it?" she asked.

"No, it may not," Chiun said. "But she walked the earth for thousands of years before she found her home in that statue. She may yet walk homeless again, not killing, not driving others to kill. The statue must be destroyed."

"You will not harm it," Ivory snapped, her eyes flashing. "You two leave and no harm will come to you.

I wish only to go with the statue. Let me go and I promise you that the statue and I will never leave Bathasgata."

"What of your people?" Chiun asked. "Do they understand what Kali lives on?"

"Some do, the wise ones," Ivory said. "The rest only want their deity returned to them. They will accept."

"Until the village runs with blood and there are no more left to kill. And then somehow the statue will leave your village and its evil will spread, as it had already spread among those foolish children who did its work."

"It is not your right to interfere," Ivory said tearfully. And in her face, Remo saw it once again, and now he was sure. She was the Weeping Woman, the face that hovered behind Kali's, the shadowy image that persisted in being seen.

"Ivory," Remo whispered, and their eyes locked. "I know who you are and I know who I am now too. I don't care what happens to the statue. I love you. I have for two thousand years."

She looked at him, then dropped the gun silently into the thick carpet and took a step toward him. "I feel it, but I don't understand it," she said.

"Two thousand years ago," Remo said, "we were lovers. I was a Master of Sinanju and you were a priestess of Kali and we loved. Until Kali separated us."

The name forced Ivory to glance again at the statue, and she said, "But I serve Kali." Her face bore a bewildered expression.

"Don't serve Her," Remo said. "Don't leave me again." He stepped forward and kissed her, and again he felt the peace of a quiet valley in a distant time. Once again he was with her, just as he had lain with her in a bed of flowers.

"Destroy it," she hissed. "Do it quickly, while there is time. Do it for us. I love—"

She stiffened.

"Ivory," Remo said. He shook her. Her hands clawed at her neck, tore at her clothing. Her eyes, round with fear, pleaded silently with him. From her lips came a choking gasp. She grasped Remo's arms, but a convulsion shook her and her hands fell limply as she sank into Remo's arms.

"Ivory!" Remo screamed. He lifted her in his arms and turned toward the statue.

The statue sprouted a small bud of an arm.

"Kali is a jealous goddess, my son," Chiun said. He took Ivory's body from Remo's arms and floated to the carpet in lotus position, gently setting the body down. The only sign of tension in the old man was in his hands as he placed them together, like a child in prayer.

He began to moan, and Remo dropped to his side.

"Chiun. Are you all right?"

"There . . . is no air to breathe," Chiun said softly. He bowed his head, his white hair trembled. Then his whole head shook in a violent spasm and lurched backward as if some invisible hand had yanked it.

Remo touched the old man briefly in panic, then rose and turned toward the statue.

"You've done this," he shouted, and threw a lethal kick at the head of the stone carving. His foot never reached it. His legs buckled and he sprawled on the floor. He rose again and tried to smash the statue with his hands, but his arms hung uselessly, refusing to serve him.

He turned toward Chiun and his mouth hung open in horror. A small blue spot had appeared on Chiun's forehead and it was growing.

The ring, Remo thought. He fumbled in his pocket. What would he do with it? He couldn't wear it. Would its mere presence be enough? He wrapped his fingers around it and pulled it out. Then, holding it in front of him as if he were confronting a vampire with a cross, he approached the statue.

His legs could barely move. Inside him was a heaviness that seemed to drag his heart into the depths of hell. He had no strength and it took all the concentration of his mind and muscles to lift his palm with the silver ring in it and move it toward the impassively malicious face of the idol.

The ring glowed for a moment, and for that instant Remo thought that the ring — Lu's ring, given to him by the woman he loved — could save him. But the glow faded and scores of small pits appeared in the silver as it melted and the molten metal burned through his skin and his flesh with a terrible searing pain.

He screamed and fell thrashing to the floor. The pain pounded through his body and the tender flesh on his palm sizzled. The bud of an arm on Kali's torso grew before his eyes, and the goddess's sickly-sweet smell overpowered the room. Remo knew that the power of the ring was as nothing compared with the foul energy that emanated from the hideous stone sculpture.

As he lay there, he looked toward Chiun. There was no pleading in the old man's eyes, as there had been in Ivory's. There was no fear, no shame, no accusation. Remo, numb in his own pain, ached for the old teacher. Chiun's eyes looked ancient and hollowed, and the blue mark on his forehead was growing, darkening. Chiun was dying, more slowly than most because he could control the responses of his own body, but dying. And there was nothing in the dying old eyes except peace.

"Chiun," Remo whispered. He tried to drag himself across the floor. If he must die, let it be with the man who had given him life. But nothing inside him worked anymore. Remo could not even lift his head from the floor.

He closed his eyes. He could not bear the sight of Chiun's proud face as it succumbed to death.

Then a voice spoke.

Its origin was not outside Remo, but somewhere in the recesses of his mind. It was more a feeling than a voice, but it carried the acrid scent of the goddess, acrid and cloying. It might have been the stink of his own burning flesh, he thought, but the pain was so great and the certainty of Chiun's death was so hard that he was forced to accept the truth: that Kali was now inside him, controlling and mocking him. Then She spoke to him in Her own tongue just as She had spoken to Master Lu two millennia before.

"This is only the beginning of your punishment," the voice said. Then it laughed, high and tinkling as a chorus of tiny bells.

"I brought her back for you, child of Lu," the voice told Remo. "A different body, but the same woman. Born to bring you a moment's joy, as Lu's woman served him. And taken by me just as quickly."

The bells were gone from the voice now, and it was rock-hard ice.

"You could have loved me as Lu could have loved me. You could have served me. But you chose to die instead. And you shall. As your woman has died. As the old man now is dying. Except their deaths will be quick. Yours will be the best that I can provide."

Remo forced his eyes open. The voice disappeared. Chiun lay on his side, unmoving. He had given up. He had waited for Remo to save him, and Remo once again had chosen to hide behind his own closed eyelids.

"You will not kill him," Remo said, pulling himself with a desperate effort to his knees. A wave of unseen energy slapped him hard across the chest. Bile rose in his throat, and he wavered, but he pulled himself up still further. "Maybe I deserve your punishment," he whispered. "Maybe Lu did. Maybe even Ivory. *But you will not have Chiun.*"

He brought himself to his full height. His hand still burned. His head still spun. His insides were water. His legs were immobile, but he was standing and he knew in that moment that he would never kneel before Kali again.

"False hero," the voice said again. "You are weak. Your teacher was weak. All are weak before me."

*But I will not bow before you,* another voice inside him said. It was a small voice, from a place very far removed from his mind, but it spoke, and Kali listened.

"No."

A sharp stab of pain clutched at his stomach. Blood spurted from his nose and mouth.

Remo stood.

The glob of molton silver in his hand sizzled into liquid again, burning down the length of his fingers.'

Remo stood.

His ears were pierced by something that felt like two hot wires jabbed into his eardrums. They filled his ears with a sound like the wail of a thousand screams.

And yet he stood, and quieted them with his will. He could feel his strength returning. He raised his head and stared directly into the evil eyes of the stone goddess.

"You are not Lu," the voice said.

"No," Remo answered coldly, speaking aloud in the silent room.

"But you have his spirit."

"And another's," Remo said.

"Who are you?" The demand was a shriek, silent in the physical room he occupied, but reverberating inside him like the keening of a banshee.

And then he answered, from the place inside himself, the place that did not make itself known even to Remo, and the voice from the place spoke its own words, the words of the old prophecy of Sinanju:

"*I am created Shiva, the Destroyer; death, the shatterer of worlds. The dead night tiger made whole by the Master of Sinanju.*"

Remo moved toward the statue. In his mind he heard a scream.

The statue repelled him with wave after wave, silent, invisible blows that pulled the skin from his face. But Remo was no longer afraid. He grasped the statue by its head. The touch of it burned him. The force inside it propelled his feet off the floor and sent him hurtling across the room. He crashed against the glass wall and went through in a sunburst of light and sound.

But he held the statue.

It moved. It twisted as if it were made of the softest clay. Its arms seemed to flutter and dance until they were around Remo's neck, clutching, squeezing, infecting him with their poison.

"You don't frighten me anymore," Remo said aloud. "I am Shiva." He let the arms twine about him. With each twist, he compressed the statue more tightly between his two burned hands. With a final gasp, it spewed a yellow vapor from its nostrils. The vapor hung like a pall, thick and foul, for a moment in the clear Colorado sky. Then it dissipated like so much morning mist.

The stone crumbled in Remo's hands. He crushed the head to powder, then broke it all apart and threw the other pieces over the side of the cliff. They made little thudding sounds as they struck the earth and rocks below.

He walked back inside the room. Fresh air poured into it through the shattered picture window, and there was no trace of the foul odor the statue had always carried with it.

Sadly Remo knelt beside Chiun. He placed a hand

gently over the blue dot on the old man's forehead.

The forehead was cool and smooth to his touch. Tears streamed down Remo's face and he asked whatever gods might hear him: "Let me die so well as the Master of Sinanju."

The forehead beneath his palm wrinkled. There was a fluttering of eyelashes and then Chiun's squeaky voice:

"Die well? You will die immediately if you do not remove your big barbarian hand from mv delicate skin."

"Chiun."

Remo sat back. The old man straightened himself with great dignity, and as he did, the blue spot on his forehead slowly faded until it was gone.

"How are you still alive?" Remo asked.

"How?" The Korean's hazel eyes widened. "How? How indeed, considering that I am always burdened by you."

"I . . .?"

"Yes. You," Chiun snapped. "I was halfway into the great Void and you performed as usual. You did nothing."

"I—"

"You should have used the ring as I told you."

"I did use the ring. I held it—"

"You did nothing," Chiun said. "I watched."

"But my hands." Remo offered his burned palm for Chiun's examination. There was not a mark on it. "The ring . . . I saw . . . It burned . . ." He reached into his pocket. There was something there. He pulled out a pitted ring, cheap and impure, fashioned of silver.

"Was it all in my mind?" he asked incredulously.

Chiun snorted. "If it all fit into your mind, it must have been a very small thing indeed," he said.

"But I swear," Remo said. He felt something on his

hand and lifted the ring from his palm. Beneath it, in the circle of the ring, was a drop of water. He tasted it. It was salt, the salt of tears.

"Oh, Ivory," Remo said. He went to the cold, dead body of the woman. Her face was wet with tears.

Silently Remo placed the ring on her finger.

Perhaps, he thought, it would bring the Weeping Woman some peace at last.

# Twenty-seven

"Am I Lu, then?" Remo asked.

"Well, aren't you an idiot," Chiun said. "Of course you are not Lu. Lu has been dead for two thousand years. Do you not yet know who you are, fool?"

"But what about Ivory? The Weeping Woman. The ring."

They were interrupted as Dr. Harold W. Smith entered the hotel room in New York and sat down behind the large writing desk.

"Well?" Remo demanded of Chiun. "What about those things? What about the statue? It talked."

He saw Smith glance upward sharply.

Chiun said in Korean to Remo, "Such subjects should not be discussed with men of bound minds such as the emperor."

"I beg your pardon," Smith said.

"Ah, Illustrious One. Forgive me my prattle. I was merely telling Remo to remain silent about the cure for the malady which has affected his reason."

"What cure?" Smith asked.

"Something that will ease his burdened mind and make these visions of spirits within statues vanish forever, thus freeing him to be of greater service to you. But we do not wish to waste your time, O Emperor. Please do not give this a second thought."

"But, well, if there's something I could do . . ." Smith said.

"Truly, it is nothing," Chiun insisted. "While it would heal Remo in a moment, you should not be troubled with such trivialities."

Remo cleared his throat. "Well, since you asked, I guess I could use a couple of weeks in Puerto Rico."

"Pay him no heed, Emperor," Chiun said. He kicked him in the shins, out of Smith's view. "That is not what he needs."

"How do you know what I need?"

Chiun kicked him again, harder this time. "Sire, this boy is like a son to me, even if he is white. A son whose innermost thoughts find their way to my heart. I know what he truly needs."

"Really?" Smith said. He sounded even more lemony than usual.

"Indeed. But it is so minor, I will say no more."

"Very well," Smith said agreeably.

"Except that Remo wishes, above all things, to be able to give to his adopted village of Sinanju the tribute it so justly deserves," Chiun added quickly.

"I do?" Remo said.

Chiun ignored him. "A mere five-weight of gold is so little. It shames my student."

Smith sighed. "I thought you gave up the extra tribute in exchange for the trip back to Sinanju."

"That is correct, O Just and Enlightened One. And so it is not I who ask for a ten-weight of gold to replace the paltry five-weight—"

"Ten? Before, we had settled on nine," Smith said.

"Yes, O All-Recalling One. But now it is not I who ask for the ten-weight. It is Remo."

"So far, he hasn't said a word about it," Smith said.

"It is because he is a shy and reticent thing, Emperor. But in his heart, he wants above all things to see the people of Sinanju clothed and fed. Is that not so, Remo?" He looked sharply at his pupil. Out of Smith's sight, he jabbed a long fingernail into Remo's thigh.

"Ow." Remo yelled.

"You see, Emperor? So great is his concern for the village that he cries out in despair. Truly, there is no other way, lest we lose him to heartsickness."

Smith exhaled in noisy resignation. "All right," he said. "An additional five-weight of gold annually."

Chiun beamed. "He is most pleased, Emperor."

Remo yawned.

"But it has to come out of somewhere," Smith said. "For instance, Remo, these expenses you keep running up."

"Of course, Emperor," said Chiun. "Remo is willing to restrict his food intake for such a worthy cause."

"And we'll have to cut your vacation time too," Smith said.

"Now, hold on just a minute," Remo said. "After the Seagull Motel, I want to go to Puerto Rico."

"Make your choice," Smith said. "More gold for Sinanju or Puerto Rico?"

"That's easy. Ow."

"He desperately prefers the ten-weight of gold, Emperor," Chiun said, leaning forward. "Desperately."

Smith looked at Remo, doubled over and racked with pain. "I'm glad that's settled," Smith said.

"For now," Remo grumbled. "Only for now."

After Smith had left, Remo and Chiun again spoke.

"What of Kali?" Remo said. "Is she dead?"

"The gods do not die. It is as I told that woman. Perhaps it will be many centuries before Kali finds another home on this earth."

"I hope so," Remo said. "My clothes stunk for days afterward."

* * *

In the handsome suburb of Denver, little Kimberly Baynes sat in her playroom making shapes out of a mound of pink Play-Doh. She wore a tiny apron over her frock, as her grandmother had instructed her, and she worked cleanly and quietly.

Mrs. Baynes peeked in and felt the same thrill she had felt every day since she had taken custody of Kimberly. Life had been grim since the death of her son and his wife and their son. It had seemed for a while that there would be nothing remaining to fill the last years of her life, but then Kimberly had come and the little girl's laughter had made Mrs. Baynes feel young again.

Children were wonderfully resilient. After the police had found the poor little creature, Kimberly had done nothing but chant insensibilities for a week. But that had all passed. Now she was as normal as blueberry pie. She never even mentioned that terrible place where her parents had taken her and Joshua to live. They forget, Mrs. Baynes thought. That's how the young stay happy.

Mrs. Baynes left the playroom to fix herself a cup of tea. She was sipping it in front of the television when Kimberly raced in, grinning, a wad of pink Play-Doh stuck to the end of her nose.

"Come see, Grandma. See what I made."

"Oh, my," the old lady said. "So this is the grand unveiling. Well, all right. I can't wait to see."

But Grandma Baynes had to blink hard as she entered the playroom. The pink blob of Kimberly's miniature worktable was nearly two feet high and formed into the shape of a mature adult woman, complete with breasts. Its face, childishly scrawled with a pencil point, seemed strangely malevolent. But the oddest thing about the statue was the number of arms it had.

Five.

"Why did you give the lady five arms, Kimberly?" Mrs. Baynes asked gently.

"So it'll have room to grow more, silly," Kimberly said.

"Ah, I see," Mrs. Baynes smiled. "It's . . . very pretty, darling." She didn't know why, but the sculpture filled her with loathing. Still, it was Kimberly's, and the child should be allowed to express herself. Maybe during the day sometime, she thought, she could fix the face herself with a nice smile and a pair of M&M's for eyes.

"She's beautiful," Kimberly said. "She's my friend."

"Does your friend have a name?" Mrs. Baynes asked.

"Yes. Her name is Kali."

"Isn't that nice?" Mrs. Baynes said. "Shall we have some ice cream now?"

"Oh, yes," Kimberly said. She held her grandmother's hand and skipped from the room.

The sun set, shrouding the room in darkness. And there, on the miniature worktable, covered with crayons and paper dolls and smudges of Play Doh, the tall pink statue produced a small pink nub in a space between its arms.

## About the Authors

WARREN MURPHY has written eighty books in the last twelve years. His novel, *Trace*, was nominated for the best book of the year by The Mystery Writers of America. He is a native and resident of New Jersey.

RICHARD SAPIR is a writer for The Destroyer series and author of *The Far Arena*. He is a graduate of Columbia University and formerly a journalist and editor. Mr. Sapir is a native of New York and lives in New Hampshire.

## The Destroyer Questionnaire

Win A Free Gift! Fill out this questionnaire and mail it today. All entries must be received by January 30, 1985. A drawing will be held in the New American Library offices in New York City on February 28, 1985. 100 winners will be randomly selected and sent a gift.

1. Book title:_____

   Book #:_____

2. Using the scale below, how would you rate this book on the following features? Please write in one rating from 0-10 for each feature in the spaces provided.

| POOR | NOT SO GOOD | AVERAGE | GOOD | EXCELLENT |
|------|------|------|------|------|
| 0  1 | 2  3 | 4  5  6 | 7   8 | 9   10 |

*RATING*

Overall opinion of book. . . . . . . . . . . . . . . . . . . . . . _____
Plot/Story. . . . . . . . . . . . . . . . . . . . . . . . . . . . . . . . _____
Setting/Location. . . . . . . . . . . . . . . . . . . . . . . . . . _____
Writing style . . . . . . . . . . . . . . . . . . . . . . . . . . . . . _____
Dialogue . . . . . . . . . . . . . . . . . . . . . . . . . . . . . . . . . _____
Suspense . . . . . . . . . . . . . . . . . . . . . . . . . . . . . . . . _____
Conclusion/ending . . . . . . . . . . . . . . . . . . . . . . . . _____
Character development . . . . . . . . . . . . . . . . . . . . _____
Hero . . . . . . . . . . . . . . . . . . . . . . . . . . . . . . . . . . . . _____
Scene on front cover . . . . . . . . . . . . . . . . . . . . . . _____
Colors of front cover . . . . . . . . . . . . . . . . . . . . . . _____
Back cover story outline . . . . . . . . . . . . . . . . . . . . _____
First page excerpts . . . . . . . . . . . . . . . . . . . . . . . . _____

3. How likely are you to buy another title in The Destroyer series? (Circle one number on the scale below.)

| DEFINITELY NOT BUY | PROBABLY NOT BUY | NOT SURE | PROBABLY BUY | DEFINITELY BUY |
|------|------|------|------|------|
| 0  1 | 2  3 | 4   5   6 | 7   8 | 9   10 |

4. Listed below are various Action Adventure lines. Rate only those you have read using the 0-10 scale below.

|      | NOT SO |      |      | EXCEL- |
| POOR | GOOD | AVERAGE | GOOD | LENT |
| 0 | 1  2  3 | 4  5  6 | 7  8 | 9  10 |

*RATING*

Able Team . . . . . . . . . . . . . . . . . . . . . . . . . . . . . . . . . . . . . . . _____

Death Merchant . . . . . . . . . . . . . . . . . . . . . . . . . . . . . . . . . . _____

Destroyer . . . . . . . . . . . . . . . . . . . . . . . . . . . . . . . . . . . . . . . . . _____

Dirty Harry . . . . . . . . . . . . . . . . . . . . . . . . . . . . . . . . . . . . . . . _____

Mack Bolan (Executioner) . . . . . . . . . . . . . . . . . . . . . . . _____

Penetrator . . . . . . . . . . . . . . . . . . . . . . . . . . . . . . . . . . . . . . . _____

Phoenix Force . . . . . . . . . . . . . . . . . . . . . . . . . . . . . . . . . . . _____

Specialist . . . . . . . . . . . . . . . . . . . . . . . . . . . . . . . . . . . . . . . . _____

_____ . . . . . . . . . . . . . . . . . . . . . . . . . . . . . _____

_____ . . . . . . . . . . . . . . . . . . . . . . . . . . . . . _____

5. Where do you usually buy your books (check one or more):

( ) Bookstore            ( ) Discount Store
( ) Supermarket          ( ) Department Store
( ) Variety Store        ( ) Other:_____
( ) Drug Store

6. What are the names of two of your favorite magazines?
1) _____
2) _____

7. What is your age?_____      Sex: ( ) Male
                                        ( ) Female

8. Marital Status:      Education:
( ) Single            ( ) Grammer school or less
( ) Married           ( ) Some high school
( ) Divorced          ( ) H.S. graduate
( ) Separated         ( ) 2 yrs. college
( ) Widowed           ( ) 4 yrs. college

If you would like to participate in future research projects, please complete the following:

PRINT NAME:_____

ADDRESS: _____

CITY:_____STATE_____ZIP_____

PHONE: (       )_____

Thank you. Please send to: New American Library, Action Adventure Research Dept., 1633 Broadway, New York, New York 10019.